THE TIES
THAT BIND

OTHER BOOKS AND AUDIO BOOKS
BY KRISTEN MCKENDRY:

Promise of Spring

THE TIES THAT BIND

a novel

Kristen McKendry

Covenant Communications, Inc.

Covenant

Cover image *In Time* © 2009 Mark Wragg.

Cover design copyrighted 2009 by Covenant Communications, Inc.

Published by Covenant Communications, Inc.
American Fork, Utah

Printed in The United States of America
First Printing: July 2009

16 15 14 13 12 11 10 09   10 9 8 7 6 5 4 3 2 1

ISBN-13: 978-1-59811-800-1
ISBN-10: 1-59811-800-5

To Emma for the story
to my husband for the journey
and to Walter Ames McKendry, the child who is still missing

Acknowledgments

Thank you to my understanding editor, Noelle Perner, and to Kelly Smurthwaite and all the others at Covenant who have seen this project through so capably. Thank you to the many family members who have let us interview them, poke through photographs, and coax out sometimes painful memories. Thank you to my patient children, who played frisbee and had picnics in cemeteries all over Ontario while their parents searched for pieces of the puzzle. Thank you to my husband, who unfailingly supports everything I want to do. Thank you to my parents, Lynn and Kaye Garner, who taught me the value of family. Thank you to Mekinda et al. for letting me hijack their ideas for long-term care facilities. Above all, thank you to Emma Lampe McKendry, who found joy in her children. She is the guiding influence for this story.

Though inspired by actual people and events, this book was generated from my imagination and should be regarded as fiction.

CHAPTER 1

1915

"Pig ankles!"

"What?"

"You can call them ham hocks all you like, but when it comes right down to it, you're feeding your children pig ankles."

"Hannah!" Elsa Wyse straightened from chopping the cabbage and stared at her daughter, knife dangling, eyes wide. "What's come over you lately?"

Hannah pushed her embroidery hoop over the next section of her towel and tightened the screw. She didn't know how to answer. She only knew that lately everything irritated her; nothing was quite as she wanted it. The frame house that had been her home most of her seventeen years suddenly seemed too cramped, the humidity unbearable, her noisy brothers overwhelming. Even her embroidery, usually a source of satisfaction and pride, was sloppy and disappointing today. She tugged at it impatiently, and the blue cotton tangled. She tossed it in her basket before she could ruin it completely and looked up to see her mother frowning at her in puzzlement.

"I'm all right. It's just the heat." Hannah flipped back her long, red hair, which the humidity had frizzed into something resembling Moses' burning bush. When her mother continued to watch her, she stood and strode to the stove.

"I'll do the onions."

"Helga will do them. Helga!" Elsa called. There was no reply from the loft overhead. She tried again, louder.

"You know she'll put it off until you get tired of waiting for her and make me do it anyway," Hannah muttered. "You know that's how Helga is."

"Don't speak ill of your sister. What I'd like you to do is take your papa his lunch. I would send Wilhelm, but the road has been so busy lately."

Hannah pulled her hat from the hook by the door, scooped up the tin her mother had readied, and went out.

The air was hot and tasted of dust, but it was still refreshing after the confines of the kitchen. Hannah's father, Heinrich Wyse, worked in a narrow little room squeezed between a milliner and a butcher, with a hand-painted sign over the door declaring, "Shoes resoled while you wait." Heinrich was hunched over his bench when Hannah entered, and he only glanced at the tin and grunted his thanks as she set his food down.

Hannah leaned back so as not to block the light coming in the single window and breathed in the familiar, oily smell of the saddle soap her father used. She watched him pare away a rim of excess leather like an orange rind from the boot heel in his hand. She liked to watch her father's hands at work; they were thick and calloused and very strong. Deftly now he smoothed the edge of the leather and placed the boot on the counter beside its mate. Then he brushed away the trimmings of leather with his hand, pulled out a clean rag, and began to whip it around the boots, bringing out the shine. It was the extra bit of service that brought regular customers, he said. It was the way he had always done it, and his father before him, back in Leipzig.

Hannah fingered the bootlace thoughtfully. Her father raised an eyebrow at her.

"So what is their story? Who wears them? What does he do for a living?" he asked in German.

"Not today, Papa."

"You like this game."

"Not today. I can't think of anything."

Heinrich looked at the boots a moment, then changed the subject. "What is your mother making for supper?"

"Cabbage and ham-hock soup." She made a face.

"You like cabbage and ham-hock soup."

"I have nothing to compare it to," she replied.

Her father's face relaxed into a faraway smile. "Cabbage is my favorite. We owe our lives to a cabbage, you know that?"

Hannah stopped herself from making another face. "Yes, Papa," she replied, switching to English even though she knew he disliked it. "We spent all our money getting on the boat to America, and if it hadn't been for that cabbage that rolled off a cart, we would have starved to death. You've told me before." She had been an infant when they'd left Germany, but she'd heard the story so often it felt like her own memory.

"What is the matter, *liebchen*? You seem very gloomy today."

Hannah shook her head. "Did you ever think about going somewhere else, Papa? I mean, why Wisconsin? Why didn't you settle in—I don't know, Detroit or somewhere? Did we really cross the ocean and leave our family and live off a cabbage to get *here*?"

He stared at her without answering. She dropped the bootlace with a sigh and went out into the August heat.

She knew if she went home now she would be put to work peeling potatoes or chopping cabbage, and the thought of going back to the stuffy kitchen was unbearable. With a guilty little thrill, she ducked down a side street and headed up Settler Road away from home. She wasn't sure where she was going, but if she stayed out an hour or so longer, her mother would have the worst of it finished by the time she got back.

They were building a new courthouse next to the town center, and for months now the roads had been bustling with trucks, wagons, and men, hauling planks and bricks to the site and carrying dirt away. Hannah didn't usually see the work progress, as Mother didn't approve of her children wandering far from home. Church, school, and Papa's shop were usually the only places she went. But today she made her way steadily up the crowded street, veering left at the bank and into the town square. Before her was the unfinished courthouse.

They had already framed in the main structure, and now boys carrying hods scurried around the foundations while two men on rickety scaffolding bricked in the walls. Hannah stopped at a safe distance and watched the man nearest her, admiring the deft swinging motion of his trowel and the rhythm he kept as the row of bricks slowly grew. Slap, scrape, tap, scrape. He was working about twelve feet off the ground, and the busy carriers fed a steady stream of bricks and mortar up to him. The noise and bustle were exciting.

Hannah knew most of the hod carriers—boys near her own age from her class at school. Georg Eisen was one of them. He was taller than most of the other boys and strongly built, with white-blond hair. Her sister Helga was sweet on him. Most of the girls in Cobb Township were. But Hannah had never fancied the boys her age. They seemed dull and silly to her, even though at seventeen or eighteen, most of them were well on their way to becoming independent men. The boys were apprenticed out young in Wisconsin, or, as in Georg's case, carefully primed to take over their fathers' farms when the time came. She knew Georg was already responsible for his own herd of dairy cows. Of course, that didn't stop him from earning a little cash carrying bricks when the opportunity arose.

A crashing sound brought Hannah from her reverie, and she looked up to see a young carrier sprawled on his face in the mud, his tray of bricks scattered in front of him. The brick mason immediately swung down from his perch and examined not the fallen boy, but the spilt bricks. Hannah's eyes widened as she heard him swear. Cobb people didn't swear.

"You've broken four of them!" The man turned on the young carrier, who was wiping muck off his hands and knees. "That makes ten today! What are you trying to do?"

The boy hung his head, and Hannah felt a surge of pity for him. He couldn't be more than ten or eleven. When the brick mason continued to rail at him, her pity turned to indignation, and she stepped forward.

"Anyone can see they're too heavy for him. He shouldn't be made to carry so many at once!"

Both the man and the boy looked at her in surprise. She suddenly felt uncertain and foolish under the brick mason's cool, blue stare, and her chin came up in defiance.

"I can't build a wall with broken bricks," the man said.

"He's just a little boy."

At this, the boy's surprise turned to resentment. He shot her a hateful look, snatched up the handle of his carrier, and marched back toward the brick pile, shoulders back. Hannah's gaze remained fixed on the face of the man standing before her.

The population of Cobb was predominantly German, and almost everyone in town had blond hair, blue eyes, and a stocky, Germanic build. The man standing before her, however, was the exact opposite of everyone she had ever met. He was tall, slender to the point of being bony, but had the shoulders and arms of one of his trade. He had dark brown hair that looked like it had been combed with his trowel, and a heavy mustache that made him look old, though she guessed he was younger than her father. Though his eyes were blue, they were different from any eyes she had seen. They were clear and bright, like ice, and deep set with crow's-feet in the corners that made him look slightly squinty. They were eyes that could stare right through you and out the other side. She wouldn't say he was handsome, exactly, just *different*.

After a moment, Hannah had to drop her gaze, and she was surprised to hear herself apologizing.

"I didn't mean to interfere, but you didn't need to go at him like that. He's only a child."

His lips twitched. He wiped his hand across his tanned, mortar-spattered jaw. "I'll keep it in mind," he said, tipping an imaginary cap, and climbed back onto the scaffold. Hannah turned and walked away, trying to keep from running, holding her neck stiff. Somehow she knew he was laughing at her.

* * *

"Who's the gutsy girl?" James asked, jerking his head after the retreating figure. His fellow mason, Niel, narrowed his eyes and craned his neck to peer around the scaffolding.

"Hannah?" Niel asked. "She's the cobbler's daughter. She has a temper to match that fiery hair of hers. She has an older sister who would take your breath away, but the father keeps his shotgun handy, if you know what I mean."

The two men laughed and went back to work. By the time Hannah had turned the corner onto Settler Road, Niel had quite forgotten her. James hadn't.

* * *

When Hannah arrived home, the kitchen reeked of boiling cabbage, and everyone was in a foul mood. Helga sat pouting at the table, chopping the last of the onions for the stew bubbling and spitting on the stove. She cast a glare at her sister, and a twinge of anxiety ran through Hannah. Helga bore grudges to be wary of.

Her mother was rushing to get supper on. She was always rushing. She hurried from table to stove, clattering dishes and snapping at the two boys who were getting underfoot with their tin soldiers. She glanced at Hannah and pinched her lips together but didn't scold her for being late. Hannah didn't need to be scolded. She quickly hung up her hat and ushered her squalling brothers into the back room, then went to work setting the table, her burst of defiance tidily finished.

* * *

"Now this is a true contest—a German against an Irishman!" Karl Bond lifted his foaming mug to the laughing crowd, tipped his head back, and downed the beer at one go. He wiped his mouth with his hand and nodded at his opponent. "Try that, stranger."

James took the mug offered him and tipped it down just as easily. His eyes glittered in the amber light from the window. "No one can outdrink an Irishman."

Karl grinned and pushed forward to the bar. His friends and neighbors cheered as he downed his second, then his third. James matched him mug for mug, and while Karl's eyes slowly reddened and his tongue grew thick, the only sign that James had had anything to drink was the foam on his mustache. After the fourth beer, even Karl's dearest friends with whom he'd sailed from the old country had to admit that he couldn't hold his drink like the brick mason could.

After the fifth drink, Karl slumped morosely into a chair, and his friends looked away self-consciously. Money quietly changed hands. James swigged the last of his beer, nodded at his hosts, and moved in his long, steady stride out of the bar.

The sun was still setting, the color of honey as it sank below the wheat field horizon. The street was still, with almost everyone at home or in the pub. James stood and took his bearings, his brain beginning to go muzzy, aggravated by the heat and humidity of the evening. He strode casually away from the bar, crossed the square, and walked into the alley between the butcher shop and Schmidt's store, where the smell of the butcher's scraps caused his stomach to lurch. He hurried past, emerging into the road at too fast a pace and colliding with someone in the half-light. He steadied himself against the brick wall, and when his head cleared, he saw a girl sitting on the packed earth in front of him.

Hannah could only sit, the breath knocked out of her, her mouth opening and closing soundlessly. Her father's ledger, which he'd sent her to fetch, lay open on the ground, the pages fluttering. She knew her dress was hiked to her knees, but she couldn't seem to move. She wasn't sure what had happened.

Then, suddenly, she was being pulled to her feet. She looked up to see the man she had met at the new courthouse, the one with the fascinating eyes. He was holding her hands and asking her something. She closed her eyes and willed her lungs to inhale.

"I'm all right. It's nothing."

He finally released her hands, then retrieved her ledger from the dirt and pushed it toward her.

"I'm sorry," he said again. "I didn't see you."

"It was my fault. I was going too fast," Hannah replied.

James stood looking at her. Her hair gleamed in the gold light of evening, and her eyes were wide and bright. He was used to the brassy red hair of his cousins, but hers was darker, richer, like weathered copper. Her mouth was still partly open as she caught her breath. She barely came to his shoulder, but seeing her now, he decided she was older than he'd thought. If her sister were more beautiful, she must really be something. He scowled suddenly, telling himself the drink had affected him more than he'd realized. He barked an abrupt good night and strode away.

Hannah hurried toward home, gripping the book in her arms and trying to forget the sensation of the stranger's rough hands holding her own.

* * *

After a short walk, James reached his destination. He was staying in a rented room at a house owned by an old deaf woman named Mrs. Werner. It wasn't far from the courthouse site, and it was inexpensive. Beyond that, it had the advantage of being the only room Mrs. Werner rented out, so there were no other tenants to bother him. James made his way up the narrow stairs now, the swagger gone out of him. He kicked off his boots and fell on the rumpled bed with a groan. For a while he lay staring up at the ceiling. Lights and shadows cast through the single bare window flitted across the peeling painted surface. The house was quiet. He closed his eyes, but sleep wouldn't come. It was going to be another one of those nights, when his thoughts kept churning and memory wouldn't be kept at bay. He rolled over, reached under the bed, and pulled out the bottle he kept there. Only when he was alone did the serious drinking begin. Swinging his feet to the floor, he sat with his back to the wall and grimly, methodically, set about draining the bottle's contents.

CHAPTER 2

2005

It was no use trying to sleep. Daniel lay staring at the patterns of light on the ceiling and felt his own heartbeat in his ears. He knew this routine well; he'd gone through it most of his life, but the frequency of the insomnia seemed to be increasing. He wadded the sheet in his fists and tried not to resent Rose's still, peaceful form beside him. How could she sleep so soundly? Couldn't she feel the vibrations of his thoughts leaping around in his head like a frog in a jar?

Of course, it wouldn't do any good to have her lying wakeful and tense beside him. The first year they'd been married, she'd tried to sit up with him, murmuring comforting things as if she could somehow coax him into sleep, as if he were a child with a nightmare. He'd managed to convince her that there was no point, that they'd both end up exhausted for no reason and that she should sleep while she could. He was fine; he'd get up and make himself a snack or read a book. He'd be all right. And yet when she agreed and went to sleep without him, he felt disappointed. It made no sense.

When he was honest with himself, Daniel knew he wasn't motivated solely by concern for Rose's own tiredness. On nights like these, when the sleeplessness hit him like an anxiety attack, he wanted only to be alone.

His hands were damp where they clutched the sheet, and his jaw ached from clenching his teeth. His brother Charlie used to grind his teeth so hard that he woke Daniel up at night. It always sounded like he was crunching walnuts between his teeth, they popped so loudly. That memory was just about the only thing Daniel had of his brother. He remembered Charlie as being very tall, but Daniel was only seven the last time he'd seen Charlie, and any seventeen year old looks tall to a child. Daniel ended up being six-foot-three himself. He wondered, if he met Charlie again, which brother would be the tallest.

He squinted at the alarm clock glowing in the dim light. Six-thirty, and Saturday too. Blast. It was a crime to get up this early when he didn't have to be at work. He slipped out of bed now, careful not to wake Rose, and felt around until he found his moccasins. He padded into the bathroom and came out again without flushing for fear of disturbing her. He would go downstairs, sit in the den, and read until it was properly morning. He paused in the doorway, looking back at his wife's form sprawled under the blanket.

It was strange for him to think that she wasn't alone in there, that she wasn't going to be alone, just herself, again for another six months. How could she handle that thought? Daniel couldn't fathom not being alone for nine straight months—ten really, when you added it up. Unimaginable. The aloneness never really left him, ever, even when he was surrounded by friends and colleagues and Rose's boisterous family. There were times he felt so alone that he envisioned himself imploding, just caving in one day, collapsing into the emptiness hollowing his insides.

That emptiness had never bothered him much before. He was used to it. Even wanted it sometimes. But since last month it had crept into every part of him until it nearly echoed. Last month Rose had told him she was pregnant.

At thirty-five, she had begun to be anxious about whether she would ever be a mother, and now that it had happened, she spoke only of her happiness, her eager anticipation, her plans for the future.

He hadn't handled it well when she told him. He should have smiled, told her that was great, that he was pleased, but the words wouldn't come. Her smile faded and the tears started down her cheeks.

"I thought you'd be happy," she'd said. "I've been hoping for so long."

"We talked about waiting," he'd replied in a flat voice.

"We have been waiting, Daniel. Until you were out of school, until we bought the house, until the debts were paid off. How much longer do we wait? What are we waiting for?"

Now, as then, he turned away from her and went silently downstairs. His den was where he worked, but it was also a hiding place. Rose didn't enter it because she thought it was a rubbish heap. He went there now, mercilessly flicking on the light, punishing himself with the glare. He didn't consider it messy, only *relaxed*. Oak shelves loaded with books and cardboard magazine boxes crammed with newspapers lined two walls. His desk was scattered with uncapped pens, half-written articles, used courier envelopes, and printouts of e-mails. The clutter had begun to seep downward onto the green carpet, filling up chair seats and forming stacks in corners like a spreading fungus. But he could find everything he was looking for without trouble. Rose said nothing but made him keep the door closed.

Now Daniel dropped into the cracked vinyl chair where he liked to sit looking out at the backyard. The curtains were closed. He leaned forward, twitched them open, and frowned at the crimson sunrise coming over the roof of the garage.

What was he waiting for? They'd been married for six years. Rose was more than ready for parenthood. What was stopping him?

The fact of the matter was that the idea of having this baby terrified him. He knew he should feel joy. Wasn't this what life was all about? Wasn't this one of the reasons he had joined the LDS Church to begin with—the strong emphasis on family? The idea of having an eternal family—a wife and children of his own for always, not just until death—had appealed to him in a way that no other principle ever had. Here was a solution, simple and beautiful, to all the loneliness in the world. The night the missionaries had taught him about it, he'd known instantly that he was going to be baptized. Surely a religion that taught such a marvelous concept was just what he needed.

And that need hadn't changed, he had to acknowledge. But somehow in the rush, in learning about his new chosen religion, in finding a wife so late in life, in building a home with her, he had overlooked one vital thing. He knew nothing about being a father.

He leaned back in his chair and folded his arms across his pajama shirt. There—he'd admitted it. At least to himself. He didn't feel ready to be a father. He liked kids well enough; Rose's sister Abbie had three little boys, rough and tumble towheads who churned his back lawn to mud with their Big Wheels. He enjoyed it when they came. A child wouldn't interfere all that much with his work, and a journalist's hours were flexible, so he could be there to help Rose sometimes. No, it wasn't the inconvenience, the change of routine, or even the idea of having to share Rose with another, smaller person.

He just wasn't sure he could do it, at least not as well as it deserved to be done. After all, how could he do something he'd never seen done? The idea of being completely responsible for someone so vulnerable scared him silly. Wanting something didn't automatically make you any good at it.

Daniel's memories of his father were even sketchier than his memories of Charlie. He assumed his father had been tall like his sons, but he couldn't remember ever looking up into his father's face. He did remember a very deep voice. He thought maybe his father had brown hair, and he pictured his eyes as a piercing blue that scorched right through you to your backbone. But he knew that might not be a real memory, just something he'd concocted in his head, staring at his own blue eyes in the mirror.

He slumped down in the chair. Dawn was well underway now, the sun a slice of light above the garage, the sky pearl white. He could hear a car starting up and the neighbor's bellow as he called his wandering dog. Life was moving on. But Daniel could feel the depression beginning to seep over him, the energy draining from his limbs, the simmering anger starting to cloud his brain. He knew it was going to be one of those dark days when he longed to shut himself away and tell the world to leave him alone. It wasn't the ordinary don't-want-to-work blahs that everyone got. It was the kind of feeling that left him having to consciously remind himself to breathe. It made him feel like a spectator to his own life. It only hit him sometimes, usually coupled with the insomnia. Or when he tried to remember his father.

Half an hour later, Daniel got up and walked into the kitchen. Rose was there, cooking breakfast. Perhaps to try to stem the tide of depression, or perhaps because he felt he owed it to her, Daniel tried to tell Rose about his anxiety, his inadequacy in the face of what she expected of him. She frowned but remained quiet until he'd finished, his voice trailing off into uncertainty. They sat in silence but for the hum of the electric clock above the stove. The faucet dripped slowly, a Saturday project he'd put off for weeks. She pursed her lips and fiddled with her scrambled eggs, which had grown cold.

"And what am I supposed to do about it?" she finally said.

Daniel blinked at her. "What?"

"What do you expect me to do to make it all better for you? Write you an owner's manual for infants? Daniel, *nobody* feels ready to be a parent. You don't feel ready until you just jump in and do it. Going *through* it makes you ready."

"You don't get what I'm trying to tell you," he said, spreading his hands. "I'm not just nervous. It's not pre-fatherhood jitters."

She set down her fork and laced her fingers on top of her golden hair as if to keep her head from floating off like a helium balloon. "I'm trying to understand, Daniel. I really am. But have you been leading me down the garden path all this time? Have you ever intended to have a family?"

"Of course I have. I mean, I assumed we would one day."

"Well, that day is here." She stood abruptly and went to the sink to dump her plate.

"It's not like I'm doing this on purpose." He couldn't keep the irritation from his voice. "Now that it's not hypothetical, but reality—"

"What? Don't you think I'm anxious about it too? I've never done this before either, you know."

Daniel rubbed the back of his neck, trying to keep the frustration from his voice. "But the fact remains that you grew up in a big, noisy family with both parents. You had a stay-at-home mom who sewed your dresses and bathed babies and was in the PTA and provided a great role model for you of how to be a mother. You know how a mother's love feels. Rose, I don't know how to act like a father or—or *feel* like one. I've never experienced it; I've only seen it in other people's lives from a distance. You know my father left when I was small."

She seemed pacified by this and returned to the table. She bit her lips together a moment, then spoke slowly, not looking at him. "I know. You haven't told me much about it, but—"

"That's because I don't know much about it," he said softly. "I hardly remember it, and nobody ever talked about it. I never asked many questions because I knew it was a forbidden topic, and because . . . well, I didn't know what I'd find. But you see, my dad wasn't there for me. He didn't leave me any part of himself. I want to be able to give my child more than that. But just because I want it doesn't mean that I know how, or even that I can." He wasn't sure he'd explained himself at all, but Rose nodded.

"Maybe it's time to ask some questions, then. What he was like. Why he left."

"How? I know Isabel won't talk about it."

Rose brought her sky-blue eyes up to his, the expression in them dead serious. "Maybe you need to find him. Talk to him."

"Talk to him!" He froze, stunned.

"If you knew about him, if you knew more about the whole situation, maybe you would feel more ready. Maybe you could put it to rest."

"I don't know if I want to find him. It might make things even worse."

"How?"

"I don't know. I mean, what if I find out I'm like him?" Daniel said.

"What do you mean? You think you'll be a lousy father just because your dad was? You think that just because he had trouble committing and ran away, you will too?" Her voice went up a notch.

"No, not that," Daniel said hastily. He was making a mess of this conversation. He reached for her hand and shook his head. "I know I'm not like him in that way. I'd never walk out on you—you should know that by now, Rose. I love you. But I'll be honest with you. When I think about raising this baby, playing the part of dad, I look forward to it, but I get this anxious feeling at the same time. I wonder if I'll buckle under pressure. I wonder if I'll be able to give him everything he's going to need—physically and financially, that's not a problem. I'm okay there. But emotionally? I don't know."

She sighed. "Everyone feels inadequate at first."

"This is different from plain inadequacy, Rose. You're not getting it. What's that saying? 'You can't pour water out of an empty bucket.'"

She took a deep breath and let it out slowly, then placed her hands flat on the table and looked at them a moment, collecting herself. Her nails were short and practical. Rose never painted them; her hands were usually covered in clay or papier-mâché or dough or garden soil. Daniel found himself studying her hands now too, as if they anchored him and Rose to the table, to each other. Daniel had never seen her sit so still.

Finally she looked up at him. "So you're saying you feel empty emotionally," she said carefully.

"Don't take it like that—"

"Daniel." She leaned forward, gazing straight into him. He could see the muscle working in her jaw. She'd never looked so serious. "This child is coming, ready or not. Whatever it takes for you to get ready, do it, because you only have six months. And then the time is up and the curtain goes up and you're on stage, whether you know the script or not."

"But what if—"

"No. If you don't know the script by then, you'd better be darn good at improvising. Like the rest of us." She stood and left the kitchen.

* * *

After fifteen minutes of wandering around his den, shuffling paper back and forth on his desk, picking up books and putting them down unread, flipping his laptop open and closed a few times, Daniel gave up on trying to settle and went out into the yard. It was a dry August, and the lawn didn't need mowing, but there were plenty of weeds in the vegetable garden. He fetched a hoe from the shed and attacked them, expending his frustration in short, vicious whacks.

He didn't fight with Rose often, and he hated the feeling it left in his stomach. He hadn't intended to upset her. He was just trying to have an honest conversation. It was all so simple to Rose. Find his father, a man he hadn't seen since he was *five*! Find out about him, find out why he left, and presto! Everything's all better. As if knowing the details of it would somehow fill the hole in his life and instantly make Daniel ready to be a loving parent.

The fact was that the hole would never be filled, no matter how well he ever understood his father's leaving. His dad hadn't been dragged away kicking and screaming. He'd left, and nothing would ever compensate for that. At least Mom had died. She hadn't left on purpose. And what if Dad didn't want to be found? If he did, he'd have come back years ago. Rose had no idea what she had suggested. It was out of the question.

And yet the idea wouldn't go away; it buzzed around in his head like a mosquito. Was it even possible to find him? The man was probably dead. If he was alive, and by some miracle Daniel did find him, what would his reaction be, seeing the son he hadn't seen in thirty years? These thoughts were followed by others: *He won't want to see me. I don't want to see him. He threw me away thirty years ago.*

But the truth of the matter was that Daniel didn't know that his father had thrown him away. No one had ever adequately explained the situation to him. For all he knew, his father had left for a legitimate reason and something had prevented him from coming back. Perhaps he'd died or been injured and was lying in a coma somewhere even now . . .

Ridiculous. It was a romantic dream he'd coaxed along as a teenager, picturing his father lying there unable to reach him but desperate to be reunited. Surely he was too old to cling to that dream. He had to face reality. Jim McDonald had tossed away his wife and children like a bunch of old candy wrappers.

Daniel's sister Isabel was four years older than he was and presumably knew more about it than he did. She'd been nine when their father left and eleven when Mom died and they'd gone to live with the Dempseys, Mom's cousins. But Isabel didn't seem to be bothered by unfinished business or questions about her past. She was married, successful, and to all appearances content. Though they talked about Mom a lot, they had never discussed Dad. It was something they didn't mention.

Daniel chopped idly at a weed. Why didn't he call Isabel up now and ask her what she remembered? He was a journalist, after all. Asking questions and researching facts was what he did, what he was good at. What was the worst that could happen?

But he didn't drop the hoe and phone her. He was afraid of what he'd find. He was afraid he'd learn that his father had taken off without a backward glance. That Jim McDonald wasn't a nice person. But really, didn't he know that already?

He was an idiot to let the mere mention of the idea throw him into such a state. He was an idiot for considering such a search. He was an idiot for putting it off this long. He wasn't going to do it. It was much too late for all that. What good could it do? It didn't really matter now, did it, after all these years?

But it did.

His side hurt from exertion, and his breath came in gasps. Daniel leaned on his hoe and glumly surveyed the ruins of Rose's zucchini plants. If he never probed into his past, he would never have to live with whatever he found out. But could he continue to live without knowing? For Rose's sake, for the sake of his coming child, maybe he needed to finally put it to rest. Could he ever really look forward if he was always looking backward?

Daniel rolled his eyes. This circular thinking was getting him nowhere.

He dropped the hoe into the dirt and went back into the house to find Rose.

CHAPTER 3

It felt ludicrously like phoning a girl to ask her to the prom. He was so nervous his bowels were rumbling. Before he could talk himself out of it, he punched in the number, then dropped his head into his hand. The line rang twice before someone picked up.

"Skocylaks."

His brother-in-law never said hello or indulged in small talk, only stated facts. It suited Daniel just fine right now.

"Paul? It's Daniel. How are you?"

"I'm all right. You want to talk to Isabel?"

"Please."

There was a muffled sound, a child's shout, and then Isabel was on the line.

"Danny? Hey, how are you? I haven't heard from you for a while."

"Yeah, sorry, I've been meaning to call you."

"We got Rose's e-mail. How's she feeling?"

"All right. Not showing yet, no morning sickness. I think she'll come through it okay."

"We're so happy for you. The kids are the best thing that ever happened to us. Tell her that if she wants to borrow my old maternity clothes, I still have them boxed in the basement. No point in spending good money on something she'll only fit into for a few weeks."

Daniel winced, picturing Rose in Isabel's flowery maternity clothes. Why was it that women who never wore flowers or lace started doing it when they were pregnant? He cleared his throat, then said, "That's nice of you. I'll mention it to her. Your youngest is eight—why do you still have the clothes?"

"Silly, don't you know it's bad luck to get rid of them? I'll get pregnant for sure if I throw them out. I'm hanging onto the crib for the same reason."

He chuckled politely, knowing it was expected, and then there was a pause. He could picture her eyes narrowing. Quickly, before he could let himself back out, he said, "Isabel, I need to ask you something."

"Okay. Sounds serious. What's up?"

"Do you remember Dad very well?"

There was silence on the other end of the line.

"I don't mean to bring it up. I just—I don't have many memories of him. Hardly any. And I was wondering what he was like."

"Well," she said quietly, "he was tall like you. Brown hair and blue eyes. Skinny."

"Do you have any pictures of him?"

"Good grief, no. Why would I?"

"I was just hoping . . ."

"You could ask Patricia. She might have an old snapshot or something. But I doubt it."

"What was his personality like?"

"What does it matter? That was a long time ago."

"I know."

"I really don't remember," Isabel said flatly. He could tell she was lying.

"I don't want to bother you with it, but—"

"Then don't. It doesn't matter anymore."

"But it does. I'm about to become a father myself. I need to know what he was like."

"Why? Let it go, Danny. You can be whatever you want to be. It's not like you have to turn out like him."

"I know that."

"Then don't be stupid."

He couldn't help grinning. She always managed to make him feel seven years old again.

"All right, I'm sorry I asked."

"Let it go."

"I will. I just said I was sorry, didn't I?"

There was another pause, and then Isabel brightly launched into an account of her daughter Heather's latest accomplishments in piano, and the conversation was firmly and unalterably back in her control. When he hung up ten minutes later, Daniel sat staring at the phone for a while, musing. She was right. It was a stupid thing to have asked. It would accomplish nothing. He should drop the whole thing right now.

Instead, he picked up the receiver again.

"Dempsey residence."

"Patricia? It's Daniel."

"Danny!" Like Isabel, his mother's cousin could reduce him to childhood without effort. "How are you, sweetie? How's Rose?"

"She's great. Not sick at all. Already painting the spare room pastel colors and picking out names. How are you?"

"Keeping busy. Getting the yard ready for winter. I could use your help cleaning out the rain gutters."

"I wish I lived closer." Patricia was in Boulder, not far from Isabel and Paul. She'd moved to a smaller home right after Daniel left for Boise State. She'd explained that with him gone to school, Isabel married, and her husband dead all these years, she'd just rattle around in that old house.

"Don't worry about it," she said now. "Isabel's going to ask Paul to help me take care of it. So what's up with you? Anything wrong?"

Good old Patricia. She had no children of her own, but raising Daniel and his sister had honed her mothering instincts to an infallible level.

"I was talking to Isabel. I'm . . . I'd like to find out more about Dad."

"Jim, you mean? What for?"

"Do I need a reason to want to know about my own father?"

"Yes."

He laughed in spite of himself. "Just call me curious. I don't remember him very well at all. I don't know what he was like. And I don't really know why he left."

There was a pause, and then she said quietly, "Is it important to you?"

"Yes, Patricia, it is."

"I can't help you much as far as my own experience goes. I only met the man once, at your mom's wedding. She was only nineteen when they got married, did you know that? He was older, by maybe ten years or so. And then they moved off to Montana. By the time Caroline came back to Denver with you three kids in tow, your dad was long gone. She never gave me details about why they split up, and I didn't feel I should ask. Not my business, you know? Couples have problems. It happens."

"Did he never get back in touch with Mom?"

"Not that I ever heard of. And I think she would have said something if he had."

"Did Mom ever talk about him at all? She never spoke of him to us kids."

"Not much. Only a bit toward the end when the morphine made her groggy. She wrote something down on a piece of paper that she said I should keep for you. I haven't thought about it in years. I wonder where I put it . . ."

"What did she write?"

"It was a list of family members on your dad's side—brothers and sisters—and what she knew about them. She knew you'd keep in touch with her side of the family because of Mark and me, but she wanted you to be able to keep in touch with his side, too. I don't know why. I got the impression they were never there for her and your dad. She certainly never talked about them to me."

"Do you still have that paper somewhere?"

"I'm sure I do. I wouldn't have thrown it out. But it might take a day or two for me to lay my hands on it. It might be in my cedar trunk. When I find it, I'll mail it to you."

"Thanks, Patricia. I'd appreciate it."

"Daniel, you aren't thinking of tracking him down, are you?"

Daniel rolled his eyes, gripping the phone until his palm was slick with sweat.

"I don't know. No, I don't think so. I was just wondering about him is all."

"Because I don't think it would be a good idea," Patricia went on. "I mean, he left a long time ago. If he wanted to be in touch, he would be. You know? It might be better to let sleeping dogs lie."

"Yeah, I know."

"He may not even still be alive. He'd be in his seventies by now. And he was so thin and sick-looking when I met him. I doubt he's still around, honey."

"I know. I was just wondering. Um . . . have you ever heard from Charlie?"

The pause was longer this time.

"That's what you're really doing, isn't it, Danny? You're trying to find Charlie. He said he was going out to look for your dad, so you think if you find your dad you'll find your brother."

"No, that isn't it—"

"Well, all I can say is that if he hasn't talked to you since 1977, he isn't much of a brother, is he? I wouldn't waste time on him."

"I'm not even—"

"He was always getting into trouble, that one. Up to no good. There wasn't anything Mark and I could do about him. I tell you, Danny, it was a relief when he left. I'll be honest about it, and the only reason I ever felt sorry about it was because I'd promised your mom that Mark and I would watch out for you kids. But there was nothing we could do with that one. Believe me, we tried."

"I know. I'm not blaming you or Mark for anything. Don't think that I am for a minute. I'm sure you guys did everything you could for him. I mean, look at what a good job you did with me and Isabel. We turned out wonderfully."

She laughed. "Humble too, aren't you? Hey, you and Rose come see me someday, before the baby comes, okay? It's been too long."

Daniel thanked her, chatted a moment longer, and then rang off. He rubbed his hands down his face. He was overwhelmed with a feeling of sadness that he didn't entirely understand. He'd known how it was in his family for years, all his life. Why was this bothering him so much now? Was it really just because of the baby coming? If it weren't for that, would he have given his father or Charlie a second thought? Such a simple question. So why was it so hard to ask? And even harder to answer.

CHAPTER 4

1915

It was harvest, and there was threshing that Saturday. The town turned out, all the men helping to bring in the sheaves that waited in the fields. The Saturday before it had been Karl Bond's corn, and before that, Paul Muller's. Today it was Johann Eisen's wheat. He had a large spread of acreage and only Georg to help him, his other six children being girls.

While the menfolk went back and forth with the wagons and worked on the threshing floor, the women set out long tables behind the house and loaded them with food—hearty meat pies, squash, cabbage, spicy sausages, kraut, and crisp melon. Elsa Wyse had brought her famous lemon pickles, and Helga, who had great faith in the saying that the door to a man's heart was his stomach, had baked an apple pie. Hannah, who didn't particularly care where the door to a man's heart was, had brought potato salad.

She placed the dish on the crowded tablecloth and looked out over the dusty barnyard to the fields beyond. Her father drove past in a wagon, heading out for another load of bundled wheat. Her brothers, Erik and Wilhelm, had joined in a game of tug-o-war with the other younger boys under the poplar trees. The air was filled with friendly laughter and cheery gossip, most of it carried on in German.

Hannah walked back to the porch, where her mother sat with the other women, buttering soft rolls for the picnic. Emmaline Eisen pushed a knife and the crock of butter over to Hannah, and she sat down to help. Emmaline was a cheerful woman with a face like a frying pan and the same husky build as her husband and son. Helga sat beside her, listening attentively to everything the woman said. Ingratiating herself, Hannah knew, to get to Georg.

"Not a day over fifteen," Emmaline was saying now. "And she had a babe in arms and another on the way, from the look of her."

"Well, Gertrude never did pay enough attention to her children," Annie Muller piped up. "What can she expect?"

"Especially when she takes in boarders," Pauline Kohler agreed. "It's just asking for trouble."

"If Jack would just lift his hand to work occasionally, she wouldn't have to take in boarders."

"Ella Werner has a new boarder now," Annie Muller added. "A brickie from Ireland. He's working on the new courthouse with Niel."

"Oh, I wondered who that was," Emmaline said, nodding.

Hannah dropped a buttered roll into the basket and cut open a new one. "He seems rather nice," she said to no one in particular.

There was silence, and Hannah looked up to see all the women looking at her.

"And how do you know him?" her mother asked quietly.

Hannah returned their stares. "I ran into him the other night, going to Papa's shop. He accidentally knocked me down, and then he helped me up."

Emmaline glanced around the circle of women and tried to steer the conversation in another direction. "Seems there are so many newcomers, more every day, and from all over the world."

"Cobb is changing. It used to be just us," Pauline Kohler said, and everyone nodded vigorously.

"When Karl and I arrived from Germany, there were only eight families here," Josie Bond said. "Seven of them were from Frankfurt, and one of them was from Essen."

Hannah dropped the knife into the butter and stood up, brushing her hands on her skirt. They were about to stampede down memory lane to Germany, and she got enough of that at home. Even Helga joined in, repeating things she'd heard her parents say, because she'd only been four years old when they'd emigrated and of course didn't remember any more about it than Hannah did. Hannah sometimes wondered why they had left Germany at all; they seemed to have brought it with them to Wisconsin.

"I'll go see if I can help on the floor," she said, and walked away from the group of women to the large shed by the barn. Chickens pecked industriously in the dirt by the door, ignoring her as she went inside.

Here the men were busy threshing the wheat as it was brought in. The noise was exhilarating, the golden air gritty with dust and chaff. There was a glorious smell of fresh wheat, damp earth, and autumn. She noted that one of the men was the Irish brick mason. He worked with his sleeves rolled up, a wet streak running down the middle of his back.

The men in Cobb still threshed the old way, beating the sheaves on the smooth floor to knock the heads of grain loose. The pile was then swept to another group of men with wide brooms. A third group of men tossed the grain in the air to let the breeze flowing through the open shed carry away the chaff. The grain fell back to the ground and was swept into sacks by a team of young boys, who then passed the sacks to Christina Baden to sew them up. Hannah knew there were machines to help farmers thresh, but such things took a long time to come to Cobb.

She stood a moment, watching the men work and breathing in the wonderful scent. Then she picked up a small broom and went to help collect the grain. She worked with efficient, precise movements, wasting no energy, but soon she began to perspire with the others. She wrapped her long red braid into a bun to hold it out of her way and surprised herself by wondering if putting her hair up would make her look any older.

* * *

James, pausing in his work, watched the redheaded girl from across the shed floor. Tendrils of hair had worked themselves loose from her bun and curled about her face. Dust clung to the hem of her long dress and small boots and made her sneeze from time to time. She didn't look quite like the others. Her hair was such a cheerful color, and her features were delicate, not broad and sturdy like the faces around her. And—mercifully—her slender frame didn't echo the other women's sturdy figures.

As she straightened to wipe her eyes of dust, she caught his gaze. For a moment she returned it, then turned back to her work. He grinned and seized the next sheaf of wheat.

* * *

When the threshing was finished and the evening was cooling, everyone gathered around the long tables behind the house. Johann Eisen thanked everyone for their help, and then Karl Bond gave a blessing over the food. Hannah snuck a glance at the brick mason where he stood on the lower step of the porch and was surprised to see that he hadn't removed his hat or bowed his head for the prayer. *Not a Christian, then,* she thought. *Or at least not a Lutheran.*

She helped six-year-old Erik load a plate with food and settle himself to eat under a pine tree. Then she stepped back in line to serve herself. Having surveyed the selections, she knew exactly what she wanted. Spicy sausage on a bun with tangy kraut, baked beans, deviled eggs, and apple pie . . . but not Helga's. She peered ahead to see what was holding up the line. The yard hummed with eager voices and clinking plates. There were several large boys ahead of her. She hoped there would be pie left by the time she reached it.

"Hello again."

She turned and looked up into piercing blue eyes. Her hands folded themselves tightly together.

"Hello."

"Recovered from our bump the other night?" the man asked.

She faced forward in the line again. "Oh, yes, thank you."

"A nice day for a picnic."

"Yes, it is." Now that she knew to listen for it, she could hear Ireland in his voice.

The line finally shuffled forward. The sausage was gone, so Hannah dished herself cold chicken, ham, beans, and potato salad, being sure to take some of her own. There was nothing more humiliating than taking something to a potluck and having no one eat it.

"My name is James McDonald," the man said suddenly. "I don't believe you've told me yours."

"Hannah Wyse," she replied. She knew her mother's eyes were on her, farther down the table. Without another word, she snagged a piece of the apple pie and carried her plate to a tree some distance from the milling crowd. She sat down on the grass, tucking her skirt over her boots. A moment later Mr. McDonald followed and sat beside her with his own meal. She wasn't sure what to make of it, but she wasn't displeased.

For a while they ate in silence, listening to the laughter and shouting of the others scattered about the yard. Hannah noticed he had taken the same food she had. He balanced his plate on his bent knee, eating with obvious enjoyment.

Hannah searched for something intelligent to say, but all she could come up with was, "It's a good turnout today."

"Mmm." He glanced at the group milling around the food tables. "I can only take noise and crowds for so long, and then I have to get away."

"I'm the same way. There are only six of us in our house, but sometimes even that seems like a crowd, and I have to escape out for a walk and just *think*."

"Where do you usually walk?"

"Along the river, usually. I follow it out of town where it widens, and there are trees. It's shady." She stopped, deciding she sounded stupid. Of course it would be shady if there were trees. He must think her an imbecile.

"And what do you think about while you walk?"

The question charmed her. It wasn't often she was asked what she thought.

"Mostly I think about going away from here," she said after a pause. "Traveling, seeing new places. I'd like to see the ocean. I saw it once when I was a baby, of course, when we came from Germany, but I don't remember it at all. I've read about faraway places quite a lot. There are so many places I'd like to see."

"Is Cobb such a dreary place? I think it's nice." He was smiling at her now.

"Oh, it's all right." Hannah brushed a loose hair away from her eyes. "But I've been here my whole life, and I'd like to know what else there is. How did you find your way to Cobb?"

He smiled. "I'm just traveling through. I go where there's work."

"Where have you been?"

He waved his fork as he spoke, drawing a map in the air. "Belfast, Toronto, Detroit, Pittsburgh, Milwaukee. Sometimes I'm a mason, sometimes I'm a field hand."

"Like today."

"Yes, like today."

"It must be exciting to travel to new places," Hannah said eagerly. "Which was your favorite?"

He considered. "Toronto, I guess."

"Where's that?"

His lips quirked, but he refrained from smiling. "Canada. On Lake Ontario."

"I'd love to travel."

"I don't know. Sometimes I think I'd like to travel a little less. It would be nice to have one corner you kept coming back to. A homestead."

"Do you want your own farm?" Hannah asked.

"Oh, I'm too old to take up farming," he replied, laughing. It was a contagious sound. His voice was mellow and deep and reminded her of slow-pouring molasses.

"You're not old," Hannah said, looking him full in the face.

"I'm thirty," James said, quieter now.

"Oh, that's not so bad. You're not too old to settle down." She attacked her cold chicken.

He chuckled again and glanced at her from the corner of his eye. "And you're still a baby."

"I'm nearly eighteen." It sounded ridiculously young, but she didn't like being called a baby. Her chin came up. "I'm getting older by the minute."

He chuckled and returned to his meal. For a while they sat in companionable silence.

Hannah looked up to see Helga sitting on a bench at one of the tables with Georg Eisen. Georg was leaning close and saying something, his blond hair falling over one eye. Helga was blushing a lovely pink and smiling. At that moment she decided that Helga was the most beautiful girl in Wisconsin, and she felt like a lump in comparison, with her too-large hands and feet and her prominent chin. She glanced at James and saw he was looking at her, and her rush of self-consciousness increased. Her skirt was dusty, her boots a mess, her hair straggling. She wished it were a pretty shade of brown and not so red. Why was he sitting here with her? Surely he could find better company.

As if reading her thoughts, he got to his feet and looked down at her.

"I'd better head back to town. It's a good walk." He paused, and she squinted up at him against the sunset. "Niel Muller tells me there's a harvest dance on the first of September. Will you be going?"

She blinked. "Yes, I'd planned to. Everyone goes."

He smiled, and the light of it was reflected in his eyes. Her breath started doing funny things in her throat.

"I'll see you there, then. Save a few dances for me." He nodded at her and moved away with rolling, lanky strides. He moved like a racehorse, she thought, warming up for a run. She watched him until he disappeared around the house, and only then did it occur to her that she could have offered him a ride into town on their wagon. Then again, something told her that her parents would not have been pleased to share the Irishman's company.

On the way home, Hannah leaned against the side of the open buckboard as her neighbors' farms inched past. Helga, her legs tucked neatly underneath her, sat opposite, her eyes half open, a dreamy expression on her face. Hannah watched her, but her mind was jumping from thought to thought. Why had James told her to save him some dances? Was he just making polite conversation? Was he looking forward to meeting again as much as she was? Why did she even care what he was thinking? He was only ten years younger than her father. She knew she shouldn't even be thinking about James—Mr. McDonald. She aimed a scowl at her sister. Hannah was determined never to be as moony and silly as Helga was over Georg. The whole town knew they were sweet on each other. Hannah was mortified over it. She hoped her own feelings weren't so transparent. She resolutely fixed her thoughts on last Sunday's Bible passage for the rest of the ride home.

It was "pig ankle" stew again for supper, reheated and congealing in the pot. The potluck had been late in the day and filled them all, so Elsa didn't want to bother cooking anything new. Hannah spooned at it distastefully and wished her mother would buy a decent roast, or at least a ham to chop up and add to the cabbage. It wasn't that they couldn't afford it. "It's good for the soul to sacrifice," Elsa always said.

"Marta Schultz is getting married," Helga announced suddenly. As always, they spoke German at the table. Heinrich Wyse tolerated no English in the home. "She's marrying Thomas Werner in October, on a Tuesday. Isn't that an odd day to get married?"

"She can't be more than seventeen. What are her parents thinking?" Elsa Wyse exclaimed. She placed a tray of thick rye bread on the table and swatted Erik's hand away as he lunged for a piece.

"They're thinking how glad they are that they'll have one less mouth to feed," Heinrich replied. "I believe in having children, but fourteen would be a few too many for me."

"Speak no ill," Elsa intoned automatically. She took her place at the table and clasped her hands in front of her. Heinrich said the blessing on the food, but Hannah had to bite her lip to keep from laughing aloud. Even God himself couldn't do much for "pig ankle" stew.

Her good humor died as her father turned to arch an eyebrow at her and said, "I saw you had a companion at the picnic today."

There was instant, absolute silence in the kitchen. Hannah clasped her spoon tightly, not meeting her father's gaze.

"Well?" Heinrich asked gently.

"Yes. Mr. McDonald."

"How do you know him?"

"We've met once or twice. I sat down under the tree, and he joined me. There's nothing to worry about," Hannah said. "We were only talking."

"What were you talking about?"

Hannah shrugged. "He just told me a little about his travels and said that he wanted to settle down someday. It was nice."

Heinrich sighed. "Can't you see that it isn't appropriate for you to be alone with such a man?"

"We weren't alone. We were sitting in plain sight of the whole town."

"You know what I mean."

"No, I don't," Hannah replied, surprising herself. She had never spoken to her father in such a way. "It's not like I invited him. What should I have done, got up and walked away? That would have been rude."

"You watch your tone, Hannah."

Hannah felt the blood pound in her ears. Recklessly, she switched to English. "Helga was sitting with Georg, but it didn't bother you."

"Helga and Georg are nineteen, almost twenty. That man must be over thirty."

"What does his age matter?" Hannah tried not to shout. "Why don't you say what you really mean? He could be seventeen, but he still wouldn't do, because he's not German!"

"That's nonsense. There are many good people who aren't German. The Mulvad boy, for instance," Elsa said, spreading her hands. "Now he pays you attention at church, I've noticed."

"He's from Austria. It's next door!"

"Mind you, you may wear your hair up like a woman, but you're still a little girl, and I won't have such back talk in my house!" Heinrich roared, jabbing his fork in the air like a spear. Down the table, Erik's lip jutted out, and he began to whimper. Helga put a hand on his shoulder to hush him.

"But Papa, I don't understand. What's wrong with talking to Mr. McDonald? He asked if I would be at the dance. He's very nice."

"You are seventeen, and you are living under my roof. You will not dance with him, and if you are planning to, I will keep you at home."

"But that's—"

"I forbid you to talk to him! And I know he is working at the court-house construction site. You will not go near it. You are not to see that man again—do you understand?"

Keeping perfectly still, Hannah stared at her father's livid face. Then, very quietly, she stood and walked to the stairs and went up. Elsa looked at her husband for a long moment, then dropped her hands to her lap, slowly shaking her head.

* * *

Sunday was still and hot, autumn's last stand before the cold set in. It was still a week until October, but already the trees had begun to turn; the maples were first, their leaves rimmed with salmon and crimson. At the same time the golden fields were beginning to go gray and dull. In a burst of feverish activity that promised a hard winter, squirrels raided barns and silos and sometimes even kitchens when a window was left open.

James didn't attend church, holding himself apart from formal religion as a rule, but on the other hand, he didn't work on Sundays. So this morning he bypassed the half-built courthouse and walked along the river. It wasn't much to speak of as far as rivers went. He'd seen much better ones.

This water moved slow and brown through the town, its sluggish speed picking up slightly as it moved out into farm country, flowing over smooth amber stones under overhanging willows and oaks. He wasn't much for walks, but today he strode along the riverbank, because *she* had said that this was where she went to think.

When he had left the town behind him, he sat down at the water's edge, removed his boots and stockings, and, rolling up his pant legs to the knee, dangled his bare feet in the water. The shock of the cold water instantly brought back memories of wading in the irrigation ditch behind his house as a boy. His sister Isabel would always sit daintily on the bank, with only her feet in the water, but he would wade in up to the waist, chasing water skeeters. Mud would squelch between his toes, cold in the shade, warmer in the sunlight. He would catch up water in cupped hands to fling at Isabel, who squealed and threatened. She never whined to Mama, though, except for the time James had gripped her by both ankles and pulled her all the way in. That time she'd really been mad, because of her wet dress, and Dad had made sure James couldn't sit for a few days. But most of the time Isabel had been a good sport. He missed her on lazy days like this. He missed her laughter and teasing and just the comfort of being near her. He looked forward to seeing her again . . . one day. He wasn't ready to go back home. Not yet.

There were water skeeters here, too, dancing across the slow-moving surface of the river. James kicked droplets at them and watched them zigzag away like tipsy spiders. A bird he didn't recognize was singing somewhere in the distance. The willow above him stretched its slim tendrils to dip in the water, like a delicate woman testing her bath. He leaned back on the bank, his hands behind his head, his eyes half closed, musing. Memories of Isabel melted into thoughts of the bright-haired German girl who had similar sparkling eyes and an impish smile. He imagined what it would feel like to touch her hair, push his fingers through it, bury his face in it. Would it feel as hot to the touch as it looked? He smiled to himself at the whimsical notion. And then, like a spirit summoned from his thoughts, Hannah appeared on the bank a few feet from him. He wasn't even surprised to see her. It just seemed right, somehow—a natural extension of the peaceful setting.

"I haven't seen you for a while," he said. "You weren't at the dance. I looked for you."

She stepped forward until she was standing above him. She looked very serious.

"Did you?"

"I ended up just going home," he said slowly. "There was no one else I wanted to dance with."

"I'm sorry. My father kept me at home."

"Why?"

Her chin went up. "I told him I intended to dance with you. I—I would have liked to."

He studied her a moment, then sat up. "And he objected to that, I take it?"

"He has forbidden me to see or speak to you."

He looked at her beautiful face, her parted lips, her hair lying loose in a red tumble on her shoulders. The sun was behind her, making the airy wisps of her untamed hair glow like sparks from a fire. He looked directly into her eyes and held her gaze.

"But you're here anyway," he said quietly.

* * *

Hannah arrived home before her family returned from church, and hurried up to her room. She had pled a stomachache that morning to avoid accompanying them. She quickly undressed and hid her damp boots under the bed. Then she curled up under the quilt and let her limbs sink into the soft feather tick. Her mind was a montage of bright sunlight, amber water, and James McDonald. She wrapped her arms about herself as if to protect the bubble of contentment and happiness rising in her chest. As sleep approached, the thought came to her, *What beautiful children we will have!* And she laughed.

CHAPTER 5

2005

"Lamaze classes? Don't waste your money, sis," Abbie said, shifting the toddler on her lap and reaching for another graham cracker.

"Didn't you take them?" Rose asked.

"The first time, with Jeremy, I did." Abbie grinned. Tall and slender in spite of her rambunctious brood, she had green eyes and a captivating smile. "Remember the old earthquake drills we used to have to do in school when we were kids? They'd make you curl up under your desk with your hands on your head, and that was supposed to magically stop a thousand tons of concrete from falling on your head. Really it was just a way to keep control of thirty panicked children. To make you feel like you could do something about an impossible situation. Lamaze classes are like that. A distraction, a trick to make you think you're in control and taking action while you're waiting for the ton of concrete to hit you."

Rose rubbed her barely bulging stomach, looking slightly alarmed. "Thanks for the encouragement, Abbie. I really appreciate it."

Abbie waved a hand and rescued the soggy graham cracker from her son's cream-white hair. "You'll get through it fine. The first one's easiest, actually. You don't know what you're in for. The second one, you go in with your eyes wide open."

Daniel saw Rose's face turn slightly pale. He reached over and massaged her shoulder, then gave his sister-in-law a meaningful look. "Maybe we should change the topic, Abbie."

Abbie laughed and set her son on the floor. "I should pack up my gang and get home anyway. It's Cub Scouts tonight, and I'm supposed to bring something for the bake sale."

"Making cupcakes?" Rose asked.

"Buying doughnuts. What, do you think I'm nuts?"

Rose laughed and got up to walk her sister to the door. Daniel followed. He paused by a narrow table in the hall, an antique Rose had picked up for next to nothing in a yard sale. She had refinished it with care, stripping off the hideous white enamel to reveal a delicious honey-colored mahogany underneath. She had burnished it to a wonderful soft finish and spread a lace runner on it to protect the top. It held a place of pride, just inside the door where it could be seen first by visitors. But because of its convenient location, it had unfortunately become the collecting spot for car keys, mail, newspapers, and wallets. Daniel picked up the day's mail. The top envelope looked like junk mail ("Opening this envelope could change your life!"), but the one under it was a familiar purple. Patricia always bought zany stationery. He hardly registered the fact that Abbie and her kids were going. As soon as the door closed, he tore the envelope open.

"What's that?" Rose peered over his shoulder at the single sheet of yellowed paper.

"It's from Patricia Dempsey. It's something my mother wrote down before she died. Patricia forgot she had it until a couple of weeks ago."

He carried the piece of paper carefully to the kitchen table under the light, a feeling of excitement beginning to spread over him. In careful, tense cursive—he assumed it was his mother's handwriting—it said:

> James Carlton McDonald Jr. had six brothers and sisters somewhere back east. He was raised by Jacob and Theresa Zahlmann in Helena, Montana, after his mother died.

And that was it. Two weeks of checking the mail and that was it. The only words his mother had felt compelled to write down and pass on before the cancer took her. He felt irrationally angry. Couldn't she have written down his father's birth date and birth place? Hadn't she known his siblings' names?

"That's terrific," Rose said cheerily, leaning over to see. "It gives you a lead. It says 'Junior,' so now you know his father's name, your grandfather. And the Zahlmanns. I wonder if they still live in Helena?"

Daniel shook himself. Of course she was right. What had he expected, a four-generation family tree? It was a clue, and he was good at following clues. He carefully tucked the paper into his wallet and gave Rose a kiss on the cheek.

"It's a step," she said, smiling. "What do you think of the name Carlton for the baby if it's a boy?"

"Over my dead body," he replied lightly and went into his study.

Seated at his desk, he pulled out a sheet of legal-sized paper and wrote at the top, "James Carlton McDonald." He drew a blank line next to it, for James's unknown wife. Then he sketched a quick chart below the two names with seven columns. In the first column he put the same name—his father's name—followed by Caroline Jenkins, his mother's name. Below them he wrote "Charles," "Isabel," and "Daniel." He looked at the six blank columns, wondering if he would ever be able to fill them in. He put the paper in one of the desk's drawers, under some newspapers. He didn't want Rose to see it. Her family, being of hardy Mormon pioneer stock and English heritage, had traced their history practically back to the Iron Age. He felt a little foolish with his pitiful blank chart.

* * *

Directory Assistance gave him four Zahlmanns living in Helena, none of whom had the initial J. But he realized that, realistically, Jacob and Theresa had probably passed away some time ago. They'd be a hundred by now. But maybe, he thought, a descendant would still be around.

C. Zahlmann had never heard of Jacob or Theresa. L. Zahlmann spoke little English, and since Daniel's German was nonexistent, that ended that call. M. Zahlmann had an answering machine, which informed him that the Zahlmanns were out of the country until December and wouldn't be picking up messages but that he was welcome to contact their business partner Peter Townbridge at the shop. S. Zahlmann answered on the first ring, a cheery female voice.

"Jacob and Theresa? Of course. They're my husband's grandparents. Who is this again?"

"Daniel McDonald. I'm calling from Denver. I'm so glad to reach you." Now that he had the right Zahlmann on the phone, he wasn't sure what to say. He felt suddenly shy. "I don't know if you can help me. I'm trying to find out about a boy they had staying with them back in—I don't know—I guess the 1940s or 50s. His name was Jim McDonald. James."

"Oh. A relative of yours?"

"He was my father. I'm trying to trace the family . . ." he added lamely. She was going to think he was nuts. But instead she brightly asked him to wait a moment, and he could hear her talking to someone in the room. A male voice rumbled a response, and then she returned to the phone.

"My husband says his grandparents took in foster children. Strays, you know. Could he have been one of them?"

"Yes. His mother died, and that's when the Zahlmanns took him in."

"That's it, then."

"Does your husband know anything about Jim McDonald? Does he remember him?"

"Oh, he wouldn't. Steve wasn't born until 1962. His dad would have remembered, but he died last year. Triple bypass. It was a shock."

"I'm sorry." Daniel felt his hopes begin to sink into his stomach. "Well, thanks anyway."

"Wait, why don't you just ask Grandma?"

"I—you mean Theresa Zahlmann?"

"Yes. She's not too quick on her feet these days, but her mind is still sharp as a tack. I always thought that would be the worst, to have your mind go first, but I'm starting to think it's worse to have your mind perfectly fine and your body not able to keep up."

"Theresa's still alive?"

"That's what I'm telling you. Grandma is in a nursing home now. We had to put her there two years ago for her own safety. She was always falling or setting fire to the hot pads or accidentally shutting the cat in the fridge. She's ninety-three, you know. Finally had to give up her driver's license. But she could tell you some stories, I'm sure. She remembers everything."

"That's terrific. Could I get her phone number and address?"

She gave him the information. "I hope you find what you're looking for. My name is Ellen, by the way," she added. "And good luck talking to Grandma on the phone. She's a bit hard of hearing. But that's to be expected, especially after the stroke."

After he hung up, Daniel thought for a moment and then went into the kitchen. Rose was clearing away the last of supper, tortellini with porcini mushroom sauce. As her appetite increased, Rose was exploring new concoctions and trying ingredients she'd never used before. Last night it had been fried plantains. Daniel hadn't realized just how many items in the grocery store he didn't even recognize, much less purchase. He watched her for a moment from the doorway as she moved between table and sink, humming. Her light hair was bunched up with a butterfly clip, and her feet were pushed into fuzzy red slippers. He thought she looked adorable but refrained from saying so. She didn't like being told she was cute when she was feeling fat (as if that tiny bulge counted as fat!). Instead he kissed her on the back of the neck and announced, "I think I need to go to Montana."

She turned to look at him, the empty broccoli bowl in her hands. "Montana? What for?"

"I found the woman who raised Dad. She's in a nursing home, ninety-three years old, and hard of hearing. I don't know if I can have the conversation I need to have with her over the phone. I feel like it should happen in person."

Rose considered a moment, then nodded. "I can understand that. And I can understand why you might be in a bit of a hurry if she's that old." She grinned.

"Do you mind?"

"Of course not," Rose said, reminding him why he'd fallen in love with her and making him fall all over again. "Besides," she added, wiggling her eyebrows, "maybe you can get an article out of it and count it as a business expense."

CHAPTER 6

1915

The next two months were a flurry of activity, but only two people were caught up in the rush. James laid bricks like a man possessed, causing his fellow workers to lift their eyebrows. But the walls grew steadily higher, well before schedule, and no one was about to complain if James seemed a little too focused. He was working as quickly as possible so that he could collect his pay and go.

Hannah, as far as her family could tell, had resigned herself to obedience and had turned her attention to domestic pursuits—tending her brothers, helping her mother cook, and sewing at her embroidery in the evenings. She practiced her knitting, which she had never mastered and didn't enjoy, and even began cutting squares for a quilt top from scraps her mother didn't have time to deal with. Elsa, pleased with her daughter's new interest in domestic things, was encouraging and began to think the potential crisis was past. Hannah was so young, after all, and still trusted her parents to make her decisions for her. Heinrich wasn't convinced, but his child seemed content as she went about the house, so he left the situation alone.

Hannah was stockpiling. Her trousseau, of course, was virtually nonexistent, as she hadn't planned on needing one soon. But as James's walls were rising, so was the collection stored under her bed. While practicing her sewing, she finished two dish towels, two pillowcases, the patchwork quilt, and some clothing for herself. She wanted to tat a lace tablecloth, but she knew there wasn't time, so she embroidered a plain one and comforted herself with tatting three doilies instead. She went to Marta Schultz's wedding in October and examined the trousseau displayed there. Her own seemed terribly lacking. But Marta was going to live in her mother-in-law's home. Hannah didn't know where she and James would be going, and it would be foolish to cart too much with them. She comforted herself with this thought and dreamed about how she would adorn their future home once they were settled. For he would settle down, eventually. He'd told her so.

On November first she turned eighteen. When Hannah awoke that morning, she went straight to the mirror and studied her reflection. She searched for some difference, some new maturity, but the same face stared impatiently back at her, oval and ordinary. She gathered up her hair and held it in a bun at the back of her head. She thought it made her look somewhat older, but not as much as she would have liked. Sighing, she dressed and went down to breakfast. There was a brown-paper parcel lying on her chair.

"Happy birthday," Elsa said, kissing her cheek.

"Well, don't stand there," Wilhelm ordered, poking her in the back. "Open it."

The family gathered around as Hannah pulled back the paper to reveal a lovely pink cotton dress. There were mother-of-pearl buttons and white store-bought lace at the wrists and throat. She immediately thought, *I'll wear it at my wedding!* And then it hit her. She was going away and leaving all these people who cared for her. She looked at her mother with tears in her eyes. Elsa smiled and touched Hannah's hair tenderly. Then she turned away to retrieve the eggs and sausages from the stove. Hannah took the dress upstairs and carefully laid it out on her bed before returning to the kitchen.

That afternoon, after she took her father's lunch to the shop, she daringly detoured to the town square on her way home. The courthouse rose like a great red block before her. It was solid and substantial and somehow reassuring. There were only a couple of feet left to go on the brick walls, and men were noisily at work on the interior. Hannah spied James sitting alone in the shade under one wall and went to join him. He brightened when he saw her approach and tossed away the apple he had been eating.

"Hey there." He brushed off a plank, and she sat beside him, her hands clasped in her lap. "You're eighteen."

She tried not to look smug. "Yes."

"Happy birthday."

"Thank you," she replied, meeting his gaze.

"It's almost finished, see? Two or three more days," he said. "They're finishing the floors and trim. I get my last pay on Friday morning."

"I can't believe it's almost here. This has been the longest eight weeks . . ."

James chuckled, crumpled the paper that had wrapped his sandwich, and tossed it away after the apple core.

"Friday afternoon we'll go to Briar Creek. The judge there doesn't know us. If we did it here, word would be back to your parents before the 'I do' was out of your mouth."

"I know. How will we get there? Do you have a wagon?"

"My friend Niel has agreed to take us."

"You told him?" she asked sharply.

"We'll need witnesses," he went on in a lower voice. "Niel and his wife. It's all right—they'll keep quiet."

"And then what?" she asked. "Where then?"

He took her hand in his. It was rough with his work and so large that her own hand seemed lost in it. "I've heard they always need bricklayers in Madison. We'll go there. There's an evening train from Briar Creek straight to Madison."

"That's fine." She stood up and looked down at him. "Friday afternoon, then."

He grinned. "Two o'clock sharp."

"I'll meet you here."

She gently pulled her hand free and walked away, and he watched her go with glittering eyes. He raised his flask in salute as she disappeared around the corner. "To Friday," he murmured. "I must be crazy." He emptied the flask.

* * *

Friday morning Hannah woke at dawn and lay in bed, watching the light warm the room to a rosy glow. She gazed around at all her familiar belongings—the frayed blue rag rug, the mirror she and Helga fought over, her sewing basket. She glanced over at Helga's lumpy bed, and a flash of sympathy came over her. Poor Helga, so goose-eyed over lanky, boyish Georg. Was that any future to look forward to? She shook her head, then rolled out of bed, pulled on her brown muslin, and went down to help with breakfast.

The morning went as any other morning. The boys squabbled over who got the most omelet. Helga complained that her hair wasn't curly like Anna Stollard's. Elsa bustled with the dishes because she had a Ladies' Aid meeting at Beate Woolner's that morning. Heinrich kissed each of his children and picked up his hat. Hannah watched him and wondered if he would be very angry when she didn't come with his lunch tin. Impulsively, she ran and hugged him at the door.

"What is this, now?" Heinrich chuckled, his hand on her hair.

"Nothing, only good-bye, Papa," she said in German. "Have a good day." Hannah quickly went to the sink and began drying the dishes.

One by one the family members departed for their various destinations. Wilhelm and Erik, who were still in school, went running out to join their friends, with Elsa calling after them to button their coats because the air was icy. Helga pulled on her own coat and went to see a friend who had a new Sears Roebuck catalog. Hannah watched her go, then turned from the window. Only her mother was left.

Elsa was giving her hair a final, firm pat in the mirror by the door. "You'll be sure to get yourself lunch? You're skin and bones. There's bratwurst and cheese and pickles—"

"Yes, Mother," Hannah said.

"Your father's lunch is already packed."

"I know."

"And will you put the dishes away?" Elsa added, throwing her shawl over her hair.

"Yes, Mother, I will."

"What will you do with yourself today?"

"I need to finish the book I borrowed from Berta Kohler."

Elsa paused. "I'll be home in time to fix supper."

"It's all right, Mother. I'm not a child. Go."

Elsa smiled and walked out the door. Hannah leaned back against the drainboard, closed her eyes, and waited for the tears to come. When they didn't, she put the dishes away and went upstairs. It was going to be a long wait until two o'clock.

Four hours later, dressed in her new pink dress, her hair in a slightly awkward bun, she paused to survey herself in the mirror one last time. She was pleased with the face she saw. She looked more calm than she felt. She put on her coat and gloves, picked up the blanket bundle containing her few belongings, and stepped out of the house.

* * *

Judge Warren had been a lawyer in Briar Creek for many years. He had handled many interesting and distinguished cases in his career. Since becoming a judge he had performed over forty weddings and figured he had seen about all there was to see in the sleepy town. But as he stood in his office with the late-afternoon sunlight shafting through the windows, he doubted he had ever faced a couple quite like this before. They seemed a most unlikely pair. The groom was tall, keen-eyed, and lean. He had a sharp look about him, as if he weren't completely at ease with his own thoughts. He wore work clothes, the dust hastily brushed from them, the line from his hat still clear across his high forehead. The girl wasn't much more than a child, wide-eyed and soft-skinned, with hair the color of the devil's trousers and a determined tilt to her chin. She said she was eighteen, but he wasn't too sure about that. They had no family in attendance, a suspicious thing in itself. A leather-skinned brickie and his startled-looking wife were to act as witnesses. It all seemed rather unusual to Judge Warren. But they'd paid their fee, and no one appeared to be objecting. Ah, well, it wouldn't be the first elopement he had assisted.

"Your full name please?"

"James Carlton McDonald."

"And the bride?"

"Hannah Louisa Wyse," the girl answered.

* * *

The ceremony was over quickly, the register signed and duly witnessed. It was not the parish register, Hannah thought with a strange twinge as she signed her name, but then, it would not have done to get married in the church. For one thing, the minister knew her parents. And besides, James wasn't a Lutheran. Hannah stood clutching James's hand, uncertain what to do next. James shook hands all around and thanked the judge. Then he led her out to Niel's carriage, and Niel and his tight-lipped wife drove them to the station, which was little more than a two-room shed tucked back from the tracks.

No one was out at this hour of the evening in November, but Hannah still felt like thousands of eyes were upon her as she rode along beside James in the back seat. Surely anyone looking at her would be able to tell what she had just done. Luckily the platform was empty but for the man who sat and smoked in the warm office and gave them their tickets with hardly a glance before closing the windows against the chilly air. Hannah and James shook hands with Niel, and the wagon creaked away, leaving them and their bundles on the platform.

They sat close together on the bench and waited. Hannah pulled her coat tightly around her neck and managed a small laugh. "We should have run away in warmer weather. Winter's coming fast."

James placed his arm about her shoulders. "We have a bit of a wait. We'll warm you up just fine, soon as we reach our rooming house."

In spite of herself, she blushed, and he laughed. Quickly she changed the direction of the conversation.

"Annie Muller certainly didn't look pleased to be a witness. I thought she was going to bite her lip clean through."

James chuckled. "Niel will keep her quiet until we're well on our way."

* * *

The six-thirty train finally pulled into the station, belching white clouds and hissing like a monstrous snake. Before Hannah had a chance to think, she found herself tucked into a hard seat against the window with her belongings packed in the storage compartment and James grinning beside her.

"Never been on a train before?" he asked, seeing her tense face.

"No."

"Relax. You'll enjoy it." He leaned down and kissed her. "The faster it goes, the sooner we'll be in Madison."

Hannah quickly looked around, but there was only one other passenger, a dozing middle-aged man four seats away. James grinned at her again and leaned back, pulling his cap over his eyes.

"Settle back. It won't go any faster if you lean forward."

Hannah tried to relax, but the sight of the fields flashing by her window and the feel of the train moving beneath her was unnerving. Each clack of the wheels took her farther and farther from Cobb. Her mother would be home by now. She would see Papa's lunch tin and be angry that Hannah hadn't delivered it. By suppertime she would be worried. By nightfall she would be frantic and would send her father out to search. But Niel would tell them she was all right. They would be shocked, perhaps, and certainly furious. Helga would be indignant. Her brothers—would they miss her? She missed them already.

Impatiently she pushed away all thoughts of her family and concentrated on the present and future. She was Mrs. James McDonald, on her way to Madison. She was actually on a train, hurtling through Wisconsin. It was the grand adventure she'd dreamed about, and she would enjoy every last moment of it. They would find a room, James would find work, and perhaps she would too. One day they would be able to afford their own house. She would remember every detail of this trip and write it all down for her children to read someday. This last thought caused her spine to tingle and a light to spring into her eyes. She was vague on the whole process of having children, but she liked them and imagined she'd have five or six. But not right away. She was well aware she had some growing up to do herself. Of course she hadn't discussed such things with James. She didn't know how many children he wanted. Come to think of it, there were many things she didn't know about him. But rather than frighten her, this fact only caused excitement within her. She smiled at the thought of discovering, bit by bit, just who James McDonald was.

CHAPTER 7

Daniel was on the first flight out Friday morning. Because he worked primarily from home and because he had no urgent projects at the moment, he didn't figure his employer would even notice he was gone. He'd be back by Sunday, he told himself. Just a quick jaunt. Just a few questions.

He found a Best Western near the airport, dropped his overnight bag on the bed of his nondescript room, and went right back out again. Armed with notebook, tape recorder, and three pens, he hailed a cab and gave the driver Ellen Zahlmann's address. When he'd called to tell her that he was coming to Montana, she'd insisted he stop by the house first to meet her and her husband, Steve. They lived in what turned out to be a townhouse, a cheerful yellow brick and so narrow he wondered how they fit beds in the bedrooms. He paid the cab driver and stood a moment looking up at the house, trying to calm the excitement rising in him. It was hard to believe he was here, in a state he hadn't visited since he'd moved from Montana to Colorado as a child. He was soon to meet the woman who probably knew his father better than anyone else now living. He only hoped her memory was as intact as Ellen had assured him it was. He went up the steep cement steps, skirted a pair of boots on the doorstep, and rang the bell.

Ellen Zahlmann was as cheery and bouncy in person as she'd sounded on the phone. Her white-blond hair was pulled into a pink scrunchie, and her glasses were so big they looked more like motorcycle windshields. She wore a green pin-striped tent dress that made her look as if she were about to go out to the playground to skip rope. She seized his hand and practically yanked him into the living room.

"We're so glad to meet you," she said as her husband rose from the green-and-white striped couch to shake Daniel's hand. Steve Zahlmann was nearly as tall as Daniel, had short buzzed hair, and was built like a football player. His midriff was beginning to spread, but his grip hurt Daniel's fingers.

"So you want to talk to Grandma, do you?" He laughed. "Has Ellie warned you about her?"

Ellen poked her husband in the ribs. "Be nice. She's a sweet old thing, but she does have difficulty taking care of herself now, and we really couldn't keep her with us anymore. But we found a great place for her. Please sit down. Would you like something to drink?"

"No, thanks, I'm fine." Daniel sat down in an armchair, realized he was sitting on something sharp, and stood again. A plastic action figure—dragon? Pegasus?—was stuffed into the crack of the seat. Ellen snatched it up.

"Oh, Pete's been looking for that. Sorry. Sure you don't want something?"

Daniel declined again and sat down. Steve Zahlmann plopped back onto the sofa, arms draped along the back of it, and smiled at him. Daniel couldn't help but think that Steve looked completely out of place in the delicate pink-and-green living room with its crocheted curtains and bowl of white roses on the coffee table. It was like sitting in an Easter basket. He wondered vaguely if the rest of the house looked like this room. It was as if Ellen Zahlmann had dressed to match her interior decorating. Or perhaps he had it backwards, and she'd chosen the flowery wallpaper and pink carpet to match her own taste in clothes. Hadn't someone once told him that Frank Lloyd Wright had designed dresses that women were supposed to wear in the homes he'd also designed?

Ellen settled in a pink wingback chair and absentmindedly cradled the action figure in the crook of her elbow, like a baby.

"How was your flight? Okay?" she asked.

"Yes, thanks. Not long," said Daniel.

"No, Denver isn't that far. You've been to Denver before, haven't you, Steve?"

"Twice, I think. Conventions. I sell flooring."

Daniel nodded and tried hard not to stare at the rose-pink carpet under his feet.

"What do you do, Daniel?"

"I write for a small newspaper. Articles about special interest stuff. Nothing too exciting."

"Oh, you have a regular column or something?"

"Not really, I'm just a staff reporter. They give me assignments," Daniel said, waving a dismissive hand. At the moment he couldn't even think of anything he'd written about lately. His mind was buzzing with the questions he wanted to ask Theresa Zahlmann.

"It's kind of exciting, you finding us like this," Steve said. "Imagine, your dad was one of Grandma and Grandpa's foster kids. I grew up hearing stories about them. Just mischief they got into, and things like that. I remember Dad telling us about how one of them burned down a neighbor's shed once."

"Not my father, I hope," Daniel said, smiling tightly.

"I'm sure it wasn't," Ellen said. She suddenly seemed to realize she was rocking the action figure and set it down on the coffee table. "Will you come for supper tonight? We'd love to have you."

"Thanks, that's nice of you. I fly back on Sunday morning. I got a room at the Best Western by the airport, so it would be close." He knew he was beginning to fidget. These people seemed very nice and probably meant well, but he was anxious to get on with things. He consciously relaxed his hands, spread his fingers out on his knees, and resigned himself to the conversation.

"We found a really nice place for Grandma," Ellen told him, as if afraid he disapproved of their stashing Granny in a home. "It's not like your usual nursing home, all long hallways and bare green tile. It's—what's that word the lady used?"

"Innovative," Steve said.

"That's it. They tried to design it to look like you're walking down Main Street in a small town instead of down a hallway. They have park benches along the walls so the old folks can sit and rest if they can't make it all the way down in one go." Ellen giggled, seeming to find this funny. Daniel found it rather sad to think of someone being so decrepit she couldn't make it from one end of a hallway to another.

"They built the whole thing around a central square, like a town marketplace," Steve said. "There are shops where they can get their hair done or buy little things, a mini bandstand where musicians sometimes perform, and street lights like you'd find outside. They even color-coded the halls and put up street signs so residents can find their way around without getting too disoriented."

"That is smart," Daniel admitted, interested in spite of himself. Maybe he could get an article out of this after all, as Rose had joked. It certainly sounded like an improvement on typical nursing homes. The few he'd visited had long, endless hallways with industrial linoleum floors. Each bedroom door had looked like the next, and the common rooms had been filled with cracked orange vinyl chairs and Formica tables.

"Grandma's waiting to meet you," Steve added. "We thought we'd better phone ahead and warn her she's having company. She doesn't like to be caught in her bathrobe. Whenever you're ready to go, we can take my car. It's just a few blocks away."

Daniel jumped to his feet and tried to arrange his face not to look too eager. "Thanks, that's great of you. I'm looking forward to talking to her."

* * *

Ellen walked the two of them to the door, explaining that she would stay behind to watch Pete and get supper started. Steve's car was exactly what Daniel would have expected: a black SUV with extra chrome and tinted windows. Steve backed it carefully out of the mini garage, somehow avoiding the tricycle, garbage can, hanging tools, and chest freezer crammed around it.

From the outside the nursing home was an ordinary low, redbrick building on the edge of a park. There were tall pine trees planted around it, and a sweeping cement walk led in a gentle slope to the extra-wide front door to accommodate wheelchairs. Some optimistic person had plunked marigolds under the pine trees, but they weren't doing well in the acidic soil. Daniel followed Steve in and was pleasantly surprised to find that the smell all nursing homes and hospitals seem to have—a mixture of cleaner, ammonia, and stale urine—was happily missing here. Instead, strangely, he could smell bread baking.

They came to what looked more like a counter in an ice cream parlor than a reception desk. Daniel suddenly wondered if he should have brought the old lady flowers. Steve cleared his throat, and the receptionist looked up from her book.

"We're here to see Theresa Zahlmann, please."

"Hi, Mr. Zahlmann. I'll let her know you're here." Her hand hovered over the phone, and she looked at Daniel with interest. "And your name, please?"

"Daniel McDonald."

The woman punched a button, waited, and then said in a loud, clear voice, "Tess, you have some gentlemen here to see you."

Through the receiver a sharp voice commanded, "Send them in!"

"But honey, I haven't told you who—"

"Any gentleman caller is welcome at my age, you ninny. Send them in!"

The receptionist set down the phone and said with a grin, "She'll see you now."

It felt like he was being ushered into the presence of the lady of the manor. Daniel followed Steve down a hallway with cobblestone-patterned flooring and saw immediately that the Zahlmanns' description of the nursing home had been accurate. He felt as if he were walking along a country road instead of a hallway. White wooden benches stood at intervals along the walls, which were painted with country landscapes. The ceiling was painted a swirling baby blue and white to simulate a summer sky. He noticed that the doors that opened on the left side of the hallway were all slightly recessed and that wooden railings stood halfway across the ingresses, serving a dual purpose: handrails for feeble residents, and the look of a front porch for each room. He thought the idea was terrific. Some of the homey "porches" even held rocking chairs or pots of geraniums. They passed a woman sitting on one of the benches, knitting with fuzzy blue wool.

To the right, the wall ended and opened up into a common courtyard the size of a school gymnasium. He could see the bunting-draped bandstand and a Baroque-looking fountain. Tall iron poles with arms held hanging baskets of impatiens and trailing lobelia. There were café tables and chairs at one end of the courtyard, where three white-haired women were sipping from teacups and chatting. Two men a short distance away played a game of chess at a table beneath a fifteen-foot potted tree. Brightly painted signs announced the locations of the hairdresser, the Dollar Shop, the library, the games room, the spa, and the bakery, from which heavenly cinnamon smells were wafting. Sun shone through the multiple skylights in the high ceiling. Daniel considered putting himself on the waiting list now.

He turned to see Steve waiting for him, smiling.

"Not bad, is it?" he said.

"Not at all," Daniel agreed. "I might have to write something up for the newspaper about this place. It's a well-kept secret. Do you know who the designers are?"

"A Canadian group called Mekinda Snyder Partnership. They ordered their flooring from me." Steve nodded at the floor of the courtyard, which looked like flagstone but smoother, without the bumpy seams that could trip an elderly person.

"It's brilliant."

Looking pleased, Steve turned into the next hallway bordering the plaza. This one had creamy Italian tile on the floor, and the walls were painted to look like a row of San Francisco townhouses. There was even a glimpse of the bay farther on. A street sign announced that they had arrived at Myrtle Avenue.

"Named after one of the residents," Steve explained. "She turned a hundred the year they built the place, so they called it after her. Here we are."

Certain now that he should have brought flowers, Daniel followed him into room 13B Myrtle Avenue.

The room faced east, the sunlight streaming in to brighten the blue-painted walls and flowered bedspread. A vase of pink roses the size of base-balls took up the entire bedside table, perfuming the air, and Daniel relaxed. Any flowers he might have found at a corner grocery store would have paled in comparison.

It was a private room, he saw with approval. Though the layout was like an ordinary room in any nursing home, a bit cramped—with the closet and bathroom door opposite the bed—the similarity ended there. There was a squashy armchair and an oak bookcase in the corner. The floor was soft cork, easy to clean but nicer on the feet than tile or linoleum. The bedside table was also oak, and though the bed was an iron hospital bed, the quilt on it was a beautiful bright patchwork. A bulletin board near the bed was jammed with photos, mostly of children. He saw Ellen's and Steve's faces among them. A glance at the bookshelf told him Mrs. Zahlmann had a taste for crime fiction of the more gory variety. The bed was neatly made, the pillow uncrushed, and Theresa Zahlmann was nowhere to be seen.

"Grandma?" Steve called.

The bathroom door opened and she came out.

Daniel wasn't sure what he had expected. From Ellen's description he had pictured Theresa Zahlmann as tiny and frail, perhaps in a wheelchair, her hair in one of those invisible nets old women used to hide the fact that they were balding. This woman looked ready to ride out with the Valkyries.

She was nearly his height, a height most women didn't reach much less keep in their old age. Her hair was thick and white and as sculpted on her head as plaster of Paris. Chunky red earrings weighted her almost translucent earlobes, and her bright red caftan was belted tightly around a plump waist. She walked carefully, as if concentrating on her balance, but her eyes were a clear gray as she gazed at him. He'd never seen such a wrinkled face, but he suspected the wrinkles had come from being outdoors much of her life, not just from age. He imagined that she had looked much the same at sixty.

"Hi, Grandma."

She tilted her cheek for Steve's kiss, but her eyes stayed on Daniel. "Hi, Steve. Who have you brought me?"

Daniel put out his hand. Her grip was stronger than he'd expected. He caught a whiff of vanilla perfume.

"Daniel McDonald," he said. "You don't know me."

"You're right," she said. "I don't know you. But your eyes look familiar. Have I seen you before?"

"This is the fellow from Denver," Steve said. "Remember I called you last night to say he was coming?"

"You didn't come all this way just to see me, did you?" She sat down smoothly in the armchair. Daniel stood awkwardly before her, like a boy in front of the principal.

"I did, actually," he said.

"I don't have any other chairs," she told him. "But please make yourself comfortable on the bed."

Daniel hesitated, then sat carefully on the edge, afraid of rumpling the military-tight cover.

"How are Ellen and Peter?" Theresa asked her grandson. From the way she said it, Daniel suspected she asked more out of courtesy than interest.

"They're good. I'll bring them to see you next week."

"Tell them hello for me. Did you see my roses?"

"Yes, they're beautiful," Steve said.

"They're from that Mr. Watson down in 42A." She arched one eyebrow at Daniel. "I have an admirer. He's not a bad looker when he has his teeth in."

Daniel tried hard to keep his face straight. Theresa smoothed the caftan on her knees.

"So, Daniel McDonald from Denver, do you live in that city just for the alliteration?"

He couldn't help grinning. "Thank you for seeing me. I have some questions I'd like to ask you."

She thoughtfully pursed her lips a moment, then nodded regally at Steve. "There are fresh cinnamon rolls at the bakery. Go get yourself some to take home."

Steve rolled his eyes at Daniel. "I know when I'm not wanted. Give me a whistle when you're done. I'll be playing chess in the plaza."

"*Piazza,*" Theresa said.

Daniel watched Steve go out, amused. He turned back to see Theresa watching him carefully.

"My grandson says your father was one of our foster sons years ago."

"Yes, I think he was. I wanted to see if you might remember something that will help me. I'm looking for information about him. His name was James Carlton McDonald."

"Yes. We called him Jimmy." She looked at him with new interest, sitting up straighter. "I thought those eyes looked familiar. Now that I really look at you, I can see they're just like his. Cool as ice. I'd forgotten his eyes."

"You remember him, then?"

"Of course I do. He lived with us for six years, from 1940 to 1946. I remember because he was mad that he wasn't going to be old enough to fight in the war. So when he was fifteen and it looked like the war was about to end without him, he lied about his age and went to sign up."

"He didn't!"

"He did. Joined the army. Of course we didn't know anything about it until they brought him home two days later. I don't know how he hoped to pass himself off as eighteen. He was tall, but he was baby-faced and skinny as a rail. Scrawnier than you."

"Is that right?" The idea of his father heading out to enlist at fifteen tickled him somehow.

"He wasn't content to stay at home after that, though," Theresa added thoughtfully. "He left at sixteen, that would be 1946, and we never heard anything more about him. Some of our kids kept in touch with us over the years, but never him. So you tell me, where did he end up? What did he do with his life? Something big, I bet. He was always a go-getter."

Daniel swallowed, not sure what to say. He didn't want to burst her bubble, but those sharp gray eyes demanded the truth.

"He married my mother in 1959, and they had three kids, Charlie and Isabel and me."

"What did he do for a living? Did he end up in Colorado?" Theresa asked.

"I don't know what he did for a living. I—I get the impression he didn't really work. I know Mom was always struggling for money. He—he left when I was five."

She continued watching him. Her expression didn't change, but she gave a sharp nod. "Ran again, did he? Somehow I'm not surprised. He had a tendency to do that."

"I haven't heard from him in thirty years. I don't know if he's still alive," Daniel added, hoping he didn't sound as plaintive as he felt.

"So that's why you came to see me. You want to know what he was like."

"Yes."

"Couldn't you ask your own mother?"

"She died two years after he left. Uterine cancer. Her cousin raised me and my sister. My older brother Charlie took off when he was seventeen. I think he went to look for my dad and tell him about Mom, but . . . I haven't heard from him since then either."

"It's a family trait, then, this wandering away."

"I suppose so." He tried not to squirm.

Theresa Zahlmann gave a philosophical shrug. "I'm sorry to hear it, but it's not the first time in history a man has left his family, and it won't be the last. But for your sake, I'm sorry. Jimmy was a good kid, but a handful. Rambunctious, my husband used to call him."

"He wasn't the one who burned down the shed, was he?" Daniel asked wryly.

She laughed, a great shout of a sound. "Steve told you about that, I suppose. No, that was Mike Marsden who did that. But I wouldn't be surprised if I learned that Jimmy had been behind some of the other antics the kids got up to. He was always looking for excitement. Always being kept after school. He had a thing for practical jokes, and sometimes he got into fistfights—friendly ones, you know, just roughing around—but none of it was allowed at school."

"What sorts of things did he do?"

"Oh, I don't know if I can remember all of the stunts he pulled. He glued my fork to my plate once, I remember that, and we never could get it off until we broke the plate. Just little things, you know, like any boy does. He'd eat all the dessert and blame one of the other kids. Say he was going one place when he was really going another. Once he stole some beer from his friend's father—we never kept it in the house, mind—and gave it to this dog we had. It was a big black Labrador. Got it drunk, you know. Poor thing was staggering around the yard. But no lasting harm done. The dog didn't seem to hold any grudges."

Daniel wasn't sure what to say to this. But Theresa Zahlmann didn't appear the least bit fussed by any of it. She must have been a remarkable mother, Daniel thought. Nothing shook her.

"Jimmy was a charmer, though," she added. "No matter how much trouble he got into, he could talk his way out of it. He had a way of tilting his head to one side and smiling and looking at you from the corner of his eye. It would knock the anger right out of you, and all you could do was laugh. I never could get after him like I should have. If there is such a thing as a leprechaun, Jimmy was one. Pure mischief, that one. But he never meant harm by it. He did well in school, in spite of it all. He had a head for numbers and a good memory."

"I wish I could see a photo of him as a kid," Daniel said.

"I don't know if I still have any. At any rate, I'm not sure where they would have ended up. I stored away a lot of things when I moved here. I don't know that I could tell Steve exactly where to look for my old albums."

"That's all right," Daniel said. "I don't want to put anyone out."

"Well, if it's any consolation, I imagine you looked a lot like him when you were a boy," Theresa said, eyeing him musingly. "And I suppose he would have looked a lot like you when he grew up. You know, my husband Jacob died years ago, but he would have liked to talk to you. He had some great stories about all the foster kids we had, but I think Jimmy was one of his favorites. He certainly stayed with us longer than most of the others. That's why I was sorry he never kept in touch after he left."

"I wonder why he didn't."

She shrugged again. "Not in his nature, apparently. Some folks just move on to the next stage of their lives and don't cling to any bits of the past. It isn't surprising, considering his history."

"But that's just it. I don't know his history. Do you?" Daniel leaned forward, automatically taking out his notebook and pen.

She eyed them and smiled. "You look like an ace reporter getting a scoop."

"I am an ace reporter," he replied, smiling. "The *Denver Gazette*. Not a big paper, but it's a good one. I'll send you a free subscription."

Theresa chuckled. "You do that. What can I tell you?"

"How did he come to be in your care? I heard his mother had died."

She reached over and tweaked a top-heavy rose into better position. "Well, yes, but she'd died long before we got him. As I understand it, she died when he was about three years old, and we didn't get him until he was ten."

"Where was he before that?"

"He lived with the Johnson family. Bill and Sarah Johnson—in Denver, Colorado, in fact. Back in your neck of the woods. He lived with them for about three years, I think, but when Sarah became ill with leukemia, he came to stay with us."

"How did you know the Johnsons?"

"They were friends of my husband's. He went to school with Bill. We'd kept in touch over the years. Sarah knew we took in children, so when she became ill, she sent Jimmy to us. I guess she figured Bill wouldn't be able to manage him alone when she died. We weren't what you think of now as foster parents, you know. Child Welfare didn't pay us to watch the kids like they do foster parents now. We just . . . acquired children. Some of them were the children of acquaintances who had died. One or two were runaways we picked up off the street. One woman asked us to take her son because she was having such a hard time with him. He was in and out of trouble, and she was at her wit's end. It was that or put him in the Child Welfare system, and it wasn't a good system back then, you see. Orphanages, boarding schools—not a system of foster homes like they have now."

"I wasn't aware of that."

"Oh, yes." Theresa nodded. "So you see, it was all very informal. It was just something we felt we needed to do. There weren't any records kept or anything like that. No one knew how many kids we had with us." She laughed. "Half the time I don't think *we* knew how many we had. I remember that once I woke up and found a teenage boy sleeping on the living room floor. I guess he was a friend of one of the kids who needed a place to stay for a while. He was with us for two weeks. I never did learn his last name." She seemed to find this very funny. Daniel didn't know what to think.

"How many kids have you taken care of over the years?" he asked, dumbfounded.

She shrugged, the chunky earrings nearly touching her shoulders. "We had one of our own—Steve's dad—and, oh, probably twenty others in total over the years."

"That's amazing," Daniel said, feeling another article beginning to bloom.

"Bill Johnson died about twenty years ago—heart attack. But I think their daughter is still living somewhere near Denver. Julie or Jill or Janice. Something like that. I'm pretty sure it was Jill. She never married, so her name will still be Johnson. I imagine you could look her up."

"Thank you, I'll do that." Daniel wrote the name down, but he seemed to be having difficulty holding on to his pen. "Do you know why my father ended up with the Johnsons in particular?"

"No, but I do know they didn't take in any other children. They had the one daughter of their own, and just Jimmy. I don't rightly recall how he came to be living with them. But Jill might remember."

"And you don't know where he was before that?" Daniel thought a moment. "Jimmy came to you when he was ten. If he was with the Johnsons for three years, that means he was about seven when they got him. If his mother died when he was three, there's a four year gap there."

Theresa sighed and seemed to be studying the photographs on the bulletin board. "I don't know about his father. Maybe he was with him during that time. Jimmy never mentioned his father. I didn't know if the man was alive or dead, and I didn't press him to find out. I'm not really sure Jimmy knew himself." She hesitated, looking at him from the corner of her eyes, and Daniel slowly straightened and set down his pen.

"What is it?"

"Just something else about Jimmy I just remembered. I don't know if it matters."

"Please tell me. Anything at all will help me."

She reached over and fiddled with the rose again, frowning when it continued to droop. Daniel didn't imagine many things defied her.

"Well, he had nightmares. Always did, the whole time he lived with us. Now that in itself wasn't unusual. A lot of our kids had trouble sleeping, but usually after they'd been with us a while they settled down. Like Patrick Ferguson, he was one of our boys. His father murdered his mother right in front of him when he was six, so of course he had bad dreams when he first came to us. But he outgrew them after a time, you see what I mean? Something that horrible, and yet it eventually faded. But not in Jimmy's case. He had nightmares right up until the day he left us."

Daniel felt a chill run over his arms, and he didn't think it was the air conditioning.

"Do you know what the nightmares were about?"

"He didn't tell us much, just a few details. The nightmares always had something to do with trains. He was afraid of trains, I remember, and would never get on one—not even something resembling a train. We took the kids to the amusement park once, and some of them went on the roller coaster. Jimmy watched a moment, I remember, and the laughter went right out of him and the color left his face. He couldn't even watch them ride it. He spent the rest of the day at the ring-toss booth and the shooting gallery. The roller coaster was too much like a train, you see. I never did learn the story behind those nightmares. But I don't suppose that helps you at all."

"You never know," Daniel said, putting away his notebook. "You never know." As he thanked her and took his leave, he couldn't help but feel a sort of difference in himself, a softening perhaps. He'd never thought about his father being a little boy. It changed things somehow, to hear about Jimmy's laughter and fears, to glimpse the child behind the villain.

CHAPTER 8

1915–17

They found a place to stay in a rooming house run by a Mrs. Davies, the oldest and most wrinkled person Hannah had ever met. From her white hair scraped into a bun to her long black shoes, Mrs. Davies was like a picture from a children's fairy tale. All she needed was the pointy black hat and a broom. She spoke with a broad Welsh accent that Hannah found difficult to follow, but she kept a spotless home and her rates were reasonable.

Over time, Hannah learned that a warm heart beat beneath the frightening exterior. Mrs. Davies treated her kindly. While James was out looking for work, Hannah helped around the rooming house, doing the heavier washing and lifting in exchange for a reduced rent. At first it had been awkward, working with a woman who was not her mother, doing housework in an unfamiliar home. But once she settled in and started to grasp the intricacies of Mrs. Davies' speech, Hannah found herself content enough. She began to relax into her new life, finding companionship and conversation—though often unintelligible—with Mrs. Davies. And after her pleasant hours with the older woman, there were the golden evenings spent at the kitchen table, listening to James, talking to James, just spending time with him. She liked evenings most of all.

On their eighth day, James found work at a construction site near the center of Madison, but rather than move to a boarding house closer to the place, he instead opted to leave early in the mornings to walk the long distance and arrive home later. But he seemed content and didn't complain about the distance, so Hannah didn't suggest they move. In fact, the idea of leaving Mrs. Davies seemed cruel. The elderly woman seemed to genuinely enjoy Hannah's company and favored her and James over the other few boarders who trickled in and out. She baked the treacle scones James liked best, and she included the young couple in her prayers as if they were family. And for Hannah, they might have been.

When they had been in Madison a month, Hannah borrowed paper and a pen from Mrs. Davies and wrote (in German) to her parents, telling them briefly that she had been married and was quite happy, and that her happiness would be complete if she knew she had their forgiveness and their blessing. She didn't put her address on the envelope but added that they could reach her by way of the post office on Whitley in Madison. She didn't fully expect to hear back from them yet, and she did not tell James she had written. He would only think her foolish and perhaps wonder if she regretted her hasty decision, which she most certainly did not.

But a year came and went, and there was no word from her parents. Hannah tried not to think about it or to let it sadden her. She had made her choice, and she wouldn't let regrets pull her down. She kept herself busy helping Mrs. Davies, exploring her new town, and looking for odd jobs that she could do to help supplement their income. Work wasn't hard to find; there were plenty of vacancies left by the young men gone to war. The spring of 1917 slowly began to emerge, intruding through the icy grip of winter. Hannah enjoyed watching the buds come to the trees and the birds return to the sky.

At Easter Mrs. Davies' married son Paul came to visit, bringing with him his Irish wife and four young children. The house was filled with cheerful noise, and Hannah and James were included in all of it. Easter morning they all went to church services—except for James, but Hannah had given up hoping for his attendance—followed by a wonderful meal of glazed ham, whipped potatoes, and hot fluffy rolls. That evening they all sat around the fireplace and listened to Paul sing in a clear tenor while his wife banged away at the parlor piano.

When the fire began to flicker, Paul and his wife went to put their yawning children to bed, and Mrs. Davies hobbled off to her room. Hannah followed James up the stairs to their room, but when he turned to kiss her goodnight, she stopped him, putting her arms around his neck and smiling up at him.

"I have an Easter present for you," she said.

He looked startled. "Present? For Easter? Is this a German custom? You know how I feel about presents."

"It's not that sort of present," Hannah told him. She couldn't keep a grin from sliding across her face. She'd waited three days to tell him, knowing that this moment would make it all the more special, and now she thought she'd burst with the news. "I'm going to have a baby."

His head jerked back, and his mouth dropped open. She could feel his shoulders stiffen. "You are? Are you sure?"

"You look like you've seen a ghost." Hannah laughed. "Of course I'm sure. I saw the doctor three days ago. Oh, James, isn't that the most wonderful news?"

He reached up and took her wrists in his hands, sliding her arms from around his neck. "I don't know what to say."

She pulled away, confused at his expression. "Don't you . . . I mean, aren't you happy?"

"Of course," he said quickly. "But you're still young yet, don't you think?"

"Not all that young. My mother was even younger when she had Helga. I'm sure everything will be fine."

"Yes, well," James said, turning away and unbuttoning his shirt, "I'm sure you're right."

When Hannah woke the next morning, the house was beginning to stir, and the dawn was coming gray and cold through the curtains. The bed beside her was empty. Quickly she washed and dressed, then went to the kitchen, where Mrs. Davies and her daughter-in-law were making breakfast. Two of the children played under the table, making loud noises, and Hannah gave them a wide berth.

"Good morning! Mrs. Davies, have you seen James this morning?"

"Is he not back yet?" Mrs. Davies looked up, surprised, from her griddle. "I heard him go out very early while I was still in bed. I thought he must not be able to sleep."

"No doubt," Hannah murmured. She went back up the stairs and began to tidy the bedclothes. She couldn't think why James had gone out so early. It was an hour yet before he had to leave for work. Perhaps, she thought as a smile spread across her face, he wanted to put in extra hours and make extra money now that he knew the baby was coming. She began to hum a favorite German hymn as she bustled about the room. She shouldn't have let his reaction to the news disappoint her. Of course James was happy.

But supper came and went, and he still hadn't returned. Hannah busied herself with her knitting, which she still hadn't mastered and still found irksome, and tried not to worry. When at last she heard his boots on the stairs, she set aside her work and stood to face the door, putting on a bright smile to greet him. She heard him pause, and then he entered. Her smile slowly slid from her face as he closed the door behind him.

His unshaven face was a blotchy red, his hatless hair mussed. At first she took the redness of his skin to be from cold, but the evening was still and mild. As he came unsteadily toward her, she realized with a sinking confusion that he had been drinking. She watched him slump onto the clean coverlet of the bed and close his eyes.

"Where have you been?" she asked through stiff lips. "Work ended hours ago."

"Wasn't at work," he muttered, and put an arm over his face.

"What do you mean?"

"Didn't go today."

"But . . ." She hesitated, then asked bluntly, "Were you drinking all day, then? Is that where you were, James?"

"None of your business," he replied blurrily, and fell asleep.

* * *

As summer progressed into fall and Hannah's condition became more pronounced, James became increasingly remote and surly. He spent much of his time away from home in the evenings, and some nights he came home staggering with drink and collapsed on the bed without a word to Hannah. She learned that he had missed several days of work and was in danger of losing his job, but whenever she tried to reason with him or find out what had caused this change in him, he replied roughly that she should leave him alone. Hannah didn't know what to make of it. She was torn between sympathy and anger and—she had to admit—fear. What was wrong with James? Now, of all times, they should be happy. This child should bring them closer together. But for some reason she didn't understand, she sensed it was driving them apart. She was bitterly lonely, her body ached and grew burdensome, and Mrs. Davies' kind inquiries only made her feel more awful. Hannah considered writing to her mother and then decided against it. Her mother would certainly be able to read between the lines and see her daughter's confusion and hurt, and that was the last thing Hannah wanted.

On the fifth of October, a windy day with a hint of early snow, Hannah spent the day washing clothes. Her hands were raw and chapped, and after she had carried the basket upstairs to their room, she sank onto the bed, stretching stiffly. It was nearly six, and James would be home soon, so she should think about helping Mrs. Davies with supper, but she wanted only to sleep. She closed her eyes, thinking she would give herself ten minutes before going downstairs.

When she awoke, it was dark outside, and her clock read ten-thirty. Horrified, she jumped to her feet, ready to run downstairs, but a sudden twisting pain seized her middle, and she fell back on the bed, gasping.

I've hurt something, she told herself. *I've just pulled a muscle.* But the pain gradually faded, and after a moment she was able to sit up and cautiously make her way downstairs.

The lower floor was dark, and everyone had apparently retired for the night. There was no sign of James. Slowly Hannah made her way back upstairs and put on her nightgown. She lay down again, trying to push her worries out of her mind.

The next thing she knew, she was seized with another pain like the first, but this one gripped her in a seemingly endless vise, and she doubled over and cried out. There was a shuffling sound in the hallway, and then Mrs. Davies was bending over her, touching her shoulder.

"Is it the baby, dear? Is it coming?"

Hannah fought for breath. "I don't know. I don't know!"

Mrs. Davies hurried away again, and Hannah put her hands over her face and burst into tears.

"Be still, girl," Mrs. Davies said, reappearing a while later with an armful of towels. "Everything will be all right. Where is your husband, dear?"

"I don't know," Hannah said again, panic rising. "He never came home."

"Hush now, lie still. Jesse next door has gone for the doctor. Here, hold on to the bed if the pains come again."

"The hospital . . . I can't afford . . ."

"It's out of the question anyway, dear. It's too far gone for that. It will have to be done right here. Mind you, I've delivered a few babies in my day, so never fear."

It was an agonizing experience. Hannah wasn't sure what she had expected, but it hadn't been this. There were no feelings of excitement, of motherly love, of triumph, or even of relief. There was only pain, and the awful knowledge that there was no way out of it but through. She hardly noticed when the doctor arrived in the small hours of the morning. The pain increased, and Hannah forgot all else as her child was born.

It was a boy, squalling like a banshee, and when they showed him to her, Hannah could only gape at the wide mouth, wailing like a siren, the clenched fists, the matted wet hair.

"What a strapping little man you are," Mrs. Davies crooned in delight. "Sing, *cariad,* my love, sing and fill up those little lungs. How beautiful you are."

* * *

Hannah woke feeling oddly light and dazed. For a moment she couldn't think what had happened. Sunlight filtered through a crack between the curtains. She turned her head. James slept on the pillow beside her, his face unshaven but smoothed in sleep. She tentatively moved her legs and winced at the pain that shot through her. Meekly Hannah lay still again, afraid to move. James stirred and opened his eyes. For a moment they looked at each other, and then Hannah said, "It's a boy."

"A healthy, beautiful boy," James said softly. "Thank you."

And instantly it was all worth it. Hannah put a tentative hand on his cheek, and he placed his own over it.

"I'm sorry I wasn't here," he whispered hoarsely.

"It's all right," Hannah whispered back. She didn't ask him where he had been, and he never told her. It was enough for her, at that moment, to know that he was with her now.

CHAPTER 9

2005

He could find no one named Jill or Julie or Janice Johnson in Denver. Daniel called Directory Assistance the day he got back from Helena, and though there seemed to be a million Johnsons in the city, none of them was the right one. Daniel went into the newspaper office Monday morning feeling wrung out and disappointed. He couldn't believe he'd hit a dead end already. It was difficult to concentrate on his job. When his employer, Dave Ross, called him in to give him his next assignment, he found himself having to ask Dave to repeat it.

"Your mind is somewhere else today," Dave said, leaning back in his chair with his fingers laced across his ample stomach. "What's up? Rose okay?"

"She's fine. I'm just tired, I guess. Not sleeping well."

"Maybe you should take some time off. Rest a bit. You haven't had a break since last Christmas."

"I'm fine. Just tell me again what you want me to do, okay?" He thought of telling Dave his ideas for articles about nursing homes and the history of Child Welfare but decided it would take too much energy. He would save them for another time when ideas for article topics were slow in coming.

By Friday Rose had had enough. She cornered him on the couch, where he sat listlessly flipping through TV stations without seeing what was on them.

"Enough moping," she said, standing before him with hands on hips, blue eyes flashing. "If it's really that important to you, then go try again."

"What can I do? There's nothing else to try."

"Have you looked at the different genealogy sites on the Internet?"

"Yes. There's nothing about my family. A million McDonalds but none of them related to me. It's a dead end, Rose."

"How about an ad in the newspaper asking for information from anyone who remembers Jimmy McDonald? Or anyone descended from Bill and Sarah Johnson?"

He gaped at her, feeling like an utter fool. And him a newspaper man! Why hadn't he thought of it? People did it all the time. There were always missing persons ads, lawyers looking for next of kin, Child Welfare looking for missing parents, adopted children trying to find their birth mothers.

It took him an hour to compose the tiny advertisement. He wanted to get results but not sound too desperate. When he was satisfied with it at last, he let Rose look at it. She nodded briskly.

"Send it in. It can't hurt. Then maybe you'll be able to concentrate on the rest of your life."

"Hey, you're the one who got me started on all this."

She softened and briefly put her hand on his arm. "You're right. I have no one to blame but myself."

* * *

That Saturday they went out and bought a crib.

Daniel thought it was a little early. The baby wasn't due until February, after all, but Rose had seen one she liked, and, best of all, it was on sale. He spent the weekend setting it up in the room Rose had cleared out and painted. Rose had also added a stencil border that marched around the top of the walls. He didn't point out to her that the baby would outgrow Winnie the Pooh in a year or two and she'd have to paint over it. He would let her enjoy her excited anticipation. But when she informed him she'd bought a $200 bedding set with Pooh on it, he had to say something.

"This baby is costing me a fortune, and it's not even born yet," he mumbled. "Wait until the diapers and formula and—"

"And braces and bicycles and summer camp and college and computer games and piano lessons," Rose agreed, nodding. "All of that. Welcome to fatherhood."

"I got through life perfectly well without braces and piano lessons," he said stiffly.

"Yes, but this child is inheriting my genes and will need braces for sure," she said.

"You never wore braces."

"Yes I did, for five years, complete with headgear. But thankfully I think they've got alternatives to that now."

"You never told me."

"You don't think I'd flaunt that information, do you?" she replied. She plunked the comforter in its plastic bag down on the crib mattress.

"Piano lessons, then. Why—"

"Our child will learn to play through the hymn book, at least," she declared. "I'm not letting him stop lessons before that. Someone has to be groomed to replace Ida Runciman at church. She's been wheezing at that organ for forty years. It's time someone gave her a break."

He couldn't argue with that one. Ida played everything at the same pace: funeral dirge. It took twenty minutes to sing the sacrament hymn, and by then the bread was dried out and crunchy.

* * *

Life went on, and Daniel nearly gave up on the newspaper ad. There had been no reply. To distract himself, he started compiling information on long-term care residences to have on hand, and he found himself more interested than he'd anticipated. He briefly wondered if he should have been an architect or interior designer. Then he brushed the thought away. There was likely too much math involved, and he'd never had a head for it. He had squeaked by in high school and hadn't touched the subject since. English and writing, though, had always interested him—the flow of words, the way they could put pictures in your mind, the turning of one-dimensional marks on a page into something meaningful, even life changing. It was his high school English teacher who had first suggested he go into journalism, and he was grateful to her to this day. So now, with his family search at a seeming dead end, Daniel engrossed himself in his work and found pleasure and comfort in it.

He found Mekinda Snyder Partnership on the Web and began an e-mail correspondence with their head architect, gleaning information for a future article. He read about human-friendly environments that could reduce stress, promote health, and actually help extend residents' life spans. He researched retirement communities that allowed the residents garden space where they could raise some of their own food. There had been studies done about the effect gardening had on longevity. This led him to Internet sites about retirement homes with parks and playgrounds on site, maintained by the seniors, which provided green space for city school-children. There were nursing homes that ran day-care centers and hobby shops, or even operated vineyards. Some facilities teamed seniors up with local high school kids who needed tutoring. There was even one nursing home Daniel read about where the residents raised puppies for the seeing-eye dog program. Daniel had to admit that the idea of growing old in a place like one of these homes had appeal. He felt less dismayed about aging now that he knew there were happier, healthier housing options. Living in a nursing home didn't necessarily have to mean spending his last days playing Rummy at a Formica table and watching reruns of *I Love Lucy* on TV. And, of course, with modern medicine always advancing, who was to say he couldn't stay in his own home to the end and not go into a nursing home at all? But in case it became necessary one day, he now felt better informed and prepared.

Daniel didn't tell Rose too much about his current research project. Usually he told her about everything he was learning and exploring while writing a new story. But right now Rose's thoughts were entirely focused on the impending birth of their child. It was as if her mind were slowly letting go of all else and turning inward, preparing for what lay ahead of her. Like a law student studying for the bar exam, all usual interests and concerns faded from her mind as she gathered her inner resources for the superlative event. And rightly so, Daniel reasoned. This was a time for celebrating new life, not planning for old age. His research was about facing mortality, and right now Rose was contemplating a form of immortality, the carrying on of life. So Daniel tucked the information away in his filing cabinet for the future, whether for an article or for his own use, he couldn't say.

Then, three weeks later, a phone call came that brought him immediately back to his original quest and made him realize that it had been there all along, niggling in the back of his brain, even while he researched and wrote about other engrossing topics.

Rose was at a friend's baby shower, and Daniel was out in the yard raking leaves (and wondering what effect it would have on his longevity). He heard the distant ringing, thought it might be Rose needing something, and ran to catch it on the fifth ring.

"Is this Daniel McDonald?" an unfamiliar voice asked. It sounded like an elderly woman.

"Yes it is."

"I'm Jill Johnson. I think you're looking for me."

Daniel nearly dropped the phone in surprise. He quickly groped for a pen on the counter, but there was no paper to be had. Of all times for a reporter not to have his notebook!

"Thank you so much for phoning me. I guess you saw the ad?" he asked.

"Yes. I'd thrown it out, but when I went to bundle things up for the recycling truck, it just sort of jumped out at me. My parents were Bill and Sarah Johnson, and I was five years old when Jimmy McDonald came to live with us."

Daniel finally located a paper plate and poised his pen above it. "You remember Jimmy?"

"How could I forget him? He'd been in the house three days when he cut off my braid and pretended he was an Indian collecting scalps. I cried for a month."

"I'm sorry." Daniel felt shame for his wild parent, seven years old or not.

She laughed. "It's water under the bridge. Now I'm old and gray and lucky to have any hair at all. What can I do for you?"

"Are you here in Denver?"

"Just outside it. Where are you?"

"Right in the city."

"Would you like to come over?"

"I'd love to meet you," he said. "What is Saturday like for you?"

"I'm retired, and every day is the same to me," she replied. "Come anytime."

She gave him her address and phone number and rang off. Holding the paper plate covered in scribbles, Daniel could hardly wait until Rose came home so he could tell her.

"Back on the scent," was her happy response.

* * *

Jill Johnson was more like what he'd originally pictured Theresa Zahlmann to be. She was about five feet tall, had thin, iron-gray hair that curled tightly to her head, papery soft skin, and clothes that were double knit and practical. She lived in an apartment with three cats and a dozen African violets. Looking genuinely glad to have a guest, she ushered him in and offered him tea.

"No, thank you," he replied, sitting in the rocking chair she indicated.

"Coffee, then?"

"Thanks, but I don't drink it," he said. When she looked dismayed at having nothing else to offer, he added quickly, "But a glass of ice water sounds terrific."

Clearly relieved, she went to get it, returning with a full glass and a coaster for him to set it on. He hadn't seen a coaster in a while. This one was painted with a palm tree and said HONOLULU at the bottom.

"You've been to Hawaii?" he asked politely.

"After my father died, I sold the house and took the money and went on a trip," she said, looking embarrassed. "It's the only trip I've ever taken. I don't think he would have minded."

"I'm sure he wouldn't have minded at all." He shifted to pull his notebook out of his pocket. No paper plates today. "So you knew my dad when he was a little boy?"

"I tried to recall everything I could after I talked to you on the phone the other night. If I'm right, he came to stay with us in 1937. I think that's it, because he was with us about three years, and my mother died in 1940."

"Yes, Theresa Zahlmann told me he came to them in 1940."

"Who?"

"Theresa Zahlmann. Jimmy went to stay with her family after your mother died."

"Oh. I don't know anything about that. I just know he left right before Mother died. That was a difficult time for me. I was so young. My father remarried when I was a teenager. A horrible woman. Never did like her. She always had poodles."

Daniel didn't particularly want to get sidetracked into stories of stepmothers. He pushed away a nosy gray cat that was perched on his chair arm and flipped to a clean page in his notebook.

"Do you know why Jimmy came to stay with you? I mean, your family in particular? Did your parents know his parents or something?"

"Oh, no, I don't think they knew his family at all. I mean, he didn't come directly from them. First he was with Sheriff Dunbar."

"Who?"

"Sheriff Dunbar. I don't know his first name, but he was a friend of Dad's. He's the one who took Jimmy away from his father. He kept him a while, I think, but the sheriff wasn't married, and, being a busy man, I guess he couldn't take care of a little boy. He sent him to us. But we never met Jimmy's father."

"He took Jimmy from his father." Daniel stared at the blank page before him, frowning. "Took him. Why?"

"Oh, I don't know. I imagine it was because of all the drinking. Apparently Jimmy's father was the town drunk or something. I hope I haven't shocked you."

"No, no." Daniel recovered himself and tapped his pen rapidly against his knee. The gray cat thought this was a game and pounced at him. He brushed it away as gently but firmly as he could. "I hadn't known that. So the sheriff removed Jimmy from his father's care and sent him to your family. Do you know what he did with the other children?"

"What other children?"

"Jimmy's brothers and sisters. He had six of them."

"Oh, I don't know about that either," Jill said, looking truly sorry. "As far as I know there were no other children. Just Jimmy."

Daniel nodded. "Okay. And this was here in Colorado?"

"Well, we lived in Denver at the time, but we were originally from Montana. Sheriff Dunbar was from Billings, Montana. That's where he picked up Jimmy." She hesitated, then apparently decided if she was in for a penny, she might as well be in for a pound. She leaned forward and whispered her confession. "I really didn't like Jimmy that much. It wasn't just that he cut off my hair. He used to kick our cat."

* * *

Daniel could hardly focus on the road as he drove home. This certainly wasn't what he had expected. Jimmy had lost his mother at an early age, and Daniel had figured that something equally sad had happened to deprive him of his father. But to be told that Grandpa had been the town drunk! And who knew where the other children had ended up? He wasn't sure he wanted to pursue the family tree any further. What else would fall out when he shook it?

Rose only laughed when he told her.

"Every family has at least one," she said comfortingly. She was lying beside him in bed, propped up on her pillow with her scriptures. She was punctilious about not missing a night of reading, even when it was late and she had to be up early for meetings. She was first counselor in the Relief Society presidency, and since all of them worked full time, they usually held their meetings at unearthly hours. Her book was propped on her stomach, a faintly humorous position that Daniel found endearing.

"My mother's youngest brother Stan is ours," she said. "He's been in and out of jail on drunk and disorderly charges probably twenty times. They took his license away years ago."

"Is that the Uncle Stan who grew marijuana right on the patio, and your mother couldn't figure out why his tomatoes never bore fruit?"

"That's the one."

"But this is different, Rose. No one has taken away Stan's children."

Rose reached over and gently smoothed the hair on his forehead. "Only because his long-suffering wife has been there to raise them. No one was there to raise Jimmy. His mother had died. In fact, maybe that's why his father took to drinking in the first place. He had a broken heart."

"That sounds very romantic, but what happened to the other children? Mom said he had six brothers and sisters."

"Back east," she said. "Maybe they never came out west with Jimmy and his dad."

"I need to find them," he said urgently. "They might even still be alive."

"Maybe," Rose said, smiling. "You may have relatives running around all over the place that you don't even know about." She set down her scriptures, turned off the light, and rolled over to put an arm around him.

"Don't let all this keep you awake," she murmured against his shoulder. "You'll never get to sleep if you think about lost children."

He was afraid she'd be right, of course, and that he'd be up with another episode of insomnia. But he fell asleep almost immediately, curled in the warmth of her arms.

Which was why he was so surprised and disoriented when he woke the next morning, shivering with cold.

Rose was still beside him, and the blankets on the bed were snug around his shoulders, but he couldn't get warm. He felt breathless, as if he'd been running. He *had* been running. The dream was coming back to him now. He'd been running down a dirt road, arms pumping, lungs bursting, running somewhere he didn't recognize. The dirt was hard with frost, and there were no leaves on the trees. His feet were in little-boy tennis shoes, and he was hardly taller than the wire fences he raced past. He couldn't grasp the rest of the dream. There was only the faintest echo of it, fading into the dawn light like dissolving sugar, gone before he could fully grasp it.

Daniel sat up, careful not to disturb Rose. The clock said six fifteen. He got up, put on his bathrobe, and crawled back into bed, still shivering. He didn't know why the dream had disturbed him so much. He wanted to remember it. Somehow it felt important, and its loss saddened him. He tried to imagine Rose's reaction if he told her about it. There was nothing frightening about the dream itself. She wouldn't understand the panic, the desperation he couldn't adequately describe. It was as if he had to find something . . . or make sure something didn't find him.

* * *

Rose wasn't happy about his proposed trip.

"This is a little over the top, Daniel. I can understand going to Montana once. At least then you had a good strong lead. But you're going to spend good money on a plane trip to Billings for scraps of information, maybe nothing at all."

"I might be able to trace this Sheriff Dunbar. Maybe there will be records of his taking my dad into care. Maybe he'll know something about Jimmy's father. If the information is out there, I need to know it."

She eyed him a moment, a smile starting to creep over her face. "You really want to know, don't you?"

"Yes. See what you started? At first I wasn't sure about this whole thing, but it's growing on me."

She put a hand on his arm. "Will it make a difference if you find what you're looking for?" she asked seriously.

He didn't answer her, but in the back of his head a voice replied, *Maybe. Maybe so.*

He called for a flight, packed an overnight bag, and then, on an impulse, took everything out of the small bag and packed a suitcase instead. Rose stood in the bedroom doorway, arms folded across her chest, watching with suspicion in her eyes.

"How long are you going for?"

"I don't know. However long it takes, I guess," he replied, not looking at her.

"What about your job?"

"That's the wonder of the Internet. I can research and write from anywhere, and e-mail it in to Dave. I'm sure they have e-mail in Montana."

"If you can research from anywhere, why are you going to Billings?"

He straightened and looked at her. "Not that kind of research. You know what I mean. I'm going to be doing interviews, hopefully access some nonpublic documents. I can't do that on the Internet. Rose, can't you understand I need to do this?"

"Yes. But . . ." She struggled silently a moment, then nodded. "I understand. And I want you to find out all you can, I really do. I'll just miss you. Will you phone me so I know what hotel you're in?"

"Of course. I'll phone you twice a day. Keep you up to date on the search."

"Don't you have an interview or something on Monday?"

"I canceled it. I'll do it when I get back." He softened at the woeful look on her face. "I won't be gone all that long," he assured her. "A quick look at the police file if I can, a search through some back issues of the local papers, that's all. There may be nothing to find. There may be something. I have to know."

"I know." She sighed. Then she rose on her toes to kiss him briefly and went back to the kitchen.

CHAPTER 10

1922

It was Christmas Eve, and the house was filled with cheerful noise. Little William was five years old, old enough to have figured out the truth about Santa, and Mary and Samuel were still too young to understand much of what Christmas was about. But both sensed their mother's happiness and were caught up in it. Hannah decorated the tree with homemade paper chains and pinecones strung on thread. She pictured her mother back in Wisconsin, stringing up pine cones in the same way, though her tree would also have the lacy crocheted snowflakes she'd brought with her from Germany.

She paused a moment in her work, imagining her family gathered around to light the candles on the tree, singing carols, with the kitchen smelling of wonderful baked things. Did they miss her? Did they wonder where she had gone? Was Helga married to Georg? How tall were her brothers now?

She had never heard back from her parents, though she had written to them a second time when William was born, again omitting a return address. She'd also omitted the fact that James had missed the birth. He seemed content with his child and with her, and she let it go at that. Most of the time he was cheerful and affectionate. If there were times when he seemed distant and remote to her, she didn't dwell on it. Sometimes she would catch him standing at the window looking out, or just gazing into the fireplace, an expression on his face she didn't understand. It wasn't sadness; it wasn't anger. If she had to put a word to it, she would have said he looked *lost*—lost in memory, or perhaps lost in time. But that look didn't come often, and she didn't pry.

Three years after William's birth, she'd written her parents a third time, with news of Mary's arrival. (James had been gone three days that time and hadn't returned until he'd spent every penny they had at the bar.) She hadn't bothered writing a few months later to tell them she and James were moving to Canada, but she'd sent a postcard the previous October telling them when Samuel was born. There was a beaver on the postcard. Let them infer from that what they would.

James wasn't back from work yet. She bent over the bubbling pot of apple cider on the stove, inhaling the scent of cinnamon and allspice. She admittedly wasn't much of a cook, even now, but she did know how to make good wassail. She replaced the lid, glanced to where the children were playing on the rug, and took the opportunity while they were quiet to slip away to her room. She retrieved the small package she had hidden under the bed. She had splurged on a new scarf and gloves for James. Surely he couldn't argue about the expense. He needed them desperately. She placed the packet on his pillow, straightened the blanket on the bed, and went back to the kitchen. The children's presents (all homemade, costing nothing, so James couldn't complain) were already tucked out of reach in the branches of the tree. Hannah didn't put James's present with the children's, because she wanted him to receive it privately, this evening. That way it wouldn't be so obvious on Christmas morning that the only person not receiving a present was herself.

The first Christmas they had spent together, she had been surprised and hurt that James hadn't given her a gift. He didn't believe in such things, he'd said tersely. But she continued to enjoy giving gifts even when they were not enthusiastically received. Over the past few years she had learned not to take his lack of reciprocation personally.

But other than gift-giving, James seemed to enjoy Christmas as well as she did. He always picked the best-shaped tree to cut and bring indoors. He had a good baritone voice and sang carols with the children. Hannah enjoyed listening to him but rarely joined in, because she didn't know many of the carols in English. As she returned to her Christmas baking, the thought of his singing brought a warm glow to her face. Those were the happiest times, when James sat by the fire with William on one knee and Mary on the other, singing. Hannah began to hum a favorite German carol as she moved about the room. Little Samuel made a squeak in his cradle, and William went over to rock him gently without being asked. Hannah gave him a loving smile, and he grinned back, pleased with himself. William had inherited his father's bright eyes, but he had his mother's flaming red hair.

When she heard James at the door, she straightened from setting the table. But her cheerful greeting fell flat as she saw his expression. He had been drinking again—a *lot*. She watched him sink onto the chair by the stove and pry one boot off with his toe, and she automatically knelt to pull off the other one. They were wet with mud, and she shuddered at the thought of the footprints he must have left across her clean hall floor. James said nothing, only blinked tiredly at her and then at the children, who had grown silent and still. Hannah stood with his boot in her hands, not knowing what to do. She had not seen him this inebriated since Samuel was born. Usually only the births of his children sent him on such a drinking spree.

When he didn't speak, Hannah turned to put his boots away. Mary came over to tug on her skirt, but she shushed her with a slight shake of her head.

Behind her, James's voice, low and rasping, stopped her cold.

"Pack your things."

She spun back to him. "What?"

"Pack your things up. I've got tickets for the two-thirty train."

She shook her head. "Where are we going?"

"We're moving to Creemore."

She dropped the boot on the floor and knelt beside him, repressing the urge to shake him by the shoulders. "Creemore? Up north? We know no one up there."

"Don't argue with me. Pack up the children's things."

"It's Christmas Eve! And you're completely drunk."

James's eyes opened wider, and he shot her a derisive glance. "I'm not drunk. I can outdrink anyone in Wisconsin."

"No doubt. But we don't live in Wisconsin. Why are we going to Creemore?"

"Work there."

"You have work here."

"It's finished."

"You said nothing of that to me." She jumped up and began to pace the floor, squeezing her fingers open and shut, trying to quell the fear and anger rising in her. "Did you know your work was ending?"

"They told us three days ago."

"Why didn't you tell me?"

"I didn't want to ruin your holiday." James leaned forward with a groan and rested his elbows on his knees, running his hands through his spiky hair. "Toronto's too big now. Growing too fast."

"I would think that's a good thing for a bricklayer."

"There's work to be had in Creemore. Sawmill. I heard about it today. We're going."

"What will I tell the landlady?" Hannah felt tears start to flow and forced them back with a hiccup. "We've paid the rent on this house for two more months."

"The devil with the landlady!" James suddenly snapped. "What does she have to do with anything, with us?"

Hannah bit her lips tightly together. There was no sense arguing with him when he was like this. She picked up Samuel from his cradle, took Mary by the hand, and led the children out of the room. Wordlessly she laid Samuel on the bed, retrieved two suitcases from the closet, and began to pack, her hands trembling. Her belongings seemed pitifully few. She was confused, angry, and suddenly frightened of the unknowns that lay before her. Fiercely she scowled at herself. She had known this was only a temporary position at best, hadn't she? She had to go where her husband found work, didn't she? They never stayed in one place for long.

She dumped one full bag on the bed beside the baby and began filling the other, including the wrapped gloves and scarf she'd placed on James's pillow. She wouldn't give them to him now, but maybe in Creemore. William had two extra outfits, Mary three, and there were the diapers and William's toy wooden train. Her belongings included a Bible, the quilt she'd made all those years ago for her trousseau, her combs, and a Sunday dress. She worked furiously, ignoring Mary's whimpering and William's stunned expression. She buckled the bags shut, carried them out to the kitchen, and dropped them on the floor in front of James. She collected the children's gifts from the tree and put them in her apron pocket. Then she went to the stove, turned it off, took the pot of bubbling wassail (how heavenly it smelled!), and tipped it out the back door into the snow. It ran away in a steaming golden rivulet, disappearing into the mud around the steps. She set the pot down and returned to stand in front of her husband.

"I'm ready," she snapped. "The kitchen things all belong to the landlady, except the kettle, and I can't fit that in the bags."

He looked up at her with bleak, red eyes, and all anger seeped out of her as quickly as it had come. She dropped to her knees and took his head against her shoulder, smoothing his hair with her fingers.

"I'm sorry," she said softly. "I'm sure Creemore will be a very nice place."

He didn't reply, but his arms went around her and pulled her close.

CHAPTER 11

2005

The air was crackling hot with no sign of the relief September should bring. Daniel's back stuck to the vinyl of the rental car's seat, and the black steering wheel was painful to touch. He cranked the windows down and, following the hotel manager's directions, turned the car toward the highway. Drive across Billings, take the exit after the giant McDonald's sign (he didn't miss the irony), go south, turn right at the crooked pine tree, and right again on Westchester.

The sheriff's office hadn't been able to help him. He'd gone straight there from the airport, eager to begin his search. They'd informed Daniel that Sheriff Dunbar had died back in 1970. Any records that might have been kept were strictly confidential. And no, they couldn't say whether the sheriff had any family in the area. He had never married.

The police station had no information either, or at least none they would give. They referred Daniel to Child Welfare Services, whose office was situated in a crowded space overlooking a shopping mall. Child Welfare Services refused to say whether there was a file on Jimmy McDonald or not.

"Even if there were, we couldn't share it with you," the woman behind the front desk informed him firmly. "Even with a file that old, the information is not in the public domain. You would be required to obtain the signed consent of everyone connected to the file."

"Fine. Give me the names of everyone connected to the file, and I'll do that."

"Nice try."

There was only one more source Daniel could think of: newspapers, of course. If anything out of the ordinary had happened, there surely would have been mention of it in the local newspaper. The more gossipy, the better. He stopped off at the Holiday Inn long enough to dump his luggage, but went out again immediately to find the newspaper office for the *Billings Morning Herald*.

The teenaged receptionist, popping her gum in boredom, informed him that the back issues were housed on microfilm at the central city library. With much prodding he coaxed directions out of her.

By the time he reached the microfilm room of the library, it was four in the afternoon, and he was crumpled and exhausted. He hadn't eaten anything since the bagel he'd nibbled that morning before leaving for the airport. But food could wait. He was hot on the scent of his quarry now, and his journalistic instincts were revving, heightened by the smell of archived paper, dust, and ink. His flagging spirits began to rise.

He found the reel containing the issues from 1937 and fed it through the fussy reader, fighting with the awkward spool. His fingers were too large to fit through the small space properly. He fiddled with the dial, and the words slid into focus, laid out in the neat symmetry and logical lines of a newspaper. He felt himself immediately relax. This was familiar territory.

Spread before him was the private life of the town. He was gratified to see that the *Billings Morning Herald* was a gossip rag. There were blurbs on who was visiting from out of town, the closing of a bankrupt clothing store, engagement announcements, and the merits of Burkbank's Lemon Balm to keep mosquitoes at bay. Someone had found a goat running loose in the street (and urged the owner to identify the animal and pay for the ad). Someone else had donated a large collection of travel books to the library. It took him just three minutes to find what he wanted, in half-inch type: "Man Arrested for Public Drunkenness." There was a brief segment that gave only tantalizing snippets. James C. McDonald had been arrested for the third time in one month for disorderly conduct and public intoxication. Daniel slowly turned the spool. Two weeks later there was another small notice, easy to miss, down in one corner.

> Mr. James C. McDonald of no fixed address has been incarcerated for the fourth time this summer for public intoxication. He was found shouting and causing a public disturbance in the middle of Hampton Street at 2 AM wearing only his nightshirt. When approached by concerned citizens, he assaulted one man, who luckily sustained only slight injury. The editors of this paper encourage the law enforcers of this good community to notify the proper authorities to do their duty, as it has come to this paper's attention that there is a child involved in this sad situation.

Daniel ran a hand over his face, trying not to smile. The wording was so old-fashioned and self-righteous. He was glad, though, that the paper hadn't minded its own business. From the sound of it, James McDonald hadn't been a jolly drunk.

An issue of the paper a week later contained something else. In inch-high type, the paper demanded whether anyone had seen the little boy pictured. James "Jimmy" McDonald had run away from the boarding house where he and his father were staying. Daniel sat staring at the small black-and-white photo, studying the pale oval face, the fringe of shaggy dark hair, the solemn round eyes that looked gray in the paper but that he knew were vivid blue. The neck looked too fragile to balance the head. His shoulders were scrawny, even for a seven-year-old, and it looked like he was wearing a shirt far too large for him. Daniel reached out a finger and slowly traced the child's features on the screen. Too solemn for such a young boy. Could this possibly be his father? Was this the imp who had cut off Jill Johnson's hair while playing Indians? Already running, even at this tender age. It had indeed been a lifelong tendency.

Daniel wiped his palms hard down his face and then twiddled the reader's handle. The article was repeated two weeks later, with the addition of a statement from Christopher Dell, former landlord of James C. McDonald. Dell claimed the man had absconded with bedding stolen from the apartment and owing a month's rent. The only useful bit of information he had been able to give police was that McDonald had driven a truck with Wisconsin license plates.

In the next week's edition there was an article that made Daniel's blood run cold.

> Authorities have located seven-year-old Jimmy McDonald, who went missing May 11th. The boy was found unharmed and in good health, living in a railroad car at the train yard outside of Billings. According to Sheriff Lawrence Dunbar, authorities are unable to return him to his father, Mr. James C. McDonald, who left town last week with no forwarding address. Police noted the child's father has been in and out of trouble with authorities since he arrived in Billings earlier this year. The child is unable to name any other relatives to contact, does not know where he lived before coming to Billings, and knows only his name and age. Anyone knowing Mr. McDonald's current whereabouts or any other family members is asked to notify the police or the editor of this paper.

That, Daniel thought grimly, might explain the aversion Jimmy had to trains. You get on, and when you get back off, your whole world is changed; everything's gone, and you can't get it back.

There was nothing else, though he scanned the remainder of the year's issues. Daniel finally rewound the microfilm and left the library, the hunger in his stomach replaced with cramps of anxiety. He had to drive for thirty minutes before he located his hotel again. Once in his room, he collapsed on the too-short bed, exhausted, and lay with his hands behind his head, staring at the ceiling.

The reality had to be faced. James McDonald hadn't perished in an accident or been incapacitated by some dread disease. He hadn't had his child taken from him because he'd been a drunk and unable to care for him. He'd simply picked up and left. He hadn't even waited around to see if his runaway son had been found. He'd just disappeared into thin air, and that took engineering. Planning. Forethought.

Why would a father ditch a seven-year-old? Had Jimmy been horrid and unmanageable? Somehow he didn't think the sober-looking child in the newspaper would have been overly loud or belligerent, despite the report of his kicking the Johnsons' cat.

And then Jimmy had grown up to do to Daniel exactly what his own father had done to him.

* * *

Daniel woke with a vague feeling of surprise; he hadn't realized he'd fallen asleep. The window was a black square, punctuated by the flash of cars going by below. The air conditioner still hummed, and the room was too cold. He groaned and sat up. The neon clock radio showed 9:25. He'd slept for hours. He ran his hands through his hair, pulling himself to wakefulness. A cold shower. Supper. Rose.

He reached for the phone. She answered on the third ring.

"I was getting ready to send out a search party," she said, smothering a yawn.

"Sorry. I meant to call you earlier."

"Did you meet with the sheriff's office?"

He told her briefly what he had found out, keeping his voice as dispassionate as he could. She was quiet a moment, and he could almost hear the hum of her brain working. But when she spoke, she didn't comment on his runaway father or his disappearing grandfather. Instead she simply asked, "What will you do next, then?"

"I'm not sure."

"Well, if James McDonald was driving a truck with Wisconsin plates, you could try that angle. See if there's a vehicle registration from back then. It might tell you something more."

"I guess. Do car registrations go back that far?"

"I don't know. It's worth a try. And you said your dad tried to get into the army under age. Maybe the military has a document or two."

"Yes, actually, I've already written to them. He was only in the army for two days before he was found out, but they might still have his application on file."

"Well, that's something, then."

"But it wouldn't list his next of kin or anything. If this newspaper article is right, Jimmy didn't remember the names of any relatives or even where he was from. It's like his life was a blank before age seven. You know, maybe that's why my mom didn't write down the names of his brothers and sisters. Maybe he couldn't ever remember them."

There was a pause. She must have picked up on his depression crackling over the telephone wire, because her voice dropped to a soothing tone, and she added, "Hang in there, Daniel. You'll find what you're looking for. You just have to keep at it."

"I think maybe I've found out all I need to," he replied, wincing at the flatness of his own voice. "He dumped me like his father dumped him. What more do I need to know?"

"That's just the result," she answered gently. "Don't you want to know the cause? The events leading up to it?"

"Why?"

"Well, so you can understand it. And maybe so you can forgive it. Maybe that's what you're really looking for with all this, Daniel. You need to forgive him before you can move on."

He gave a short bark of laughter. "This isn't the kind of thing you forgive, Rose."

"Well, maybe not right *now* . . ."

"I didn't know that my search would turn this up. I thought maybe it would help me figure out how to be a father myself."

"Right," she said slowly.

"Well, I sure figured it out, didn't I? What terrific examples of fatherhood I've found! It goes back generations!"

"All right, Daniel, but there are other reasons to keep up the search, aren't there?" Rose pointed out. He could picture her holding on to the top of her head like she did whenever she was thinking intently. "What about your brother? And all those missing uncles and aunts you have?

Jimmy has six brothers and sisters somewhere. You said you wanted to find them."

He swallowed hard. "Yes," he said slowly. "They're my family."

"Don't you want to know what happened to them? Maybe they're out there looking for you."

"They don't know I exist."

"It's just a thought," she answered softly. "You didn't know they existed until just a few weeks ago."

He drew a deep breath, his ribs expanding painfully, as if he hadn't breathed in a long time.

"Yes," he said. "You're right. There's other family to find."

* * *

The dream was different this time. He didn't know where he was, didn't recognize the wide, tree-lined street he was running down. The houses were unfamiliar clapboard, the trees thick with frightening shadows beneath them. He bolted through the pooled shadows on the sidewalk, breathless, with tears running down his face.

The road curved, and he rounded it at a full sprint, still not sure where he was going. A woman stood on the sidewalk ahead of him. He was going too fast to really look at her, but he caught a glimpse of red-brown hair the color of an old penny, and a plain house dress like Aunt Bea wore on the *Andy Griffith Show.* As he passed her, he turned his head and looked up into eyes of the purest blue he'd ever seen. They were fixed on him in kindly concern, and even as he ran past her, she raised a graceful hand and pointed down the road. *That way. Run, child. Run fast.*

He zoomed down the road, his wet tennis shoes making squishy sounds on the pavement. He was growing tired, his breath painful, but he was afraid to slow down. He turned at an intersection and smacked hard into a sudden brick wall. Dazed, he put his hands out to keep from falling and felt the rough brick beneath his palms. It was a dead end.

Daniel woke with a sharp pain in his side. He sat upright, moaning, and rubbed the stitch. His breath came in painful gasps. He fumbled for the table lamp and switched it on. The 70s orange and gold of his hotel room sprang into focus, along with the flea market paintings and the laminated furniture. He squinted at the clock and saw it was four in the morning. Still holding his side, he swung his feet to the floor and stood. His legs trembled, and he felt as if he'd run a great distance. The dream was already receding, but he remembered the running. His bedclothes were tangled on the floor where he'd thrown them off.

Blast! Would he never get a decent night's sleep? He stumbled into the bathroom, used the toilet, and automatically went to wash his hands. The cold water struck his palms with a horrible pain, and he jerked his hands out of the water. What on earth? He felt for the light switch and flipped it on. The glare blinded him a moment. When he regained his sight, he looked down at his palms. They were scraped raw. Angry red abrasions covered his hands from the base of his thumb to the middle joint of his fingers.

Daniel carefully wrapped his hands in toilet paper, round and round, until he looked like a boxer. Tucking the wounded appendages under his armpits, he slid back in bed and curled up on his side against the pain. His head ached, he was exhausted, and he felt ridiculously like crying. What was wrong with him? A little scrape. He wasn't a little boy, falling off his bike and scraping his knee. He was a grown man, for heaven's sake, and surely there was an explanation for his injuries. The wall at the head of the bed was brick. He must have rubbed it in his sleep.

Suddenly Rose seemed far away. He was alone in the middle of Montana with no one to comfort him. He was a fool for coming on this goose chase. He tried to think what Rose would say to him if she were here. *That's what you get for going to sleep without saying your prayers.* He almost chuckled at that. It was just the sort of thing she'd say. His body began to relax. *It will all be better in the morning. You'll be home soon. Go back to sleep, liebchen.*

Since when does Rose speak German? he wondered muzzily.

Just as he drifted toward sleep again, he remembered the red-haired woman in his dream. He felt an odd yearning to see her again, to examine her more closely, but he was already losing the shape of her. Even as her form faded in his memory, he imagined that a feminine hand gently touched his forehead, soothing the creased skin, smoothing back his hair. He felt his pulse slow, his breathing deepen. He felt as he did when Rose touched him, her hand cool and peaceful on his head. It was immensely comforting.

He fell asleep with the shameful tears forgotten on his cheeks.

CHAPTER 12

1930

"You didn't steal it, did you?"

William's face turned a dull red, but whether with embarrassment or anger, she couldn't tell. He was thirteen and tall for his age, but he hadn't grown into his ears yet. They stood out like red handles on each side of his head. He struggled to find his voice for a moment and then burst out, "Of course not, Mother! Mr. Barnwell said we could have it because it hadn't sold and was going to go bad."

Hannah looked at the paper-wrapped lump on the kitchen table and fought with herself. It had been ages since they'd had a ham, but her pride warred with her need. The whole town probably knew there was little food in their house. After a while, need won out.

"Tell Mr. Barnwell thank you," she told William in a low voice. "And take him a dozen eggs from the henhouse." Despite the shame of it, she was grateful for William's job at the butcher's. It helped them survive.

He nodded, hesitated, and then went out, letting the screen door swing and slam behind him. Hannah carried the ham to the sink and unwrapped it. It was small—she'd seen larger chickens—and smelled just on the edge of going off. But if she cut it up and boiled it with cabbage and carrots, then threw in a few onions, it would taste all right. Wryly she smiled at herself as she pushed the wrapping paper into the garbage. She'd sworn she'd never feed her children pig ankle stew, but this was certainly close enough.

There was a window over the kitchen counter, and as Hannah chopped the ham she kept one eye on the little ones playing outside on the lawn. Their frame house, two rooms up and two rooms down, was in bad need of paint and threatened to fall down when the wind was strong. It really wasn't big enough for their family, and there was a rust-colored stain spreading over the ceiling above the window, where the damp came in. But the rent was low, and there was a lovely patch of grass in front with a willow tree where the children liked to play. It was right on the main thoroughfare of Collingwood, too, so she didn't have far to walk to the stores or to church. She attended the Methodist church, since there wasn't a Lutheran one, and she bundled the children up and took them with her. James always remained at home. He made up all sorts of excuses at first, but after a while he didn't bother, only shaking his head when she suggested he accompany them. Finally she stopped asking. It was difficult hauling the children with her, but William and Mary helped her, and the small ones seemed to enjoy the children's class. Hannah enjoyed the company of the other women, too. Being on the main road at least kept her from being as isolated as she had been in the farmhouse in Creemore. There she'd had no visitors, not even James's sister Isabel, who made the trip twice a year from Toronto to Collingwood to the resort on the Bay. When she came to town, she would sit in Hannah's small parlor and make dutiful, polite conversation for fifteen minutes while her narrow eyes darted disapprovingly around the shabby room. Hannah never knew quite what to say to her, and her presence always caused Hannah to feel self-conscious of her German accent and much-mended clothing.

After the cabbage was set to boiling, Hannah asked Mary to keep an eye on it and went outside. What would she do without Mary? Though only ten years old, she was a willing and obedient girl and of great help to her mother. Without her, Hannah thought she'd never have a moment's peace.

Anna came running to meet her, her blond braids flapping and coming undone. Her hair was slick and thick, as hard to trap in a braid as honey. She held up her find—a small smooth stone the color of a pearl—and Hannah bent down as well as she could to examine it and exclaim over its beauty. She was carrying this baby very low, and even bending a little was difficult. She wasn't very far along and worried about how she would manage when a little more time had gone by.

"Let's go for a walk," Hannah suggested, straightening and easing her back. A little exercise sounded like just what she needed.

Anna immediately took her hand, but two-year-old Matthew took some coaxing to leave his play. He was building a road for his toy car in the dirt under the willow. Finally she had his little hand firmly in hers, and they set off down the road at a suitable pace, more of a crawl, really. Hannah's lips quirked in a smile, wondering if the slow pace was to accommodate Matthew's little legs or her own lumbering gait.

There was a lovely grassy area along the river, not a far walk from their house. Trees grew along the water, and the river made comfortable chuckling sounds as it ran over the rocks. It reminded her of the river she'd walked along in Cobb. There was a stone bench near the riverbank where she could sit and keep an eye on the children as they played tag. The air smelled of newly cut grass and fresh-baked bread, wafting from the bakery on the corner. Hannah silently vowed that one day she would splurge and buy her bread instead of making it.

But when they arrived at the park today, there was someone else already sitting on the bench. Hannah didn't know the woman. She was pretty, with an elegant face, now turned up toward the sun. Her hat had been removed, and the sun glinted off her blue-black hair. Her eyes were closed, and pure enjoyment was written in her slight smile. She simply sat and soaked in the light.

Hannah hesitated, then turned away, not wanting to disturb her pleasure, but the woman's eyes popped open—Hannah saw they were a clear Irish blue.

"Caught me napping, did you?" she said, laughing. "Please don't go. Come sit down."

"I don't want to bother you," Hannah said.

"It's no bother. Surely we'll both fit on this bench."

Hannah glanced down at herself with a rueful smile.

"Well, for a little longer, maybe." She chuckled and sat down carefully. The woman gave a nod toward Hannah's stomach.

"Another one on the way?" She glanced at the two children, who had gone to collect rocks at the water's edge. "That's lucky, to have three children."

Hannah laughed. "This will be my seventh, actually. I have others at home." She didn't mention the fact that one of them had died, two years ago. She couldn't speak of it, even now. She glanced toward Matthew in automatic reflex, making sure he wasn't straying too close to the river.

"Seven!" The woman gaped at her a moment, then sighed and settled back on the bench more comfortably. "I don't have any. We've been married for six years and nothing. Ah, well." She fiddled a moment with her hat and then tossed it back onto the bench beside her as if giving it up for a bad job. She stuck out her hand. "Martha Reid."

"Hannah McDonald." Hannah shook the proffered hand a little reluctantly, knowing her own was rough and red from work. Martha's hand was soft and the color of cream.

"You have an accent of some sort. I can't place it."

"German. I grew up speaking German," Hannah said. It wasn't something she mentioned often, since the war. But Martha didn't seem to care.

"Really? Not in Collingwood, surely. It must be seventy percent Irish."

"Wisconsin. My parents moved there from Germany when I was two."

"How interesting! I've never lived outside of Collingwood myself."

"It's a nice town. We've been here about three years."

"You have lovely children. The little girl has a face like a china doll."

"Thank you. I don't know what I'd do without them. They're my greatest joy."

Martha looked away over the grass toward the bakery and the road beyond. When she looked back, Hannah was surprised to see a flash of pity in the woman's eyes. But it vanished in an instant, and Martha gave Hannah a broad smile. "I'll just borrow your children once in a while, then. I have a wonderful yard for children, fenced away from the road. You'll have to bring them over to play, and we can sit and chat while we watch them."

Hannah cautiously returned the smile. "I'd like that."

* * *

Martha Reid, Hannah was astonished to learn, was twenty-nine, just four years younger than Hannah, although Martha looked closer to twenty. Hannah thought her very beautiful and was amazed Martha took any notice of her, but Martha took to the stubborn German woman from Wisconsin, and they became the best of friends. Hannah often packed the children over to the Reids' spacious white house by the river, and while the children played in the fenced garden, she and Martha talked and laughed and looked over the latest Hudson Bay advertisements in the *Streetsville Gazette*. Martha could play the piano, and the Reids owned one, right in their front parlor. Hannah could imagine nothing more wonderfully decadent than reclining on the long horsehair chesterfield, listening with half-closed eyes to Martha's charming music while the children danced on the rug.

She never invited Martha to her own house. It was partly out of embarrassment, for though she kept their tiny house clean as glass, it was far from elegant. The wood floors were scuffed, the light hopelessly dim, and there was really no place to entertain a guest, because the parlor doubled as William's bedroom. And it was partly out of worry that James would come home while Martha was there.

* * *

Although Martha suspected she knew why she had never been invited to the McDonald home—James McDonald had secured quite a reputation in their small town—she never let on. She was content to let Hannah and her children come to her, and she took great delight in watching Hannah's enjoyment of her children. They were a handsome group, all of them tall and straight and with their father's striking eyes. But in temperament they resembled Hannah—a blessing, Martha thought, though she'd never say as much aloud. They were cheerful, willing, and generous with each other, though they had little. The older children liked to run three-legged races or play kick-the-can in the road, but they were also happy to include the younger ones in a game of tag or statues. Most of all, Martha liked to watch Hannah's expression as she watched the children dance to the piano. She knew Hannah's life was not a comfortable one—she had her suspicions about what went on behind closed doors—but Hannah never gave anything away. Always she was smiling, gentle, and kind, and she played as hard as any of her sons did. Martha didn't pry, but she did manage to find small things she could give her friend—a basket of vegetables from her garden, a length of fine cloth left over from her sewing, a book she'd found at a sale, a tiny bag of ball-and-jacks for the children.

Martha also talked to Hannah about the things she was learning at her church. She knew Hannah had been raised Lutheran and wasn't completely satisfied with the Methodist church she attended in Collingwood. Martha and her husband had made friends with another couple the year before who were Mormons. Martha had joined their church not long after, and her husband had followed last Christmas. There were only a handful of LDS Church members in the area, and they met on Sundays in a small room in the back of a pub. It wasn't an ideal meetinghouse—they had to sweep away cigarette butts and clear away bottles and glasses before they could meet, and the room was drafty in winter and hot as an oven in summer. But there was still a wonderful feeling in their meetings and a closeness in their friendships that Martha had experienced nowhere else. Martha wished she could share her convictions and happiness with Hannah, perhaps even bring her out to meet the rest of the group. But Hannah declined every approach with a polite smile. She was resigned to being Methodist now, she said, and saw no reason to change.

* * *

As the summer went on, the friendship that had blossomed between the two women continued to grow. Martha continued to extend invitations to church, and although Hannah could see that her friend was sincere, she still felt no desire to join herself with another religion. "I'm glad you've found something that makes you happy," she said, hoping she hadn't offended Martha by turning down so many of her offers. But she needn't have worried. Martha never took offense at anything.

"It could make you happy too," Martha said, linking her arm through Hannah's as they strolled through the park with the children.

"But I *am* happy."

"If you say so." Martha shot her a look from the corner of her eye and then said gently, "I think I know you well enough by now to say that things could be . . . better for you at home. Couldn't they?"

Hannah let her breath out in a puff, making her bangs flip. Matthew always laughed when she did that, but he was up ahead, racing Sam on his short little legs. It never occurred to Matthew that he couldn't do everything his older brothers did.

"I have my children. They're enough for me."

"All the more reason to come to church with me," Martha declared. "I know you love them more than anything. Don't you want them to be yours forever?"

Hannah frowned. "What do you mean? Of course they're mine."

"Only for this life. Until they die, or until you die."

"Well, I suppose, of course . . ."

"It doesn't have to be that way," Martha said. "You can be sealed to them, and they'll be yours forever, even after death."

Hannah stopped in the middle of the path, staring at her friend. "What are you talking about?"

"Wouldn't you want that, Hannah?" Martha asked earnestly. "Isn't that a beautiful thought, that you could *always* be their mother, no matter what?"

"Yes," Hannah said slowly, thinking of her little lost Charlotte. She swallowed hard. "It's a beautiful thought."

Martha gave her arm a squeeze and resumed walking. "Then let me tell you about it," she said.

* * *

The late summer heat had been horrible all day. Matthew was cutting his two-year molars and had been cross and whiney since morning. Hannah was worn to a frazzle trying to deal with him. She'd been planning a stew for supper, but the heat had driven her out of the kitchen, so she gave the children bread and milk and tucked them into bed early with only light sheets over them to keep the flies off. At last the house fell silent. She cleared away the last of the dishes and tried to settle at the kitchen table with some sewing, but the heat made her as irritable as the children, and her fingers were too sweaty to hold the fabric. The baby she carried kicked mercilessly whenever she tried to sit still. At last she put down her sewing and peeked into the room where Matthew, Samuel, Anna, and Mary slept, piled into two beds like a litter of puppies. The crib stood waiting, ready, in the corner. Smiling, Hannah crept away and let herself out the back door. Surely it wouldn't hurt to step out briefly, just long enough to catch a breeze. They were settled and wouldn't wake now, but if they did, Mary was there. And William should be home soon.

She walked along the yard, past the rubbish heap and the shed where she kept her rake and clippers—James did no yard work—and out the back gate into the lane. The sun was down, but the air was still gray and murky, and she could see perfectly well to walk. There were lights and noise coming from Queen Street, but she wanted coolness and solitude, and the best place for that was the river. The air was always cooler there, with a breeze blowing from the north and the trees making soft sounds. There was a comforting smell of water and damp earth and fresh green growing things. Her feet found the path without trouble, she had been along it so often. She loved her children, loved playing with them and caring for them, but it was also nice to be on her own sometimes.

She walked slowly, feeling the heaviness of the baby about to come. She felt big as a plow horse these days and about as attractive. She didn't let herself indulge often in thoughts of Wisconsin, but for a moment she let her mind dwell on her mother. How Elsa would have loved to see her grandchildren! Samuel was almost eight now, already strong and with the promise of height in his lanky limbs. He would take after his father in that way. Anna was bossy and self-assertive—not one to be ordered around by her older siblings. She rather reminded Hannah of herself at that age. Yet in many ways she was also a miniature Helga. Even at five, she was always looking at herself in the mirror and fussing if her fair hair slipped from its braid or the elastic was loose in her stockings. Hannah put a hand on her belly, fingering the shadowy shape of the child there. Soon. This time she would write a proper letter to her mother, telling her all about the children, and this time she would give her return address. Surely Elsa would write back. Surely they missed her as much as she missed them.

Hannah gave a sigh, then frowned at the wistfulness in the sound. It wouldn't do to think about it, especially not now when she needed to face the coming birth. The last thing she needed was to feel sorry for herself. And really, why should she? She had a home—albeit a cramped one—she had friends, she loved the bustling little town by the river, and she had James. Frustrating, charming James. She sighed again.

She emerged from the path under the trees and stopped beside the river, listening to the clink and hollow ripple as it flowed past. She loved the sound of rivers and the rush of wind in the trees. There was only a slight breeze now, and she moved farther along the bank, craving coolness. There was a log where she liked to sit sometimes, and she needed to rest now. She also wanted to think.

She had done a lot of thinking since her talk with Martha in the park. The things she had told her—the idea of families being sealed for eternity—had flooded her mind, and she'd had a hard time thinking of anything else these past weeks. It was more than a beautiful thought. It was a vital energy, coursing through her blood. She knew without any hesitation that this was how things were meant to be, that this was what she wanted. She could see Charlotte again, have her little girl back with her someday. She wouldn't have to fear losing another child. It was *right*. But how could it ever be hers?

James would never consider joining any religion. He'd laughed at her for taking the subject so seriously. And the idea of James, sober and in a suit, sitting on a folding chair in the back of a pub for Sunday meetings, was ludicrous. Hannah scrubbed her fingers over her face, so depressed she couldn't even cry. It all rested on James, and she couldn't even approach him about it. She remembered Martha's serious face, her gentle voice as she'd asked, "Tell me honestly, Hannah. Would you *want* to be sealed to James forever?"

Hannah knew she was foolish. She knew the other women in town thought she was stupid for staying with him. She knew they thought she was a coward, and she'd even heard them say she was trapped with him because of the children. But the truth of the matter was, she loved him. In spite of the disappointment, the drinking, the constant moving, the frequent lack of money, the loneliness, and even in spite of her little lost Charlotte, Hannah had given him her heart, and she couldn't take it back. So she had been able to look Martha straight in the eye and say, "Yes. I want it more than anything."

CHAPTER 13

2005

It took some cajoling and several long waits on the phone, but Daniel finally found someone in the Department of Motor Vehicles who not only knew how to find the ancient information but was also willing to share it with him.

"James Carlton McDonald . . . here it is. There are a lot of McDonalds, but only one with that middle name. We won't have a truck registration that old. You said 1937, right? If it ever existed, we would have purged it after so long, see? But there's a driver's license. He gave his address as 233 Washburn Avenue, Madison."

Daniel wrote it down and thanked the man profusely.

"No problem—I'm sure it's okay since it's so old. Hey, this gives a description of him. Want it?"

"A description? Yeah!"

"Six-foot-one, brown hair, blue eyes, a hundred and sixty pounds. Skinny guy, wasn't he?"

Daniel automatically glanced down his own lean frame. He wasn't much heftier himself. He felt rather smug, though, that he was two inches taller than his grandfather had been.

"Does it give a birth date?"

"April 14, 1885. No birth place. I think that's all we have."

"Thanks again for your help," Daniel replied.

"Hey, no problem. He's your kin, after all."

* * *

There were probably a million McDonalds living in Wisconsin. It was still worth looking, though, wasn't it? Something of his family might remain. Provided, of course, that Madison was where his family had originated. Who was to say where they had lived before that? If James McDonald had scarpered from one town without paying his rent, what were the odds that he'd done it before somewhere else? Feeling faintly ridiculous, Daniel set up his laptop and began to search the white pages of Madison by surname. He came up with forty-one McDonalds, none of them on Washburn Avenue.

"Why couldn't I have been named something unusual, like Skocylak?" he muttered, waiting impatiently for the printer to spit out the list. His brother-in-law wouldn't have had this kind of trouble, finding needles in the haystack. Daniel sighed. It was going to take him forever to contact all of these McDonalds. And besides that, what on earth was he to say?

Daniel went out to grab a plate of scrambled eggs and buckwheat pancakes at the Golden Griddle next to the hotel. When he got back, he kicked off his shoes, sprawled on the bed, and dialed the first phone number. An elderly voice answered promptly.

Daniel cleared his throat. "I wonder if you could help me. My name is Daniel McDonald."

"McDonald?" the voice said sharply. "That's my name too."

"Yes. I got your name from the phone book. I'm trying to locate someone who remembers a James Carlton McDonald who lived on 233 Washburn Avenue in Madison back in the early 1930s."

"James, hmm?" The elderly gentleman rambled to himself for a while, remembering the names of all of the relatives he knew who had lived in Wisconsin back then, but none of the names were familiar to Daniel— most, in fact, were female. It took Daniel a while to politely extricate himself from the one-sided conversation, thank the man, and hang up. He ran his hands through his hair. If all the people he contacted were this talkative, he would be ninety by the time he talked to them all. Should he try again? He closed his eyes. *Yes.* He muttered a brief prayer before dialing, hoping for some sort of help in wading through the forest of McDonalds. He knew his wife was a patient woman, but he'd spent enough time and energy on this search already.

The second number didn't answer. The third number was a small child who didn't seem to grasp the meaning of the phrase "Get your mommy for me," and Daniel finally hung up in frustration. The fourth call was different.

"McDonald?" the voice responded with interest when Daniel introduced himself. "I'm Alex McDonald."

Encouraged, Daniel briefly explained what he was looking for. There was a long pause on the other end of the line, and then Alex McDonald said, his voice an octave higher, "You're James's grandson?"

"Yes."

"Your dad was named James Carlton too?"

"That's right." Daniel gripped the phone. "Do you—"

"Oh, my gosh. Kathy, come here!" Alex called to someone. "It's my brother Jimmy's kid on the phone!"

Daniel sat up quickly on the edge of the bed. His heart was pounding so hard he felt it in the ear pressed against the phone.

"Brother? Did you say Jimmy was your brother?"

The voice grew louder as Alex came back to the phone. "If you're the son of James Carlton McDonald the second, I'm your uncle. I was born after him, in 1933. He was born in 1930. But it's a long story. Where are you calling from? Where are you?"

"I'm in Billings, Montana, right now, but I live in Denver."

"Colorado? How the heck did you end up way out there?"

"Oh . . . that's a long story too," Daniel said with a laugh, but it came out sounding rather strangled. He felt like a sponge, soaking up every drop of his uncle's voice, trying to memorize it, internalize every little clicking consonant. The voice was warm like honey, deeper than his own, and with the slight twang of Wisconsin.

"Well it's good to hear from you! My word! How did you find me?"

"I didn't. I mean, I didn't mean to. I mean, I didn't know you existed. I was just going through the phone book, really, looking for someone who remembered my grandfather, a distant relative maybe. I traced him back to Madison but I . . . I lost the trail there."

"What do you mean?"

Daniel laughed again, heartily this time. "I guess I don't sound very coherent, do I?"

"Not really."

"Sorry. To make it short, my dad left us when my brother and sister and I were little. I don't know anything about him or his family except that his dad's name was also James Carlton, and they were from Madison, or at least lived there a while. I'm trying to trace the history, figure out where I came from."

"Left," Alex murmured, sounding stunned. "Left you. You mean . . ."

"Never to be seen again. I'm sorry I can't tell you more than that."

"But is Jimmy still alive?"

"I really don't know. I haven't seen him since 1975."

"Is that so!"

"But what about you?" Daniel asked. "Did the family originally come from Wisconsin?"

"What? No."

"Then how did you end up there? Was Grandpa just passing through?"

"Well, sort of. He left me here with Aunt Helga after my mother died. Helga was Mom's sister."

His mother. Jimmy's mother too. My grandmother.

Alex was still talking. Daniel had to force himself to drag back his wandering thoughts. "After she died," Alex was saying, "Dad brought me and Matthew and Mary down here to stay with Aunt Helga. Mom was from here, you know, originally."

"No, I didn't know . . . Matthew and Mary?"

"My brother and sister. You mean you don't know anything about our family at all?"

"No," Daniel said, deflated, apologetic. "I was really little when Dad left. I never heard him say anything about his family. I know he had six siblings, though."

"Yeah, I was Mom's seventh. Eighth, actually, but one died young. You say Jimmy had three kids?"

"My brother Charlie, my sister Isabel, and me."

"It sure would be nice to get together with you and talk. There's no way I can leave right now, though. My wife, Kathleen, is due to have hip surgery soon. I gotta be here. You know how wives are, I guess? You married?"

"Yes. My wife—Rose—she's expecting. But not until February."

"Hey, that's great! Is this your first?"

"Yes."

"Congratulations. We have three ourselves, two boys and a girl. They're all married now, but they all live around here. Listen, do you think you could possibly get away and come visit us? Stay for a bit?"

"Of course," Daniel said instantly, not knowing if it were true. He would go today. "But your wife may not be up to company."

"Kathleen's a good sport. She's standing right here by me, nodding like crazy."

"I'll stay in a hotel, anyway, to make it easier."

"No need; it really isn't a bother. And hey, I'll call Mary and Matthew and tell them. They'll want to come too and meet you."

"Do they live near you?"

"Mary got married and moved to Detroit. Her husband died a few years back, though, with lung cancer. They had two children. Now Matthew, he stayed here in Madison and married a local girl. They have three boys. Two of them are married and living here in Wisconsin, but Aaron, he's a different kettle of fish." Alex broke off, chuckling, and Daniel could hear a soft murmur in the background as Kathleen said something.

"Yeah, *different* is the word, all right. He's probably about your age, Daniel. What is he now, Kathy? Thirty-seven or eight? Aaron's been through a lot, but he always manages to land on his feet. He's divorced, nasty breakup a while ago. Has one kid he never sees. He moves around a lot. Right now he's in New York. Can't seem to hold a job. He's been in and out of trouble, drunk driving, that kind of thing."

"Ah," Daniel said, because there really wasn't anything to say to that. He had cousins. And apparently they'd inherited some of the drunk-and-disorderly gene.

"But Matthew and Mary will be thrilled to hear from you. I bet Mary comes down."

Daniel hesitated, then asked the question he couldn't hold back. "Do you know why Grandpa left just you and Matthew and Mary with . . . Aunt Helga, and took the other kids somewhere else?"

"It wasn't by choice, that's for sure," Alex replied. "Apparently he asked Aunt Helga to take the whole crowd, all of us. But she couldn't, not with her own kids to care for and everything. So she agreed to take me, since I was just a baby, and she agreed to take one other so I could grow up with a brother. Matthew volunteered, and Mary stayed on to help out until she got married. Since Aunt Helga couldn't take all of us, Dad left, taking the rest with him. We always assumed he went back to Canada, but we never heard another thing from him, or any of the other kids. Until now."

"Wait, say that again. Back to *Canada?*"

"Well sure, that's where we were all from originally. Didn't you know?"

Daniel scrubbed the back of his neck with his knuckles. "No."

"Well, sure. Mary can tell you more about that, though, since of course I don't remember that at all. But I do know that we were all born in Ontario, Canada, except the older two, who were born here in Wisconsin. Mom and Dad married here, see. Eloped."

"They did?"

"I'll back up." Alex chuckled. "I don't mean to overwhelm you with information. Mom was from Wisconsin. Dad was an Irishman who'd immigrated to Canada. They married here, apparently against Mom's parents' wishes. They had a couple of kids here and then went back to Canada, where the rest of us were born."

It was too much for Daniel to take in at once. He realized he hadn't written a thing in his notebook. He told Alex he would be on the next flight out, if that was okay. Alex assured him it was. Daniel didn't know how long he could stay, but he'd do his best to get some time off work. He wrote down Alex's address with the hotel room pen (why couldn't they ever give guests pens that worked right?) and promised to phone again as soon as he knew his flight information.

"It was great hearing from you, Daniel," Alex said. "I can't believe you really called, but I'm glad you did. I've been trying to find your father for years. I looked all over Canada, but it never occurred to me that Dad might not have gone back home."

* * *

"You're going where?" Rose's voice rose shrilly.

"Wisconsin. Madison. Just for a little while," Daniel repeated. "I'm sorry to be gone so long, Rose, really I am. But . . . but this is my family. I've found them."

"Of course, you have to go," she agreed, recovering herself. "I know this is important. It just seems like a long way to go. But it's so great you've found them. I'm excited for you, honey, believe me."

"Me too," he said, and it felt as if the hole in his heart that he'd lived with all his life was suddenly starting to fill. "Me too."

CHAPTER 14

1933

The nurse was shouting in her ear as if she were deaf. "The baby's coming, Mrs. McDonald! Sit up just a little, and the doctor will be here in a moment. You're all right now."

Hannah fought for breath, thrashing her head on the pillow. "There's something wrong this time!" she cried. "I don't know what. It's just not right."

"Now, Mrs. McDonald, you've been through this before."

"This is the eighth time I've been through it," Hannah snapped back. "I know what I'm talking about."

The woman hurried away again, muttering under her breath, and Hannah pulled the blanket over her head and tried not to cry. She felt an overwhelming sense of panic. If something were to happen to this baby, she wouldn't be able to handle it. She had lost one daughter. She couldn't lose another. They weren't sealed together as a family yet. She thought of the other children waiting at home, thirteen-year-old Mary in charge, and imagined herself having to look at those little expectant faces and tell them the new baby wouldn't be coming home. If only James were here, she might feel more brave. She'd hoped with each child that he would handle it better, that he'd be there for her. But every time, as her pregnancy advanced, he became more and more withdrawn and remote, until by the time the birth came and he disappeared on one of his drinking binges, it was a relief to have him gone.

She'd finally understood it after the birth of little Jimmy, three years earlier. James had at last told her what was wrong. He'd come creeping in to her bedside, face awash with tears and red with drink, as she lay there holding Jimmy to her breast. James had put his head down on the bed and told her everything, the words pouring out as if a dam had broken. He told her of his first wife, Laura, a person Hannah had never suspected existed. He spoke of how beautiful she'd been, with hair like thick maple syrup and a laugh that gladdened his heart. How he had loved her! She'd lived on the next farm over, the only daughter among five sons, and James had loved her from the time they were children. They'd been married when they were twenty-three. Laura had died having their first child. She had bled to death in the bed, an abrupted placenta the doctor had called it. The child, a girl, had died too, bleeding to death in the womb.

Lying stiffly in the bed with Jimmy in her arms, Hannah hadn't reacted to the fact that he'd had a first wife and hadn't told her all these years. She wasn't astonished to think he'd fathered another child with someone else. Her only thought was relief: *Finally, I understand.*

But even though he'd confessed it all, even though it was all clear to Hannah now, it didn't stop him from running in the same pattern. As her latest pregnancy had advanced, James had once again withdrawn. The only difference had been that now Hannah understood the fear that made him do it. She hadn't seen him at all in the last two days. Yes, she understood him all right. But she still wished he were here.

Her thoughts were shattered now as hands tugged the blanket away from her head, pulled down the sheets, and pushed towels underneath her. Someone gripped her nightgown, and she pushed them away.

"Hold still, Mrs. McDonald; you're soaked to the bone. Hold still, I said. Dr. Spink is on the way. Is your husband waiting outside?"

"No. Something is wrong, nurse!" Hannah cried again, the panic rising. "The baby isn't lying right."

"It's fine. Take deep breaths."

Hannah gripped the head of the iron bedstead with her hands and waited, trying to take deep breaths to calm herself. The next pain came about three minutes later, even stronger than the last. A few moments later, Dr. Spink arrived, and the nurse busied herself around the room, covering Hannah with a clean sheet, straightening out towels beneath her, and bringing basins of steaming water.

"Doctor, please do something. The baby isn't lying right," Hannah gasped, reaching out to clutch his coat sleeve. "I'm not due for another month."

"Now, Mrs. . . ."

"McDonald," supplied the nurse.

"Mrs. McDonald. I've delivered plenty of babies, and I can assure you that you're all right. Everything looks fine to me."

Hannah thrashed her head back and forth on the pillow. Surely her eighth child shouldn't put up such a struggle as this, especially being so early. The room receded, and all sound faded. There was only pain, blinding and sharp, that turned her world white.

It was a boy. William, Sam, Matthew, and Jimmy had come screaming their way into the world. But this one mewed like a cat, a pitiful sound, and when the doctor laid the white-wrapped bundle on her stomach for her to inspect, Hannah felt only stunned bewilderment. He was small, terribly small. She looked at the delicate limbs, the soapy white scum that covered his skin, and felt total disbelief.

"He's a tiny one," Dr. Spink pronounced, as if it were her fault. And perhaps it was. If she'd eaten better, if she hadn't worn herself out with work . . .

"Will he live?" she asked, tears running freely down her face.

"I'll be honest, Mrs. McDonald. It's not often you can save them when they're this small. But he's only a month early, not more, and he's breathing on his own. We'll do everything in our power to help him. You just relax now and rest a little."

"What will you name him?" the nurse asked, helping her to slide up farther on the pillows while another nurse whisked the baby away.

"Alexander," Hannah said. "Alexander Heinrich McDonald. After both his grandfathers."

"A good strong name," the nurse replied.

* * *

The next morning, Hannah woke up feeling empty, both physically and emotionally. Doors closed quietly in the hospital corridor outside her room, and she heard footsteps and low voices. They had brought the baby to her once in the night to nurse, but that was all, and he hadn't fed well. She reached for the bell by the side of her bed, but the door opened and a nurse entered before she could press it.

"Good morning, Mrs. McDonald. How are you feeling?"

"Like a horse has trampled me," Hannah replied. "Will you please bring my son to me?"

The nurse hesitated, and Hannah felt every instinct jump and jangle like electric wires. Instantly she was fully awake and sitting bolt upright.

"What's the matter?"

"The doctor thinks it would be better if the baby were hand-fed for a while," the nurse said. "He didn't nurse well last night, and we can't afford for him to lose any weight. He's being kept warm now."

Hannah nodded, swallowing hard. "May I come see him?"

"Certainly. Do you feel well enough to get up?"

Hannah threw back her sheets and swung her legs to the floor. "Of course."

Later, Dr. Spink told Hannah that the baby would have to stay in the hospital for some time. "If he gains weight well, he could come home soon, but if not . . ." he left the sentence unfinished, but his kindly face was troubled. "And you should remain here in bed for at least three days."

"I'm afraid that's impossible," Hannah replied. "If I'm not nursing the baby, there's no reason I need to stay in the hospital. I'm needed at home. I have other children, and only my oldest daughter to care for them."

"But you won't recover well at home," Dr. Spink protested.

"I won't get any rest here in the hospital," Hannah insisted. "I'll only fret and worry. I need to go home to my children. I'll feel better if I'm with them."

"Well," Dr. Spink said, "I will come to see you tomorrow, and if I think you're fit, I will send you home. But return to bed now."

Hannah went back to her room, her thoughts on the tiny baby she'd just seen, and the size of the hospital bill that was to come. She'd never be able to pay it. Her family would hardly have enough to live on now if it weren't for William coming home and slipping her part of his pay whenever James was away. William still brought home a turkey or a goose for them sometimes. But only when he knew James wouldn't be at home.

* * *

The next morning, the doctor pronounced Hannah fit to return home, but only if she promised to put her feet up and do no heavy lifting. Hannah packed her small overnight bag and prepared to leave. She'd brought only one baby sleeper with her, and Alexander was wearing that—though it was much too big for him. There was a box of baby clothes at home, and perhaps something smaller could be found. She would ask Mary to sort through it. Perhaps she already had; she was a conscientious girl.

Hannah picked up the bag and carried it out of the room, then down the green-painted hall to the nurses' desk. Dr. Spink was there, writing in a chart, and when she paused beside him, he looked up and smiled.

"Ah, yes, Mrs. McDonald. Something else?"

"I just wanted to thank you. For letting me go home. And for all the care you're giving Alexander."

"We'll be in touch, and of course you can visit any time. You'll come see me on Friday?"

"Yes."

"Good, good."

He smiled again in his friendly fashion and headed away down the hall. Hannah shifted her grip on her bag and looked at the nurse, wondering what sort of papers she needed to sign, her thoughts already leap-frogging ahead to dinner, laundry, and finding change to pay the taxi. Something warm and wet slid down the inside of her thigh, and she looked down, surprised.

There was a puddle of blood around her feet.

CHAPTER 15

2005

The taxi brought Daniel from the hotel to Alex's redbrick house in less than fifteen minutes. He paid the driver and stood on the sidewalk, looking at the house, suddenly nervous to walk up the steps and knock. He hadn't taken time after his flight to wash up or change. He had simply dumped his suitcase and come straight here. He'd called Alex when he'd gotten his flight information, but the line had been busy, and he'd just left a message on the machine. Now he was actually here, about to burst into the life of someone who was, for all intents and purposes, a total stranger. Some of the questions in his life were being answered, but new ones were springing up in their places. Why had James McDonald left Matthew instead of Jimmy behind with Aunt Helga? Why hadn't he gone back to Canada where he'd come from? How on earth had he ended up in Montana with only one child in tow? What had happened to the others? Where had James himself ended up?

And where was Jimmy McDonald now? Was he still alive? And if so, would he want to be found?

They must have seen him from the window. The front door opened, and a man came onto the porch. He was tall and thin, and wore black slacks and a button-down white shirt. His sandy brown hair had faded almost gray, but his eyes, even at this distance, shone a clear summer blue. Jimmy McDonald's eyes. Daniel's eyes.

"Daniel?" The man's voice was deep and raspy, as it had been over the phone, but there was a strain to it now.

Daniel took a deep breath, smiled, and nodded.

Alex came down the steps and crossed the little yard. He was seventy-two, by Daniel's calculations, but his handshake was vigorous enough to bruise Daniel's fingers. As they greeted each other, the men examined one other in sideways glances, each seeking something in the other's features. The resemblance was strong, not just in coloring and height but in the way they smiled and moved.

"I can't believe it!" Alex exclaimed. "I can sure see you're a McDonald. Come in and meet the rest of the gang." He ushered Daniel indoors, calling out to his wife and children. They came eagerly, en masse, from the kitchen. Kathleen was a self-conscious but pretty woman in a Hawaiian-print blouse, and she moved slowly with a cane. She pumped Daniel's hand enthusiastically.

"It's all Alex has been able to talk about since you called yesterday. We're so glad you're here," she declared, grinning.

"These are our kids, Greg, Tom, and Kate." The "kids" were about Daniel's own age, the boys darker haired, and Kate strawberry blond. *A handsome bunch,* Daniel thought, pleased. He came from a good-looking family. "We sent the grandkids next door to play for a bit. Didn't want to overwhelm you. There are six of them."

"Four of them mine," Kate said with a smile that was half proud, half embarrassed. She put a hand on her stomach, and Daniel suddenly realized she was expecting again. He hadn't noticed because of how petite she was. But now he could see it in the careful way she carried herself, in the glow on her face that reminded him of Rose. He gave her a grin.

"I look forward to meeting them," he said.

"We'll bring them back in a bit. Let you get settled first."

The house was neat and countrified and smelled of baked apples. The couch in the living room sagged with crocheted throws and patchwork pillows, and a child's crayon drawing was framed on the wall beside a Rembrandt print. A plastic bucket of Legos stood on the coffee table beside a glass dish of cashews. Daniel sat on the couch with his hands cupping his knees, and his uncle sat opposite him on a recliner with rubbed-bare arms. Greg, Tom, and Kate arranged themselves around them, looking eagerly back and forth between their father and this stranger who looked so much like him. And suddenly, with so much to say, there was nothing to say. Daniel and Alex looked at each other and both laughed at the same time at their mutual shyness. Laughed for the sheer joy of staring at each other.

"Mary screamed when I phoned and told her," Alex said after a moment. "She couldn't believe it. I think she took it especially hard when Dad took the other kids away. I mean, she'd practically been a second mother to us all. She told me a lot, growing up, that she felt more like our mother than our sister. And then to lose track of everyone like that . . . anyway, she's flying in tonight. I have to go pick her up at seven-fifteen."

"And Matthew?"

Alex grimaced apologetically. "He's out of town for a while. He's tied up with something."

"You can say it out loud, Dad. We're adults now," said Kate. She wrinkled her nose at Daniel. "Matthew's son Aaron is getting out of jail tomorrow morning, and he wants to be there."

"Ah."

"He's supposed to be in court on Tuesday." Alex sighed. "But at least Mary's coming."

"Yes."

"The grandkids and I baked cookies to celebrate your arrival," Kathleen said. "Tom, be a dear and bring them in, will you? And the milk, too." She grinned. "I should offer you something to drink, but the only thing that really goes with chocolate chip cookies is milk."

"Milk is fine," Daniel said, grinning back. He leaned forward, elbows on his knees, and asked Alex, "So do you know anything at all about the other kids? Your brothers and sisters? You've heard nothing?"

Alex swallowed the cookie he'd popped into his mouth. "The only news we've heard was about my brother Sam." He paused, seeing if the name rang any bells, but when Daniel shook his head, Alex said, "He was the third one, just younger than Mary. Sam was maybe eleven when Mom died. I don't know what happened, really. All I know is that in July 1990, I read his obituary in the paper. He died right here in Madison, of cirrhosis of the liver. He was only sixty-eight when he died. But the obituary gave his name and birth date and said he was born in Toronto, so I know it was our Sam. I couldn't believe it. He was right here in Madison, maybe all this time, and I didn't even know it."

"But you're sure it was your brother?"

"Yes. Samuel Wyse McDonald. Born October 1, 1922, in Toronto, Ontario, Canada. Had to be him. I called the paper to find out who paid for the obituary. It was his employer at the foundry." He shook his head mournfully. "All this time he might have been here, and I didn't know it."

"The only surviving family member listed in Sam's obituary was Anna Peterson of Michigan," Kathleen chipped in. "Alex's sister was named Anna. Of course we tried to follow up on that, but you know how many Petersons live in Michigan. We didn't find her."

"Sam's middle name was Wyse?" Daniel asked, consulting the notes he'd started jotting down.

"It was Mom's maiden name. She was German. She was from Wisconsin—grew up here, I mean. She was born in Leipzig, Germany."

"What was Grandma's full name?"

"Hannah Louisa Wyse McDonald." He paused, and again grimaced apologetically. "I don't have any memories of her, of course, but Mary told me all she can remember about her. She had a slight German accent, wasn't very tall—we get our height from our dad—and she had blue eyes and red hair."

Daniel felt something start to close over his throat, and he had to remind himself to breathe. "Do you have a photograph of her?"

Alex blinked. "Of course." He got up from his chair and went to a cabinet across the room, then came back with a battered photo album, which he reverently placed in Daniel's hands. Alex moved to sit beside Daniel on the couch and carefully opened the album to the front page. And slowly, page by page, Daniel's family came to life before him.

A gray-and-white snapshot of Hannah Wyse, her face a perfect oval, her hair swept up, gazed steadily at him from the page. She looked about sixteen, and her lips were slightly parted as if she were about to say something humorous to the photographer. She was beautiful.

He turned the page to see a series of snapshots of various solemn-eyed children of different ages, with the anonymous, noseless look of all small children. They wore overalls, button-down blouses, bobby socks, and Easter hats. None of them were smiling in the pictures but instead stared at the camera apprehensively. He looked at each of these photos carefully, wondering but not sure if one of the small faces belonged to his father.

He came to a photo of an older woman, sharp-faced and frowning, in a print dress. Her hair was pulled back severely, and her gaze clearly told what she thought of the experience of having her photo taken.

"Aunt Helga," Alex supplied, and Daniel began to wonder if his father had been one of the lucky ones to escape being raised by this stern-eyed woman. He saw little if any warmth in her.

And then there was another picture of Hannah Wyse. She looked considerably older, her hair lighter, her dress a plain gray. She stood, slim to the point of being skinny, in clunky shoes. She held an infant in her arms, which one he couldn't tell. The baby was wrapped in a white blanket that looked like a hospital towel, and the tiny face was screwed up with crying. Hannah looked, not at the camera, but at the baby, her finger lightly touching the round cheek, and her face, despite its lines, was gently radiant.

Daniel touched this photo carefully with one finger, tracing the changes wrought by age and perhaps something else. Hannah looked as if she'd lived a difficult, demanding life.

She also looked exactly like the woman in his dream.

* * *

After much persuasion, they convinced him to stay at the house instead of a hotel, insisting that Kathleen had already gotten a room ready for him. When Daniel rode with Alex to the airport a few hours later, he stopped to collect his suitcase from the hotel and cancel his reservation. At the ARRIVALS gate, he stood right up at the front of the crowd waiting for disembarking passengers. His stomach was jumpy with excitement. Without question, he recognized Mary as a McDonald as soon as she stepped out of the gate. She was tall, painfully thin—and her blue McDonald eyes shone like headlamps, visible from fifty feet away. They skimmed the crowd and landed on him, and he saw delight spring into them. She hurried over at a speed he hadn't thought possible for a woman of eighty-five. Right there in front of everyone, she dropped her carry-on bag, spread her arms, and cried, "You look just like I thought you would!"

He climbed over the velvet rope, and she hugged him tightly. She was very light, and he felt her ribs creak as he squeezed her. He didn't know this woman, had never met her, hadn't even known her name before yesterday. And yet he knew her, thoroughly and utterly.

After a moment, he pried her away and held her at arm's length. Her eyes were drowned in tears now, but her smile was bright and her hands patted his face, exploring, claiming, rejoicing.

"My little Jimmy's boy. My word, you're tall! You look just like Alex when he was younger."

Other people were trying to squeeze past them, like a stream around a rock. Mary guided him back to the velvet rope and stepped nimbly over it, not letting go of his hand, as if afraid he'd disappear if she let go. Alex gave her a quick hug and retrieved her bag.

"Follow me. Let's get out of this crush," he said.

Once at the car, Daniel sat in the back seat with Mary. Alex, looking back at them in the rearview mirror, couldn't stop grinning.

"I told you she was excited," he said.

"I thought I'd have a heart attack when Alex told me he'd found you. Or rather, that you'd found him," Mary said, nodding repeatedly. "I'll never forget the day Dad drove away with Jimmy and Sam and Anna in the truck. It was a beat-up old thing, and I could see Jimmy, your father, kneeling on the back seat, his hands pressed against the back window, looking at me. I just bawled and bawled. I felt like I was losing my own children."

"There's so much I want to ask you. You'll remember more than most of the rest of the children because you were older," Daniel said.

"There's a lot to tell. But you first. Alex told me you're living in Colorado."

"Yes. Denver."

"Married?"

"Yes. Her name is Rose. We've been married about six years, and we're having a baby in February, our first."

"Terrific! And what do you do for a living?"

"I'm a journalist for a small newspaper in Denver. Nothing terribly important."

"So you managed to go to school?"

He smiled. "Yes, I managed." No need to tell her about the two part-time jobs, the exhausting night shifts, and the hefty loan from Rose's father that had created a rift between them deeper than either of them cared to admit. The loan had been paid off two years earlier, but the rift hadn't completely healed.

"And what does Rose do?"

"She teaches arts and crafts at a community center in Denver. After the baby's born, she'll take a break and then maybe just teach a class one or two nights a week. She makes beautiful painted glass ornaments, and she likes to restore old furniture." He felt a twinge of homesickness and wished Rose were there to meet these people—his family. She would like them, and he knew they'd like her.

Mary was stroking his hand unconsciously with her own, as if he were a cat. Anxiously she asked, "And how did you end up where you are? What happened to Jimmy?"

He hesitated. "I don't know much about what happened, but I do know that Jimmy was left in Billings, Montana when he was seven."

"Left? What do you mean?"

Daniel squirmed. "I found the account in an old newspaper article. Jimmy ran away from home when he was seven. While the police were looking for him, James—Grandpa—left town, skipping out on repaying his debts. He didn't come back. I don't know what happened to him. When they found Jimmy, he was living in a railroad car. He was fine, but they had nowhere to put him, no known family to give him to. He was placed in the care of a family named Johnson in Colorado, friends of the sheriff who found him. And then, when Mrs. Johnson became ill, he was sent to their friends the Zahlmanns in Montana. He was with them for a few years and then struck out on his own."

In the shifting shadows of the car's interior, Daniel saw that Mary's face had gone still and white. Alex's eyes held his in the rearview mirror.

"So Dad never went back to Canada, I guess," Alex told Mary. "We've always assumed he did."

"I don't know what Jimmy did during the intervening years," Daniel said. "I talked to Theresa Zahlmann, his foster mother, and she hadn't heard from him since he left at the age of sixteen. But in 1959, Jimmy showed up in Colorado and married my mother, Caroline. My brother, Charlie, was born in 1960; my sister, Isabel, was born six years later; and then I came along in 1970."

"That's good, then."

He hated to tell her, but there was no use avoiding it. "Dad left us when I was five."

She drew her breath in sharply. "You too?"

"Yes. But at least we had Mom . . . for a while. She died two years later of cancer, and her cousins raised me and Isabel. Charlie left home. I think he went looking for Dad, but we never heard from him again."

"What is it with the men in this family?" Mary asked, and her voice was bitter. "Your father, my father, Charlie. They wander around like stray dogs."

Daniel cleared his throat. "But it turned out all right. I have a good life."

"I should have insisted that Helga take Jimmy in too. He was only a little boy. He needed me."

"Why didn't your father leave Jimmy instead of Matthew?" Daniel asked. "Do you know?"

"Matthew volunteered. I think Helga was happy to have a boy a little older. Two tiny ones would have been too much, on top of her own children."

"Well, there's no point in regretting things now, I guess. No one could have known how things would turn out." He paused, then said, "Now you know my end of it. What happened in your life?"

She coughed and said quietly, "Well, I suppose Alex has probably told you just about everything. I stayed at Helga's with Matthew and Alex after Mother died."

"I'd like to learn more about that. How did Grandma die?" The word *Grandma* felt strange on Daniel's lips.

"She . . . she died shortly after Alex was born, in 1933. You wouldn't know about that, I guess. Jimmy was only three then and wouldn't have remembered."

"No." Daniel closed his eyes. "No, I didn't know that. I don't know if Jimmy—Dad—remembered her or not; he didn't tell me either way." He felt a pang of sadness for little boys separated from their parents at such a young age—himself, Matthew, Alex, Jimmy.

"I'm sorry," Alex added quietly.

"For what?"

"I've always felt a bit responsible, you know. Her dying because of me."

Daniel swallowed hard. "That's ridiculous. It's not your fault."

"Of course not. I've told him that a hundred times over the years," Mary said peacefully. "Anyway, I stayed with Aunt Helga for a while, to help out. When I was twenty-three, I got married to a man named Oscar Lewis; we had two children, a boy and a girl. Oscar was a manager at a power plant in Detroit." A wistful look filled Mary's eyes. "He died four years ago. Millie, our daughter, is married and lives in Detroit, near me. John never married. He lives in Lansing and works as a mechanical engineer. Just had his fifty-fifth birthday last week."

"And you never heard from your other siblings? Samuel and Anna and—who was the other one?"

"William. He was the oldest. But he had left home by the time Mother died. He stayed in Canada and didn't come with us. I've always felt bad about that. We were quite close. He was tall, like you." Mary shook her head sadly. "Alex told you what we learned about Sam, didn't he?"

"Yes—that he ended up in Madison, but you never even knew."

"A pity. When we talked to his employer at the foundry, we were told he'd worked there for ten years. No idea where he'd been before that."

"And his obituary mentioned Anna?"

"Yes, and gave her married name. But it only listed 'Michigan' as her place of residence and didn't narrow it down. We looked in all the directories and made a lot of calls, but we never found her, and after a while we just gave up. We'd been searching so long already," she added apologetically.

"Of course. I'm so sorry Sam died before you could find him. It was cirrhosis of the liver, wasn't it?"

Mary nodded. "Yes. I was sad to hear it but not overly surprised."

"No?"

"Well, look at what he came from. Matthew's son Aaron is another one like him."

"Sorry?"

She drew a sharp breath. "But of course you don't know where he came from, do you? Your father wouldn't have remembered, so I suppose he never told you. Well, I guess you don't need to know all about it. But I'll tell you this: Alcohol played a major role in our family. Still does, I think."

"Ah. I got that impression," Daniel said quietly. "But I think maybe I do need to know all about it."

"Maybe so, but not tonight. Tonight let's just be happy."

CHAPTER 16

When Daniel phoned Rose that evening, she was just leaving for class, but even their brief exchange warmed him. Later he would tell her everything, but for now it was enough just to hear her voice.

The adults stayed up late, eating chocolate chip cookies and talking endlessly, until Kathleen sagged with exhaustion in her chair. The grand-kids, who had long since come home from the neighbors, had fallen asleep like kittens on the throw rug. They were beautiful children, three girls and three boys, all with strawberry-blond hair and cream-white skin spattered with freckles. In spite of Alex's warning that they were a handful, they were well-behaved and polite children. The oldest was about seven, and the youngest was a chunky toddler of two. This last one, whose name was Eli, stared at Daniel for a while with one finger in his mouth, and then solemnly climbed into Daniel's lap, lay his head back against his chest, and proceeded to stay there the rest of the evening until he fell asleep. Daniel sat, afraid to move for fear of waking him, and no one removed the boy. But the warm, limp weight of the child was comforting somehow, like a hug.

Daniel soaked up every detail about Alex and Matthew's life living with their German relatives. What it had been like to grow up on a farm with cousins and chickens. How they had stuck apples to the electrified barbed-wire fences and waited for the cows to bite into them. How Matthew had fallen off a haystack and nearly impaled himself on a pitchfork. How they had driven the tractor up and down the fields at the age of eight. How they had learned to keep Aunt Helga happy by blending into the background as much as possible.

"She was a generous woman but overworked and tired, and her husband, Georg, wasn't very helpful. I'm sure we were a burden to her," Alex told Daniel while Mary nodded slowly. "But she tried to be kind. I did hear her cursing our father a few times, though, when she thought no one was listening."

At last Alex stood and stretched and declared the day over. "I'm too old to stay up late anymore," he apologized. "But we can talk more tomorrow." He paused with a hand on Daniel's shoulder. "It's good to have you here. It's almost like finding my brother."

Kate came to take her sleeping son from Daniel's lap. Daniel's legs were cramped from holding still, but his lap felt empty and his chest cool without the little boy snuggled against him. For a moment he felt a sense of loss. But as Alex had said—there was always tomorrow.

Daniel glanced at his watch and considered the time difference. Best to call Rose back tomorrow. Instead, he sent her a text message for her to find in the morning. "I love you. All is well."

* * *

Daniel didn't expect to sleep with his mind so keyed up from the day's events, but he sank like a rock into oblivion as soon as he lay down on the soft bed in the guest room, and when he awoke in the morning, it was with only the vaguest memory of dreaming. He knew he'd dreamt of the red-haired woman again, but the details of the dream were fuzzy. Now he knew—perhaps—who the woman was. As he looked around the room, at the family pictures—his family—on the wall, he felt a deep sense of contentment, excitement, and satisfaction.

The children had already had their breakfast, leaving the kitchen a dazzling display of dirty cereal bowls, spilt milk, and scattered Cheerios. He could feel granulated sugar underfoot as he crossed to the table. He wondered if his own child would be this messy.

Kathleen, her hair snagged back in a rubber band like a teenager, greeted him cheerily. "Don't mind the mess. I'm just whipping up some waffles. They'll be ready in a few minutes. I hope you don't mind drinking out of a plastic mug," she added. "We don't have much glass left. Alex ran down to the store for some more milk. He won't be a jiff. And the kids will take the grandkids home this morning, so it will be calmer here."

"I don't mind at all," Daniel said pleasantly, and discovered it was true. "Where are they all now?"

"Out in the backyard terrorizing the squirrels."

Daniel pushed open the back door and walked onto the porch. The morning air was clear and cool, and the birds were going wild in a stand of birches next door. Alex's yard was huge, much bigger than he'd expected. A nicely trimmed lawn ran slightly downhill to a playground, where the six children swung on swings and played in a sandbox. There was a dilapidated shed with a wheelbarrow tipped on its nose against the side, and along one fence ran a flowerbed, thick with mums and day lilies the color of salmon. A gigantic pine tree stood in one corner, the ground beneath it bare but for a layer of ancient pine needles and a wooden bench overlooking the play area. A stone planter full of geraniums stood next to it, and Daniel saw that someone had parked a Tonka truck among the flowers. He walked through dew-wet grass to sit on the bench. In the shade he almost wished for a sweater. Summer was over.

Eli looked up from the hole he was digging in the sand. He was squat-ting as only a toddler could do, in a position Daniel would have found impossible to maintain. After a moment the little boy rose and came over. He held out a sandy pine cone for Daniel to inspect.

"Very nice. Did you find it under the tree?" Daniel asked politely.

Eli nodded.

"Are you building a sand castle?"

Eli contemplated the word for a while and nodded again.

One of the other children, a girl of five called Barbie or Brandy or Betty—he couldn't remember now—was swinging upside down by her knees from the monkey bars. Her socks didn't match, and her long hair dragged in the sand. She gave him a gap-toothed upside-down smile.

"Eli doesn't talk," she informed him.

"Eli's only two. I'm sure he'll learn," Daniel answered, feeling somewhat defensive.

"He wears diapers, too. Mom says he's got to hurry and get out of them before the next baby comes."

"I'm sure he'll learn that too," Daniel said.

"I want the next baby to be a girl. We already have three boys. I want a sister."

"I'm sure you must."

"We could share a room, and I could braid her hair. I can braid already," she added proudly.

"I don't think a baby will have enough hair to braid for a while."

The girl gave herself a push and swung peacefully back and forth. "I can wait," she said. "Mom says you're my long-lost cousin. Why were you lost?"

Daniel chuckled. "I don't know."

"Who lost you?"

He hesitated, not sure how to answer. Eli stuck a sandy finger in his mouth and looked up at him, wide-eyed.

"Don't eat sand," Daniel told him.

"But you're found now," the little girl added, giving herself another push.

"Yes," Daniel said quietly. "I'm found now."

The back door opened, and Kathleen stuck her head out.

"Breakfast, Daniel!"

Saved by the bellow.

As Daniel seated himself at the table, Mary came in. She wore gray knit pants and a yellow blouse that reminded him of boiled egg yolk. She looked like she hadn't slept well, but her smile was warm, and she came over to kiss first Kathleen's cheek and then his own.

"When I first woke up, I was afraid it had all been a dream and you'd be gone," she confessed, sitting beside him at the table. She examined her plastic mug. "Daffy Duck. My favorite."

Daniel smiled and admired his own mug—Tweety Bird. Kathleen offered coffee, but he opted for milk without bothering to explain that his religion forbade coffee. There was enough to explain about his life without complicating it with religion at the moment. But maybe, he thought, he'd have an opportunity to talk about it later. He would like that.

"Strawberry jam or maple syrup?" Kathleen asked.

"Syrup," Mary and Daniel answered together. They smiled at each other.

"What else could I expect from two Canadians?" Kathleen chuckled, opening the fridge.

"That's another thing. I had no idea Dad was born in Canada," Daniel said. "Does that mean I'm entitled to Canadian citizenship?"

"You probably would have had to apply for it before now," Mary said. "But I don't know for sure how it works."

Daniel pushed half of a waffle into his mouth and found it to be the most delicious thing he'd ever eaten. When he was able to talk again, he asked, "Where was Dad born exactly?"

"Collingwood, Ontario. It's a nice little town on Georgian Bay, which is kind of a piece of Lake Huron that sticks out." She turned to her sister-in-law. "Do you have a map, Kathy?"

Kathleen rummaged around without result, and finally produced an inflatable toy globe from the den. It didn't give much detail, but Mary was able to give him a general idea. "There, north of Toronto. I remember it had nice beaches that were always crowded in the summer, and the water was shallow for quite a ways out, so even little kids could swim safely. We would play on the sand and swim for hours. There was an ice cream place that a boy at school once took me to." She frowned. "Listen to me. I sound like an old granny remembering her first box dance." Then the frown quirked upward. "But it was fun. His name was Toby McNamara. I wonder what became of him. Anyway, Dad married Mother down in Wisconsin, where he was working." She slid her eyes sideways at him. "One of the few times he did work. Mother was only eighteen when they married. Eloped, because her parents disapproved. Dad was thirty."

"That's quite an age difference," Daniel remarked. "I can see why her family objected."

"It wasn't just the age difference. A lot of girls married young to men much older than themselves. Mother's parents thought Dad was . . . unstable. Not suitable. They wanted their daughter to marry a nice German boy, and Dad was an 'Irish gypsy,' as Aunt Helga put it."

"He was Irish, then? I would have thought that, with a name like McDonald, the family would be Scottish, not Irish."

"They were once. A lot of Scots moved to Northern Ireland in the 1700s. It was part of England's plan to move Protestants into the area to help keep the Irish Catholics under control. A land grab, that's what it was."

"Yes. I know that bit of Northern Ireland's history. I just hadn't realized that our family was a part of it."

"I don't know exactly when the McDonalds moved to Ireland. But even though they may have been Scottish at one point, after a few generations in Ireland they counted themselves as Irish. Dad was born in County Antrim in 1885, and I never heard him call himself anything but Irish. He came to Canada when he was only ten, with his parents. They both died in the early 1930s. Dad was a brick mason."

Mary speared another waffle from the plate that Kathleen had just set gently before them. She helped herself to butter and a large quantity of syrup. For someone so thin, she certainly ate well. She was matching Daniel waffle for waffle. Kathleen sat down with her own plate but didn't interrupt the conversation, just listened with a smile on her face.

"I asked Mother once about how they'd met, but she didn't like to talk about it. She just said he'd followed the work down to Wisconsin. Their first two children were born in Wisconsin. William and myself."

"I want to make sure I have all the information right," Daniel said, pushing aside his plate and reaching for his notebook. "What year was William born?"

"In 1917. I came along in 1920—don't gawp—yes, I'm old. Then we went to Canada, and Sam was born in—let me see—it would be 1922. Anna was born in 1925. Matthew was born in 1928. Jimmy came along in 1930, and then Alex was born in 1933. Mother died right after."

"Alex seems to think it was his fault."

"Alex takes the weight of the world on his shoulders," Mary replied peacefully.

Daniel's pen paused midair. "That's seven."

"What?"

"That's only seven. Alex told me he was Grandma's eighth child."

"Oh. I'm forgetting Charlotte," Mary said blankly. "She was born between Sam and Anna. She died a week before Matthew was born. I think the shock of it is what sent Mother into labor." She paused a moment, then noted, "Sam was born in Toronto. Charlotte and Anna were born in Creemore, just north of Toronto. And the rest were born in Collingwood, north of that. We moved around a lot," she added vaguely. "I can write down everyone's birth dates and places for you properly."

"Thanks, I'd appreciate it. You mentioned that your father wasn't employed much?"

She stirred a little pile of fallen sugar with her finger, leaving a soft indented pattern. She didn't look up as she shook her head.

Daniel said, "According to the newspaper articles I found, Jimmy was the only child with James McDonald when they reached Montana. Sam and Anna weren't with them."

"Then they were dropped off somewhere between here and Montana," Mary said, and took another bite of waffle. "Probably not far away, if Sam ended up back here and Anna ended up in Michigan."

"Do you think we might be able to find Anna, William, and Jimmy now? Then the family would be complete."

"I've looked." She gave him a smile that was meant to soften the pathos of that statement but only ripped at his heart. "I put ads in the paper in Toronto years ago, and I've searched phone books."

"I'm going to keep looking," Daniel said. "I'm a journalist. I'm good at ferreting out information. Maybe I'll even find out what happened to James McDonald."

Mary straightened a little, and Daniel saw her exchange a swift look with Kathleen.

"What?"

"What, what?" Mary responded, smiling.

"That little exchange just now."

Mary drew a deep breath and let it out slowly. She set down her fork and reached to touch the back of Daniel's hand with her fingertips. Her nails were short, and the skin on her hands was papery and soft.

"Not all the information you'll find will be happy," she said quietly. "Maybe you should just be content with what you've found so far."

"I don't understand. You just said you'd looked for them. Why shouldn't I?"

"You don't know. It's different for you . . ."

Daniel spread his hands. "I mean, for all I know, my dad is still alive. I may have another aunt and uncle living somewhere. James McDonald would have long since passed on, though."

"Oh, I should hope so," Mary responded fervently, and then blushed.

Daniel stiffened, staring at her. Carefully he drew his hand away from hers.

"What aren't you telling me?" he asked. "I have the right to know."

Kathleen glanced over, holding her fork up like a scepter. "He does, you know," she told Mary. "Better that he hear it now, from you, than find it in some hospital record or newspaper account someday. It's his heritage too."

Daniel looked from Kathleen's solemn face to Mary's pinched one and felt a knot of fear begin to form in his stomach. "Tell me," he said. "I'm not a kid. You don't have to protect me."

To his dismay, Mary's face crumpled into tears. But when he went to put his hand over hers, she yanked it away, and he saw she was trembling.

"That's all I ever did was protect those kids!" she cried. "Jimmy and Sam and Matthew and the lot of them! Even little baby Alex. I spent my life protecting them! You're Jimmy's son. I want to protect you too. It's not such an easy thing to stop."

The waffle was a cold lump in his belly. Daniel slid his chair back a few inches, physically bracing himself. "I need to know it all," he said.

Mary scraped at her eyes with the backs of her hands. "I'm sorry," she said in a calmer tone. "I didn't mean to have a meltdown."

Kathleen gripped her cane and moved to sit opposite her sister-in-law, reaching out to put a hand on the older woman's arm. Mary gave her a watery look and then breathed deeply again, her composure restored.

"All right, it's your history too, in a way. You should know, if for no other reason than to make sure you turn out differently."

Daniel waited, his pen forgotten, his eyes on hers.

"Dad wasn't always a good man," she said after a moment. "When he was working he'd spend all his wages on drink. He'd sit around the house and . . . well, we preferred it when he went out drinking, because then at least he wasn't home where we could see it. Sometimes he'd go on benders that lasted weeks at a time. Once he was gone for three months. Mother was the one who held it all together. As soon as we kids were eleven or twelve and old enough to work, we got jobs and brought the wages home to Mother. I worked three days a week in a neighbor's dairy. William worked for the butcher, doing deliveries. Mother cleaned house for some people in town and took in laundry. She washed it by hand, too—no machine. I don't know to this day how she managed to keep body and soul together for us, but she did. William got away from home as soon as he could. But I stayed, even when I could have gotten a job waitressing or something and moved into town. I stayed because I knew Mother couldn't do it on her own."

Daniel shifted uncomfortably, suddenly not wanting to hear but knowing he must. When Mary paused, he nodded encouragingly but did not speak.

"Mother was in the hospital twice, other than when she had us kids, I mean. Once with a broken arm. Once with a gunshot wound."

"Gunshot!"

Mary glanced at Kathleen as if for support. "She was hanging out sheets to dry in the side yard. I was maybe nine or ten at the time. Dad was sitting on a chair on the porch with a rifle, shooting holes through the sheets as she hung them out. He wasn't yelling, wasn't angry, nothing. He just sat there and took shots. And Mother . . ." Mary swallowed and went back to fiddling with the spilled sugar. "Mother kept right on hanging those sheets. I was in the kitchen, looking out through the window over the sink. I remember thinking how stubborn she looked, her lips pressed tight together, frowning, but she kept bending down to the basket and snapping the sheets out straight and pinning them up on the line. And then, suddenly, she stopped and fell to her knees, holding her shoulder. I remember there was a lot of blood. I hollered for William, and between us we picked Mother up and carried her to the neighbors, who had a car, and they took her to the hospital. And Dad just sat on the porch and kept right on shooting holes through that laundry."

Daniel pushed his fingers through his hair, trying to grasp this. "Did he get arrested or anything?"

"No. No police ever came. The next day Mother was home again with her arm in a sling, and nothing was ever said about it. Dad took off, though, the next day. I think he was gone two weeks that time."

"Unreal," Daniel muttered.

Mary picked up her fork and stabbed another waffle. Without looking up, she spread it with butter and reached for the syrup. "When William was fourteen, he wanted to get a job with the railroad. You had to be sixteen to work for them. There was a paper that a parent had to sign, stating he was sixteen. Mother signed it. I guess she figured he was better off working on the railroad far away than he was living at home." She gave a wry smile, blue eyes bright. "But William needed his family—or most of it, anyway. He came back to Collingwood and went back to work at the butcher's, and he'd smuggle us hams and chickens and turkeys. But he wouldn't come back to live with us."

"Did your father . . ." Daniel found he couldn't ask the question. He looked at Kathleen, then at Mary, trying to form the words. "Was it only his wife?"

"Did he hurt the children?" Mary prompted gently. "Is that what you mean?"

He nodded.

"When he'd been drinking, yes. He would go after anything that drew his attention. You learned to keep your head down and mind your own business, and then it was all right. It took a while for the younger ones to learn that, though."

Daniel fought the constriction in his throat. "And so you drew his attention. To keep him from going after the others. You drew his fire."

Mary shot him a sidelong glance and then looked away. "Oh, well," she said, waving her hand dismissively. She sounded tired. "Somebody had to, and Mother couldn't do it all the time. Even she had her limits to what she could take. The older boys were out working most of the time, so I was the oldest one left. I did my best for Jimmy, Daniel. I really did."

"I know you did," he murmured, distressed.

A faraway smile drifted across Mary's wrinkled face, and her eyes turned misty.

"When Dad was sober, things were different. He was a different person. He had the most wonderful laugh. He was charming. He would come home at night and sit on the porch and whittle. I would sit beside him and watch him work a piece of wood in his hands, carving it into—oh, anything. A horse, a rabbit, a snake. And he'd tell stories, just bits of Irish fun and nonsense, you know. I liked it when he wasn't drinking."

"I'm glad you have some good memories of him."

"Of course I do. But not many. Mostly, Dad was just . . . absent." She sniffed and felt for her napkin. "We were always hungry. I remember neighbors bringing us a chicken one Easter and telling Mother to cook it up for us quick before that man of hers came home. I was so humiliated. Mother was very gracious, thanked them nicely, and she did up that chicken that very hour. We had eaten it and cleared the evidence away, even the smell of it in the house, before Dad came home. He came home just a bit drunk that time, and he was angry because there was no supper ready for him. He yelled at Mother because of it, but she never did tell him about the meal she'd given us children. She just fixed him a tin of soup and said nothing, and Sam buried the chicken carcass in the backyard. Mother went from a beautiful eighteen-year-old to a worn-out old woman in a matter of a few years. Did Alex show you her photos?" He nodded, and she continued.

"Then I'm sure you saw for yourself. Mother was only thirty-six when she died, but she looked fifty."

"And she died having his child."

"His eighth child," Mary agreed. "It was in 1933. Something went wrong after Alex was born, and she hemorrhaged. When they sent the man around to tell us—we didn't have a phone—Dad thanked him very politely. And then he walked down to the local bar and came home two hours later and fell into bed and stayed there for three days. He didn't—"

"Didn't what?" Daniel urged.

She shook her head. "He didn't claim Mother's body. He left her there in the hospital, and the baby too. They buried her in the common ground of the city cemetery. There's no marker for paupers' graves, you know. And baby Alex was left in the hospital, and me with my hands full with four other little ones, well, I didn't think I could take on a newborn too. But what else could I do? There was no one else. Mother had a friend named Martha who tried to help us, but Dad wouldn't let her. He drove her off. It was up to me. So I went to the hospital with our Radio Flyer wagon and collected Alex. He'd been lying in one spot for so long that one side of his head was flat."

"And you took care of him," Kathleen murmured gently.

Mary nodded. "He was so small. Nowadays they can save most babies that small—only three pounds—but back then it was rare to have one so tiny survive. I fed him cow's milk with an eyedropper and oiled his skin because he was so dry. It was like holding a snowflake. Anna helped me some, but mostly it was up to me."

"How did you manage to go to school at the same time?" Daniel asked.

She gave an apologetic shrug. "I didn't have much choice. I dropped out after the seventh grade. And we got along all right. But then when Alex was about five months old, Dad suddenly took it in his head that Mother's family should have the care of us. He piled us all in the truck, and we drove down to Wisconsin. I remember making Alex a little bed out of a box and placing it on the floor of the truck at my feet. I cried most of the way down. I don't know if I was crying because I'd never see my home and William again or because I was so relieved I would finally have help with the children."

"And James knew where to find his wife's family after all those years?"

"Yes, they were still in the same town. Of course, Mother's parents were old by that time, in their late sixties or early seventies, maybe. There was no way they could take us in. But Aunt Helga was nearby and married and had four children of her own already. She agreed to take on two of the children, and I stayed to help out. Dad put the rest of the children back in the truck and left again, as I told you, and that was that. I thought they'd all gone back to Canada, but I never could learn what happened."

Daniel digested this a moment, then shook his head. "Hannah was so young to die. What a life she must have led! Why did she stay with him?"

"Things were different then. Women didn't strike off on their own, especially with so many children. And remember, she'd burned her bridges pretty thoroughly behind her back in Wisconsin."

"Wouldn't her family have forgiven her for eloping and taken her in?"

"I don't know. Mother had no contact with them at all. She never heard from them once after her marriage, though I know for a fact she wrote a few times. If Dad had written to Mother's family for help instead of just showing up on their doorstep, they may not have lifted a finger, for all I know. But it's harder to turn away children from your very door, if you know what I mean." Mary shook her head again. "So you see why Mother stayed put. She didn't feel she could rely on her family, and she probably felt she had nowhere else to go."

"Hannah couldn't have been any worse off," Daniel pointed out angrily. "She should have left him. She should have tried appealing to her family, at least."

Mary sighed. "There are two other reasons, I think, that she didn't. One reason was that she was so stubborn; she didn't want to give her mother the satisfaction of saying, 'I told you so.' She'd married him against their wishes, and Mother had a certain pride. A combination of the German blood and the red hair."

"And the second reason?"

"She loved James McDonald," Mary said simply.

Daniel shook his head. "How could she, if what you say is true?"

Kathleen and Mary exchanged another knowing look that excluded him entirely.

"Women are weird," Daniel muttered as he carried his plate to the sink.

CHAPTER 17

He phoned Rose Sunday afternoon, when he knew she'd be home from church. She sounded tired but assured him she felt fine.

"The Gordons invited me over for dinner tonight, so I don't even have to cook," she said. "And I spent most of yesterday lying around reading a novel and didn't do a lick of housework. So don't worry about me. Now enough of that. Tell me what's been happening. What are they like?"

"Wonderful people," Daniel told her. "They've made me very welcome. And they've told me a lot of things. I know where four of the seven kids ended up. Now I'm just missing Anna and William . . . and Jimmy, of course. I've met a few of my cousins and their kids. They're nice people. Especially Mary. She's eighty-five and acts fifteen, and she's like the granny I never had. I know it sounds weird, but it's as if I've always known her. When she walked off that plane, I recognized her right away."

"Blood runs strong," Rose murmured. "Tell them hi for me."

"I will. After the baby's born, I'll bring you out here to meet them."

"I'd like that. When do you think you'll be home?"

He hadn't thought about that. What sort of guest was he, that he didn't even know how long he was staying? And Kathleen and Alex hadn't said a word about it, they were so gracious.

"I don't know. Soon," he told Rose. "I have a lead or two to follow on Anna and William. Maybe Jimmy, too. Dad, I mean."

She made a sound that told him she was sucking on her lower lip.

"What?" he asked.

"Nothing. Just hurry home, sweetie. I miss you."

"I miss you too."

"Your boss checked in on Friday. I think he's a little antsy."

"I'll be back soon."

They said their good-byes. After he replaced the phone on the hook, Daniel went into the kitchen, where Kathleen and Alex were sitting. Kathleen was sipping a cup of tea, and Alex was reading his newspaper. With the sunlight drifting in the window and the smell of Sunday dinner still in the air, it made a cozy domestic scene. He was reluctant to bother them, but they both looked up, smiling, when he entered.

"Mary around?" Daniel asked, snagging a cookie from the plate on the counter and sitting beside them.

"She's lying down for a bit. She's not a spring chicken, you know, our Mary." Alex chuckled.

"I thought I'd talk to you about my visit. How long I've stayed, I mean, and how long I'll be here," Daniel began awkwardly, but Kathleen anticipated him.

"You are welcome to stay as long as you want to, but if you need to get home, we understand."

He grinned. "You're the perfect hostess. I've barged in on you out of the blue and stayed for three days, and you haven't said a word about it."

Kathleen put her hand on his arm. Her eyes were shining. "I haven't seen Alex this animated in years. It's been good for him to have you here. It's been a delight to meet you. And we really wish you luck with your search. I—I just hope you don't get your hopes up too high. You may not find them. And, like we mentioned earlier, you may not like everything you find." She glanced at Alex and away.

"Told him about that, did you?" Alex said, looking a bit sad but not angry.

"I thought he had the right to know, and Mary thought he should be prepared for whatever he finds."

"Well, I agree." Alex gave Daniel a rough pat on the shoulder and hauled himself to his feet. "You be sure to pass along whatever you find out, happy or not. If William, Jimmy, and Anna are alive or dead, I want to know."

"Of course," Daniel said. "I'll keep in touch."

* * *

He flew home Monday evening. Rose was out, but the house was welcoming, the porch light on, the lamp in the hallway on low, a pot of stew cold on the stove and ready to be heated. She'd left a note on the counter. "Gone to class—home by nine. Can't wait to see you!"

To be honest, he was glad to have the house to himself for a bit before Rose came home. Daniel tossed his suitcase, unopened, into his closet and stretched out on the bed, his arm across his eyes. He told himself that he'd made so much progress so quickly that he should be grateful. He should be content. But he wasn't. The sense of urgency he felt was stronger than ever. He needed to find the rest of the missing pieces of his family. It was a need, not just a happy wish. Now that he'd found Alex and Mary, now that he knew what it was like to have extended family, the desire to find the rest had turned into a physical ache.

He didn't remember falling asleep. One moment he was on his familiar bed, and the next he was sliding, the walls changing, and he was standing on the dirt road from his dream. Standing this time, not running. The road stretched endlessly in both directions, and he had no idea which way to run. The sky was bright blue overhead, and there was a smell of dry grass and— he supposed it was cows. There was a light crunch of footfalls on gravel, and he turned to see a woman approaching. It was the redheaded woman he'd seen before. He knew her name now, but at the moment couldn't recall it. It was on the tip of his tongue. He stood looking up at her, hands dangling at his sides, and the woman smiled kindly down at him.

"Which way do I go?" he asked. He had to tip his head back to look up at her.

"You're a newspaper man," she said, and her voice was light as silver, rippling with laughter. "You're a newspaper man."

He awoke to find the bedside lamp glowing and Rose beside him, her arm around his middle. She was sound asleep.

Carefully Daniel extricated himself from her embrace and went out to the kitchen, flipping on the light. Rose's coat was draped over a chair, her shoes on the floor under it. The pot of stew had been put away. He blinked at the clock and discovered he'd been asleep for hours. Poor Rose, so looking forward to his return, had come home to find him zonked out on the bed. Shaking his head ruefully, he opened the fridge and found the stew. He heated himself a bowl in the microwave and sat at the table. A few minutes later, he heard shuffling in the hall and Rose came in.

Even rumpled and half asleep, she looked wonderful. He started to get to his feet, but she gently pushed him back and bent to kiss the top of his head.

"I'm sorry I fell asleep," he said. "Thanks for the stew."

"How was your flight?" She settled herself on the chair opposite him, tucking her bare feet beneath her. He thought she looked a little stouter already, moved a little more stiffly. He'd been gone less than a week, but he could see the changes in her. Apparently she could see changes in him too. She studied his face a moment, then put her hand on his.

"Are you okay?"

"Fine. How are you feeling?"

"All right. I have a routine check-up with Dr. Abramson tomorrow. He's going to let me listen to the heartbeat, if you want to come with me." She hesitated. "But I guess since you've been away, you'll need to get into the office tomorrow."

"I wouldn't miss coming with you for anything."

Rose smiled, her whole face relaxing. "Thanks." She stood, got herself some stew, and joined him at the table. For a while they ate in silence. Daniel savored the taste of rosemary and bay, feeling the warmth of it comforting him, nearly putting him to sleep again. He looked up to see his wife watching him, a smile on her lips.

"So what's the next step, Sherlock?"

"I want to find William, Anna, and my dad."

"Who are William and Anna, exactly?"

He realized he hadn't filled her in on everything he'd learned. He sketched the details for her, including what Mary had told him about the alcoholism and violence in the family's past. Telling her about it brought back the goose bumps he'd felt listening to Mary. There was so much to tell Rose.

"Apparently it runs in the family," he ended. "Matthew's son Aaron—he'd be my first cousin—has been in and out of jail with some of the same problems. And don't forget Sam, who died of cirrhosis of the liver. That could have been from drink."

"That helps explain why your grandpa got the title of 'town drunk.' I think your dad was better off being taken from him."

Daniel shook his head. Jimmy hadn't been taken away from his father. He'd run away and then been abandoned . . . just like Daniel. But there was no point reiterating it. It was late, and he was tired.

Rose reached over and smoothed the hair from his forehead. "What is it?" she asked softly.

"It's just . . . I keep thinking of that awful verse in Exodus. The one about how the iniquities of the fathers will be brought upon the heads of the children."

She looked at him a moment, then said quietly, "But that can be cured, you know. Healed. There's that other verse in Malachi: 'He shall turn the heart of the fathers to the children, and the heart of the children to their fathers, lest I come and smite the earth with a curse.'" Her lips quirked in a little smile. "I always wondered what the curse was."

"It's loneliness," Daniel said.

* * *

He didn't get a chance to do much more about his search for a while. Things became busy at work, and he was given assignments that took most of his time and attention, even if they didn't spark his interest. After being away so much, he threw himself guiltily into his work, determined to make up for lost time. But Daniel's heart wasn't in it. While he researched and wrote and interviewed, his mind constantly turned back to his own personal puzzle. What should he do next? What had Hannah meant in his dream, that he was a newspaper man? Was there something he was missing?

The weather began to turn cold, and by the time the last week of October rolled around, there were no leaves left on the trees, and Rose's garden had turned black and limp from frost. The crisp taste of coming snow was in the air, and he guessed it would arrive in the next week or so. It was the time of year when Daniel started craving hot chocolate and a good book beside the fireplace.

"Just think. Next year at this time we'll be dolling up our own kid to go trick-or-treating," Rose mused one night as she readied for bed. She'd grown steadily plumper, but Daniel thought it looked great on her. Her skin glowed with health, and her hair seemed shinier. She'd had none of the nausea Abbie had experienced with her pregnancies, and Abbie was madly envious about it. He couldn't help going to Rose now, putting his arms around her from behind to cradle their child between his hands. Since hearing the steady, surprisingly fast heartbeat in the doctor's office, Daniel found that the baby had become more real to him—an independent little being. He kissed Rose on the back of the neck.

Rose tipped her head back to look up at him.

"You're different," she said.

"How so?"

"I don't know. Just different. Happier, maybe. Not so stressed out about the baby."

"You're right; I'm not as stressed out. The idea is growing on me," Daniel said. But as he climbed into bed and reached for his book to read a while, the thought niggled in the back of his brain, *Not as stressed out. But there's still trepidation.* What sort of family was he bringing this child into? How deeply did the family heritage of alcoholism and violence run? Was it possible to completely end it with him? Could you overcome genetics?

Well, yes, of course you could. Alex and Mary and their kids had clearly turned out okay. Their grandkids were healthy and affectionate. And he and Isabel had turned out all right in spite of everything, hadn't they? He wasn't so sure about Charlie, though. He had little memory of his big brother, but he did seem to recall one night when the police had brought him home. Had it been about underage drinking? He couldn't remember now. Maybe Isabel would. Not that he felt he could ask his sister. She clammed up every time he mentioned Charlie or his father. He had tried to tell her over the phone the things he had found out about the family, but she hadn't shown any interest. To her it was all water under the bridge and was not to be discussed. He wished he could somehow convey to her that it was all right to talk about the family. Maybe she had her own fears, her own doubts about the persistence of genetics.

* * *

"I've been going through some ideas in my head," Daniel told Rose Halloween morning. "Ways to find William and Anna. The census is no use, because the last one published isn't recent enough. If William's still alive, he's eighty-eight. My relatives all seem to be a long-lived bunch, but there is a chance he's passed away."

"It's a likely possibility," Rose agreed. She was sorting through the bags of candy she'd purchased for the trick-or-treaters that night, trying to estimate how much she could give each child who came to the door. Last year she had run out early. This year it looked to Daniel like she'd bought enough mini chocolate bars to feed a small country.

"I'm going to post an ad in a few newspapers in Ontario, Canada, to see if anyone knows anything about William. If that doesn't produce any results, I'll start looking for a death certificate. For a fee they'll search ten-year periods for you. The last time anyone heard from him was in 1934, when he told Mary good-bye right before they left for Wisconsin."

"And he remained behind in Canada," Rose said.

"Yes. Newspapers get results. It's worth a try."

"I thought you told me Mary had tried that already."

"She did, but that was years ago. I got the address of the *Toronto Star* off the Internet. I'll locate another paper in Collingwood and place an ad there, too."

"While you're waiting for those results, here's another idea you could try," Rose said. She carried the big bowl of candy over to the counter, snagging a Snickers for herself as she returned to the table. "I mentioned your search to Susan Larsen. You know, Sister Larsen with the ten kids, always dresses them in homemade clothes, and has served in nursery for the past three years, poor woman?"

"Yes, I know who she is." He always thought of her name in hyphens: Sister-Larsen-in-nursery-poor-woman.

"She said to try looking at the U.S. Social Security Death Index. She used it while she was researching her husband's line. We might find something there."

"That won't help me with William. He may have been born in the U.S., but his family left for Canada when he was very young. I doubt he'd have a U.S. Social Security number."

"No," Rose said, popping in the last of her chocolate bar. "But Anna and your dad apparently grew up in the States. Maybe they became citizens. If they worked here, they must have had Social Security numbers, and if they're deceased, they'll be listed."

Intrigued, Daniel brought his laptop out to the kitchen table. He brought up Google, typed in "Social Security Death Index," and a moment later he was on the Roots Web site. Feeling rather numb at how simple it was, he filled in Anna McDonald Peterson's name and hit SUBMIT. Three seconds later the results were splayed across his screen.

"There she is," Rose said with satisfaction, reaching for another Snickers. Her face remained carefully calm, but he could see the laughter sparking in her eyes.

"I can't believe it was that easy." Daniel reached for his notebook and pen, his eyes on the screen. "Anna McDonald Peterson, born March 13, 1925. Died November 18, 1990 in Alma, Michigan. That has to be her. She was only sixty-five. She died just four months after her brother Sam. I wonder what she died of."

"You can click there to order a birth, marriage, or death certificate," Rose observed, coming to hang over his shoulder. "Of course, you won't be able to get the birth certificate this way if she was born in Canada, but the marriage and death certificates would be worth ordering. It will say on the death certificate what the cause of death was, and maybe next of kin."

"Not only that, but now that I know she was from Alma, I'll be able to use Directory Assistance or look at the white pages on the Internet to see if there are any Petersons still living there. And I'll be able to look up her obituary in the local paper now that I know the date of death. It might list next of kin. Obviously she married a Peterson. She probably had kids."

"A whole new branch. I'm glad for you, honey," Rose said happily, and handed him a Snickers.

But Daniel wasn't finished yet. In a corner of the site he'd seen a link to the Railroad Retirement Board records, which dated back to 1937. Hadn't Mary said William briefly worked for the railroad? He might have returned to that work as an adult. That wouldn't have been in the States, of course, but perhaps there were similar records kept for railroad workers in Canada. He made himself a note to look. Every little lead helped. The more he found, the more he realized the search would never be completely over. The branches kept on branching, further and further. But it was definitely a good start.

Next Daniel typed in "James Carlton McDonald," knowing it might bring up his grandfather as well as his father. But no, the search brought up no results. Puzzled, he typed the name in again, more carefully this time. Still nothing.

Rose, who had been watching quietly, put a hand on his arm. "I guess that means your dad is still alive."

"Maybe so. But why doesn't it bring up Grandpa? He was born in 1885. He certainly isn't alive anymore."

Rose shrugged. "Maybe he went back to Canada and died there, and his Social Security number was never canceled. Maybe he never had one to begin with. Maybe back then things weren't so regulated and he just walked across the border and got a job and didn't have a number."

"Great. Not only was Grandpa the town drunk, he was an illegal immigrant and a tax evader too."

Rose laughed, the warm sound filling the kitchen, and after a moment Daniel couldn't help laughing too.

* * *

Halloween had always been low on Daniel's list of favorite holidays. Cherub-faced children dressed as devils and monsters shuffled to his door while their parents waited on the driveway. As he doled out the candy (two pieces per child, no more, according to Rose's strict instructions), he wondered what sort of parents would dress their darlings as vampires and grim reapers. Didn't anyone dress up as cowboys or firemen or ballerinas anymore? Daniel vowed that when his child went trick-or-treating, he was going to insist on a bunny outfit.

"Some of these kids are just way too old to be out going door to door," he complained to Rose when she came to relieve him on door duty. She sported a witch's pointy hat and long fake red fingernails. Her billowy black graduation robe did a good job of hiding her stomach. She called herself the witch of lower campus. "When a kid comes to your door smoking a ciga-rette, he's just too old to be trick-or-treating."

"Yes, dear."

"And one kid came to the door jangling his car keys. He *drove* here. That's way too old."

"Yes, dear." Rose laughed. "When someone over the age of twelve came to my parents' door to trick-or-treat, Dad would give them a zucchini instead of candy."

"Zucchini?"

"Well, they always had so much in their garden . . ."

"That's just wrong."

He kissed her cheek and left her to greet the next giggling arrivals.

CHAPTER 18

The *Alma Herald* wasn't available online, and the *Weekly Gazette* didn't have archived copies older than 1995. Giving up on finding an obituary, Daniel tried Directory Assistance and was given the name of eighteen Petersons living in Alma. With a depressing feeling of déjà vu, he began calling.

It was on Peterson number twelve that he hit pay dirt.

"Anna? She was my mother." The voice sounded suspicious. "Why are you calling, again?"

Patiently, and trying not to sound too eager, Daniel repeated who he was and that he was looking for his aunt's family.

"Well, you've found us," the woman said. "I'm Phyllis. This is actually my brother Scott's phone. I'm just visiting, but he isn't here, so I answered. I'll tell him you called."

"Wait, please," Daniel said quickly, afraid she was going to hang up. "Please, I've been looking for you for weeks. Could I just ask you a few questions?"

"I guess so. I don't know if I can help you."

"Your mother was born in Canada?"

"Yes. In 1925."

"And her mother died when Anna was about eight years old?"

"I think so, something like that, yes."

"Do you know what happened to your mother after that? Who raised her?"

There was a pause, and then the voice returned, sounding somewhat angry.

"I'm not sure what you want to know that for."

Daniel quickly took a different tack. "My father, Jimmy, was Anna's little brother. He was three when their mother died. Some of his siblings were left with a relative in Wisconsin, and he ended up out in Montana. But Anna and her brother Samuel got dropped off somewhere between the two states. I want to find out what happened to them and who raised them."

"Samuel. Yeah, I had an uncle named Sam. We used to kid about it, you know, Uncle Sam, and he was in the army and everything. It seemed funny at the time," Phyllis added with a verbal shrug.

Daniel wrote himself a note: *Military records.* "Did he serve in World War II?"

"Yes. He was decorated for being injured in action. He was in France for most of it."

"Did he and your mother keep in touch, then?"

"Of course. In fact, Uncle Sam stayed with us for a few years when I was small. See, my mom had previously been married to a guy named David Keller, but after they divorced she married my dad, Joseph Peterson. After Scott and I were born, they divorced too. And then Uncle Sam came to live with us and help Mom with me and Scott. When I was in junior high, Sam went to live in Wisconsin. He got a job there. We kept in touch, though, and he visited sometimes."

"Did Sam ever marry?"

"No, he never did. He was injured in the war. It was just a leg injury, but it kind of affected Uncle Sam mentally, you know? He was always a bit . . . jumpy. Odd. Oh, I don't mean to speak ill of him. He was a great guy, lots of fun to be around. But the war messed him up a little, you know? It made him drink too much. He never had a steady income."

"I understand."

Phyllis had apparently warmed up to Daniel now. Her voice took on a chatty tone. "You wanted to know who raised my mother and Uncle Sam," she said a little aggressively. "I'll tell you. They grew up in an orphanage. A state-run place with separate dorms for girls and boys, so they didn't get to see each other often. Mom told us a bit about it, but Uncle Sam never talked about it once. It wasn't a happy time, you know? Then he went off to war and Mom got married. Uncle Sam died years ago, and Mom died not long after him, of an aneurism. And I've told you the rest."

"I'm sorry to hear it. Thank you for telling me. You've helped me a lot."

"So you said your dad ended up in Montana? I knew we had other aunts and uncles, but mom never knew much about them."

"Yes. He was raised in foster homes. I have an older brother and an older sister. I don't know where my father is now. He left us when I was young."

"Ah. Sorry."

"It's all right. Listen, I really appreciate you talking to me. It's nice to find a cousin, you know?"

"Cousins? Yeah, I guess that's what we are." She seemed to be puzzling it out.

"If you'd like, I can send you what information I've collected about the rest of the family—Anna and Sam's other brothers and sisters."

"That would be okay, I guess. I suppose . . . how much will that cost?"

"No, no. I'm not researching all this for money," Daniel assured her. "I'm just trying to put the family tree back together. I'm happy to share with you any information I've got, if you're interested."

"Well, I don't know, but Scott would probably like to see what you have."

"That's great. I'll mail you a copy of what I've found so far, then," Daniel said.

* * *

After he'd hung up, Daniel went out into the living room. Rose was sprawled on the couch watching a crime drama on TV and eating the last of the Halloween candy. He watched a few minutes of the show with her, thinking that Theresa Zahlmann would probably enjoy it. He couldn't help smiling to himself, imagining introducing Rose to her. Maybe they'd go visit in the spring, after the baby was born.

"What are you smiling about?" Rose asked, poking him in the ribs. "This poor lady just got knifed in the closet, and you're smiling."

He shook his head. "I wasn't smiling at the show," he said. "I just talked to Anna's daughter."

* * *

Two weeks later, Daniel came home from the library, where he had spent the day researching the history of Child Welfare. He was finally getting around to doing an article on it for the paper. His boss had been enthusiastic about the idea and had suggested some human interest angles to work into the article. It was an interesting project and had temporarily driven other thoughts from his head. But now, as Daniel entered the house to find Rose waiting by the door, grinning madly and waving a piece of paper, his personal project leaped back to the fore.

"You had a call while you were out," she said. "The phone rang half an hour ago, and you'll never guess who it was."

He snatched the paper from her and read it eagerly. "Edward Goldthorpe? Who is that?"

"Yet another cousin. Or second cousin, I think. I'd have to stop and figure it out."

At his dumbfounded look, Rose began to laugh. "Come in and take your coat off, and I'll tell you all about it. And then you can phone him back."

Edward Goldthorpe, Rose told him over a hasty supper, was the son of Isaac Goldthorpe. Isaac was the son of Isabel McDonald Goldthorpe. And Isabel was the sister of James Carlton McDonald.

"My grandfather had a sister named Isabel too? How weird is that?" Daniel nearly choked on his pasta. He took a quick drink of grape juice and reached for a napkin. "So Edward saw my ad in the *Toronto Star*?"

"Yes. He was very excited when he saw it. Apparently he grew up hearing all about our side of the family and thought it a shame that all the kids were split up when Hannah died."

Daniel smiled, hearing her say "our side," instead of "your side." It gave him a funny, happy feeling.

"Why are you grinning so goofy?" Rose asked, but went on without waiting for his reply. "Edward has been researching the family himself but hasn't gotten very far with it. So when he saw your ad he couldn't believe it. Now I'll excuse you from helping with the dishes, so go off to your den and make your call."

Daniel blew her a kiss and was on the phone two minutes later. He held his pen over the notebook, nearly vibrating with excitement. Maybe this was the break he needed. All the pieces were falling into place so quickly, so smoothly. It was almost as if they'd been there, poised, all along, just waiting for the first domino to tip so that the others could fall neatly into place. Each person he talked to had one more piece to the puzzle. He could feel a guiding hand in all of this, subtly nudging him in the right direction. What were the odds of a second cousin seeing the ad and knowing enough about the family to recognize that the ad was meant for him? The blank slots in Daniel's hand-drawn chart were nearly filled.

Edward Goldthorpe sounded about his own age and equally anxious.

"You have no idea how good it is to hear from you," he greeted Daniel. "I've been working on this line for a year now with little success. It's like Great-Uncle James went down to Wisconsin, and then his kids all just disappeared."

"They sort of did," Daniel agreed. "I didn't know that James had a sister named Isabel. It's weird, because my sister is named Isabel."

"Your wife told me that when I spoke to her earlier. A little uncanny, isn't it?"

"That's what I thought too. So you're in Toronto?"

"A small town just outside of it called Oakville. I was raised in Toronto, but I moved to Oakville last year when Mom and Dad bought a condo in Shelburne, south of Collingwood," Edward said.

"Collingwood. That's where a few of James's children were born, including my dad. James had seven kids: William, Mary, Samuel, Anna, Matthew, Jimmy, and Alex."

"That's what I've learned too."

"I've found out about all of them now except William—and my dad."

"Rose told me about that too. I'm sorry to hear you had such a rough childhood." Edward paused a moment. "Hey, maybe I'm wrong, but aren't you forgetting Charlotte?"

"Oh, yeah, the daughter who died young. You know about her?"

Edward gave a low whistle. "It took a while, but I found her birth record, baptism record—they were Methodist—and the death record."

"How old was she when she died?" Daniel asked.

"Five. She died a week before Matthew was born."

"That's awful. It must have been hard on her mother. I guess things weren't so secure back then. They didn't have all the vaccines and medicines and things we have now."

"What do you mean?" Edward asked. "A vaccine wouldn't have helped Charlotte."

"I—I just assumed she died of some childhood illness. That happened a lot more often in those days. Why? What did she die of?"

Edward sounded distinctly uncomfortable. "I found notice of her death in a back issue of the local newspaper. It sounded odd to me at the time. It just said she died of 'accidental causes.' I thought maybe she'd been hit by a car or something; you know, the ordinary sort of stuff. But it didn't give details, eh? So I sent for a copy of her death certificate. It said she'd died of a brain injury."

"Oh. Well, she could have gotten that being hit by a car, right?"

"It still sounded strange to me," Edward said, his voice growing quieter. "I went to my father about it. He squirmed a bit but eventually admitted he'd heard rumors about what had happened, growing up. The family story is that Charlotte died from a blow to the head. When the police looked into it, Hannah told them the little girl had been accidentally kicked by their horse, out in the barn. There was no further inquiry."

"That's terrible, but I'm sure it happened once in a while."

"Except, you see, according to my grandmother, James and Hannah never had a horse."

Daniel gripped the phone, feeling his fingers turn cold and bloodless. "That can't be right."

"My father grew up with the understood but unspoken implication that James hit Charlotte once in a rage. Drunk, most likely, or I'm sure he'd never have done it, eh? I'm sorry to drop it on you like that, Daniel. Especially over the phone. But there are other family stories about James McDonald that sort of verify he had a bad drinking problem and a temper when he was in the drink."

"No, I know about all that," Daniel said quietly. "But, if he did do such a thing, why would Hannah cover up for him?"

"I don't know. Humiliation, maybe. Fear of losing what support he provided. Maybe she excused it as an accident because she felt sure he'd never do it again. Who knows? But the authorities couldn't very well press charges against James if his own family was covering up for him, despite what they may have suspected."

"That's—that's awful." Daniel could think of nothing else to say. It was much worse than he'd ever suspected. Was that what Mary had been warning him about? Had she known the truth? She'd been, what, eight years old when it had happened? Certainly she would remember the truth. He swallowed and tried to speak, but nothing came out. He felt slightly sick.

"Sorry," Edward said again. "Not the sort of thing you want to find when you go searching out your family tree."

"No."

"I'll tell you, though, every family has something unsavory they'd rather keep hidden. My mother's side had its secrets too. Great-Uncle Archie thought he was a turkey hen and spent his days clucking and scratching around in the yard."

"I suppose every family has *something*," Daniel muttered. "Though harmless insanity isn't quite the same as finding out your grandfather was—"

"Yes, well. I—uh—do you want to hear the rest?"

"I do. Please."

"I also found snippets in the local paper about James being brought in for public intoxication on more than one occasion, and a hospital record for his wife—"

"The gunshot wound? Yeah, I know about it already."

"How do you know?" Edward sounded relieved.

"James's daughter Mary and his son Alex. I've met them, stayed with them a few days. They still live in Wisconsin."

"Hey, that's great that you've located them! They're still around, eh? Can I get their addresses and numbers? Grandma Isabel died about fifteen years ago, and Dad died last spring. I haven't been able to find any more information since. I've been kind of on my own here."

"Yeah, I know about being on your own," Daniel said quietly. "Listen, I have quite a bit of information I've managed to collect over the last several weeks. I'm happy to send you a copy of everything."

"That would be terrific! Thanks. It would be great to get together and talk about your visit with Mary and Alex and . . . and everything. I don't know if I can get away, though. Work is hectic. I'm a landscaper, and our busy season is just wrapping up. I have one more big project to finish before the weather turns bad."

"I understand," said Daniel.

"What do you do?"

"I'm a journalist for a local newspaper." Again, Daniel heard Hannah's voice: *You're a newspaper man.* That was the tip she'd been trying to give him, he thought. The ad in the paper that had reached his cousin in Toronto.

"That sounds interesting."

"Hey, if you can't come here, maybe I can come there." The words were out before he could stop them. Suddenly he was dying to see Canada, to see where his father had been born, to see where his grandmother was buried. "Would it be a bother if I came up? If you're too busy—"

"I don't work round the clock, eh? I'm still home in the evenings," Edward said, laughing. "I'd love to have you. But you'd be on your own during the day, I'm afraid."

"I'll find out about flights and hotels and call you."

"Forget hotels. You can stay with me. My apartment has a spare room. I'm bacheloring it, though, so don't expect great cooking."

"Not married, huh?"

"I will be in April. Her name is Gwen, and she's terrific. She runs the greenhouse where I order all my plants. She's marrying me out of gratitude. I'll introduce you. Do you really think you can come? That would be great."

"I don't know how soon I can get away, but I'll call you when I know the details. I couldn't stay long, but I'd like to see Collingwood and Creemore if they're not too far away."

"Two hours' drive. I'll take you up on a Sunday when I don't have to work."

"Sounds good," Daniel said. "In fact, it sounds perfect."

* * *

"The trip to Montana was an adventure," Rose said. "The trip to Wisconsin was a necessity. But another trip is just an extravagance, Daniel. What could this cousin tell you in person that he can't tell you on the phone?"

"It's not just that," Daniel explained. "It's not just for information. I want to see these places. I want to walk the streets my grandparents walked and see where they lived."

Rose tucked her hands under her arms, hugging herself. She was leaning against the fridge, wearing an old blue track suit, her hair hanging straight on her shoulders. He thought she looked tired; there were smudges under her eyes.

"But it's so far away."

"Remember a few years ago when your whole family drove out east and toured the Church history sites? Kirtland, Nauvoo, Palmyra . . ."

"Yes."

"That was visiting your roots, Rose. That was seeing the places where your ancestors lived and worked and died. You know how you felt about that trip and what it meant to you."

"Yes," Rose said again, softly. "It made my family history very real to me."

"Well, this is that kind of trip for me. My ancestors didn't build temples in Kirtland and camp at Winter Quarters. They laid bricks and played on the beach and shot holes in their laundry in Ontario, Canada. I need to feel closer to the people who came before me, and seeing where those things happened would be a start." He gave her a sheepish smile. "Now that I've found my family, I can't be satisfied until I've found *all* of them. Until I know them."

"I understand all that," Rose said after a moment. "I think I know what it means to you, and I'm so happy for you, making contact with your family. I don't mean to whine, but it just sounds so far away."

"You could come with me," Daniel urged. "I'm sure Edward wouldn't mind. In fact, he'll probably welcome you with open arms if you'll agree to cook for us once in a while."

"I can't just drop everything. I have to teach all next week. And I'm almost seven months along, you know. I don't think the airline will even let me fly."

"We can find out. Please come with me."

She thought a moment, eyeing him, then shook her head. "This is your journey, Daniel."

"What do you mean? You're the one who got me started on all this."

"Maybe so. But somehow when I first encouraged you to look, I didn't envision you racing off all over the country." Her lips curled in a wry smile, and she shrugged. "I think this is something you have to do yourself. And I have my own job to do, here at home." Rose slid her hand over her stomach as if caressing the tiny form within. "I'll wait for you here."

Daniel stepped closer, looking down at her intently but not touching her.

"Rose, I don't want you to feel like I'm leaving you behind or leaving you out of anything. You're everything to me."

"I know," she said softly.

"No matter how many other family members I may find, you're my family first and foremost, for always. You and the baby. You're the reason I'm doing this at all."

Rose nodded but didn't reply. Daniel bent slightly to look into her downturned face.

"If anything, this search is making me love you all the more," he said. "It's making me start to look forward to this baby with anticipation instead of fear."

"Is it?" She looked up at him, her hopeful eyes bright with tears.

"I feel like I'll have something more to offer him."

Rose shook her head. "That's what I haven't understood through all of this. You have so much to offer him already."

"But I want to be able to give him a history, a past. It may not be much; there may be both good and bad in it. But it will be his."

"I guess I understand that."

Daniel hesitated, then said, "I know it might sound strange, but sometimes I feel like I'm being encouraged and helped along in this search. Like someone is nudging me in the right direction when I need it. I—I think my grandmother wants me to find her children."

Rose's eyebrows flew up, and she scanned his face in astonishment. "You really feel like that?"

"Yes. It's a feeling that's growing stronger every day. I feel almost like time is running out and I need to hurry."

Rose nodded. "If that's so, then you need to do it. And I need to quit blubbering like a pregnant woman and support you."

He smiled. "Once I find all of her children, I can do the temple work for the ones who are deceased. And Rose, when it comes time to do that, I want you beside me in the temple. I can't imagine having anyone else in there to help me."

Rose sniffled and swiped her eyes with her fingers. "Do you mean that?" she asked in a small voice.

Daniel held out his arms, and she went into them, pressing her face into his shoulder. "I can't think of any place I'd rather be," she said.

He laughed into her hair. "Now, how am I going to explain to David Ross that I need another week off?"

CHAPTER 19

The Pearson International Airport was larger than Daniel had expected. He'd never had to go through Customs before and found it intimidating. The luggage claim area was like an echoing cathedral, and it took him a while to find his suitcase and even longer to find the stairs going up to the concourse level. When at last he emerged into bitter cold air and weak sunshine, he stood blinking on the sidewalk, feeling totally lost. A line of blue and white taxis hovered at the curb, waiting to swoop down on potential passengers. There was a concrete island between the lanes of the road and, following Edward's instructions, Daniel carried his suitcase over to it. There he waited, stamping his feet to warm them and wishing he'd thought to bring heavier gloves.

At last a zippy blue Subaru pulled up before him, and a man got out of the driver's seat. He was tall and thin, but the family resemblance ended there. He had light brown hair and eyes, a disproportionately long jaw, and big ears that made him look like a caricature of himself. He wore only a light sweatshirt with the Toronto Raptors logo on it, and the freezing air didn't seem to affect him at all. He strode forward, hand outstretched, a grin all over his flexible face.

"Daniel McDonald? I'm Edward."

They shook hands and thumped each other on the shoulder, and then Edward ushered him into the car, making observations about how cold Daniel looked and apologizing for keeping him waiting.

"I always misjudge the traffic," Edward said. "Strap yourself in."

The car shot out into the lane, circled through a mind-boggling spaghetti bowl of roads and overpasses, and launched itself into the steady stream of cars on the freeway.

"How far do you live from the airport?" Daniel asked, closing his eyes as the car crossed four lanes to the inside lane.

"If it's not rush hour, about fifteen minutes. If it's rush hour, an hour and a half," Edward replied cheerfully.

"Do you always drive at one-twenty?" Daniel couldn't help gritting his teeth as a semi rushed past, rocking them in its wake.

"That's kilometers, not miles," Edward assured him. "What, don't you have freeways in Denver?"

"Of course we do. Not—not quite like this, though. So I take it this is rush hour?"

Edward looked around at the cars they were whizzing past and waved an airy hand. "Not for another hour or so."

Eventually they left the freeway and drove down Trafalgar, dropping to a sedate eighty kilometers an hour. They passed large homes on stately lots shadowed by tall maples, humbler houses on farm acreage, and several sprawling greenhouses.

"You said Gwen owns a greenhouse," Daniel said. "Is one of those hers?"

"No, hers is west of here. You can recognize it right away because she stuck a twenty-foot pink flamingo on the front lawn." Edward grinned. "She has a way of making a statement, my Gwen."

At last they came to a stop in front of a three-story white brick building surrounded by bare-branched maples.

"Third floor walk-up, I'm afraid. No elevator." Edward hoisted Daniel's suitcase and insisted on carrying it for him. The apartment was only moderately warmer than the outside air and had the sad look of most bachelor abodes: Formica kitchen table, IKEA sofa and chairs, and crooked blinds. Edward pried off his shoes at the door and tossed his keys on the window sill. Daniel hesitated, then started to follow suit, bending to tug at his laces.

"That's okay, you don't have to take your shoes off," Edward said, padding across the floor in his stockings to dump the suitcase in the spare room. But when Daniel started to follow, Edward shot him a grin over his shoulder.

"Sorry. I guess I should explain the Canadian custom. You're supposed to offer to take your shoes off as a sign of respect. I'm supposed to say no, no, it's perfectly fine, which—being interpreted—means that I respect you enough not to require you to take off your shoes. And then in the end you're supposed to take them off anyway. It's a sort of ritual we go through, eh? Kind of stupid, actually, but tradition."

"Got it," Daniel said, a bit muddled. "Just like in Japan."

"Yes. Your room is in here."

Daniel toed off his shoes, tucked them to one side of the door, and went to peer in the spare room. He was pleased to see a real bed, not a pull-out couch. A cream blanket with colored stripes was spread over it, and a bedside table held a lamp and alarm clock.

"Make yourself at home," Edward instructed him. "Are you hungry? I guess with the time difference it's not your supper time yet, is it?"

"Not yet, thanks. But you eat whenever you feel like it. Don't wait for me."

"I thought I'd grill up some Scottish sausage for supper later, eh? It's about the only thing I can really make besides scrambled eggs, which is what you'll get for breakfast."

"So explain another Canadian custom to me," Daniel said. "What's with this word *eh* you keep saying? I've heard people joke around about Canadians saying it, but I thought they were exaggerating. You really do say it."

Edward laughed, his pliable face creased in merriment. "I suppose so. I don't notice it myself, much. The way I see it, Canadians are super polite people in general. We don't ever want to forward an opinion or express a thought without making sure our listener agrees or at least has the opportunity to disagree. So we pause every so often and give them an 'eh?' so they have the chance to jump in and disagree if they want to."

"How accommodating of you," Daniel agreed, amused.

"You sort of do the same with *huh*." Edward pulled a cardboard box out of the closet and dropped onto the couch. "I can hardly wait to talk to you. What all have you found out?"

Daniel sat on an armchair, sinking comfortably into the worn upholstery like a bird snuggling in its nest. There was stuffing coming out of the arms, and the fabric was worn to an indeterminate gray. "I'd kill for this chair. Rose won't let me have anything like this in our house, not even in my own den."

"It was my dad's. Comfy, isn't it?"

With his shoes off and his body comfortable, Daniel felt he could nod off to sleep. But he made himself lean forward, elbows on knees, getting down to business. "I've located every one of James and Hannah's kids except for William and Jimmy, my dad. I haven't had any luck there yet."

"Well, William I can help you with," said Edward. "He was born in 1917, and he stayed in Collingwood when the rest of the family left. When he was twenty, he married Susannah Barker, but they didn't have any children. She died in 1978, and he died in 1987. He's buried in Collingwood near his mother."

"His mother. Hannah? You know where she's buried?" Daniel felt his pulse speed up again. "I was hoping . . ."

"Well, I know the approximate area in the cemetery. She was buried in what's called common ground, with no headstone."

"A pauper's grave. Mary mentioned that."

"Yes. But I have photos of the general vicinity if you'd like copies." Edward dug diligently through the box and came up with a few snapshots, which he handed across. "I also have a photo of William's headstone."

Daniel studied the photos. The common ground didn't look as dismal or Dickensian as he'd feared. It was rather pleasant, actually, with a maple tree spreading above a smooth lawn the color of limes. The picture had been taken in the spring, and there were dandelions here and there in the grass.

"It would be great if I could get copies of everything you have," Daniel said. "And I'll give you what I've collected. Did you ever meet William?"

"Yes, a lot of times," Edward said, as enthusiastic as a small boy. "He worked for the railroad, and a couple of times when I was younger he let me ride with him, just up and down the line from Shelburne to Orangeville and back up. My folks lived in Shelburne back then. I'm sure I have some photos of him, too. Here."

He set the box aside and pulled an album with a denim cover from his bookcase. He flipped through until he found the page he wanted.

Daniel looked eagerly at the photo and felt he was staring at his own image. William was standing next to an old Rambler, the car barely coming to his waist. He'd been very tall. The eyes in the black-and-white photo were light and deep set, and Daniel recognized them as what he had come to think of as the McDonald eyes. William's hair was light, and his ears stuck straight out from his head.

"You can see why I recognized you right away at the airport." Edward laughed.

"What was he like?" Daniel was almost afraid to ask. Had William been another victim of alcohol and violence? He searched William's face for signs of it but saw only a friendly smile and kind eyes looking back at him.

"He was great," Edward said. "Truly. He was tall and very thin and had these piercing blue eyes. He had red hair, but it was going gray by the time I came along. His hands were always stained with grease and oil from working on the train cars, and he smelled like Lava soap. Have you heard of it? It was green soap with sand in it, so it was like washing with sandpaper. But the grease never completely came off. William played the fiddle and sang. He was a true Irish tenor, and he could tell a good joke. I loved him as a kid. He always had time to talk to me. I was twenty-two when he died, so

I remember him well. He was a really great person, eh?"

Daniel felt a smile begin to creep across his face, and something loosened its grip on his chest. "It's good to hear that," he said. "I'm glad he turned out okay."

Daniel turned back to the cardboard box. "This is something you may not have either." He held out a framed photo, this one a formal studio pose. The woman wore a turn-of-the-century long dress, all tiny pleats, and the scarflike collar was held by a brooch at her throat. She had dark hair piled in a thick bun on her head. She wasn't classically beautiful, but her features were striking. Her expression was intelligent and good humored.

"Who is she?" Daniel asked.

"Laura Gray."

"Who?"

Edward blinked. "Laura Gray. James McDonald's first wife."

"First wife?" Daniel heard his voice go up in a squeak and blushed. "I—uh . . ."

"You didn't know he was married before? Yes. They were married in 1908 in Orangeville. She died two years later in childbirth, with their first baby. Bled to death. Like you said, you know how medicine was back then. There were no guarantees. The baby died too."

Daniel moistened his lips. Poor James. To lose his young wife so soon, in such a way, and then to lose his second wife the same way! Daniel imagined how he would feel if Rose were to die having this child, and he nearly had to set the picture down, his hands began to tremble so badly. He took a deep, steadying breath and studied Laura's picture again. He wondered if it had been her death that had first driven James McDonald to drink.

"She's not beautiful," Edward said, echoing Daniel's own thoughts. "But I'm sure he loved her a lot. He erected a huge stone monument for her. Here's a photo of that too."

The stone was probably six feet tall, standing against a backdrop of a dark yew hedge. The inscription was clear in the photo.

Laura Gray McDonald, beloved wife of James, born June 1, 1885, died August 3, 1910. Cherished in our hearts.

Daniel couldn't help thinking of Hannah, the woman who had borne James eight children, buried in a pauper's grave with no stone to show where. He handed the photo back and said nothing.

"According to my dad, there was a separate smaller stone for the baby girl—no name, just 'Infant Daughter.' But it was damaged and fell apart over the years, and now there's nothing to see of it. Just a stone base," Edward said. "Not long after Laura's death, James headed down to the States, and five years later he married Hannah Wyse."

"Eloped, apparently, according to Mary. Her parents were set against it."

"Oh, really? That I didn't know."

"And then he proceeded to make her life miserable," Daniel muttered.

"Oh, I don't know that her life was entirely miserable," Edward said gently. "I mean, getting shot and all, yeah, okay, it wasn't all sunshine and roses. But Grandma used to talk a bit about Hannah, eh? She knew her fairly well. They weren't all that far apart in age, and apparently Grandma went up to visit once in a while. She said Hannah took great joy in her children. I remember she used that very phrase. She took great joy in them."

Daniel leaned back in his chair and stared up at the ceiling. He remembered Hannah's expression in the photograph as she'd tenderly stroked the crying baby's cheek. Yes, he could believe she'd found great joy in motherhood. Maybe not in anything else, but certainly in that. He also felt somewhat better knowing she'd had another young woman to visit her, that she hadn't been utterly alone.

"I do have one other thing you may not have," Edward added, and Daniel could hear papers shuffling in the box. He straightened and tried to bring his wandering mind back in focus. "I have a death certificate for James Carlton McDonald."

"You do?" Daniel eagerly took the plastic-covered certificate. "How on earth did you get this?"

"Sent away for it. I started with the date he went to Wisconsin and had a ten-year search done. Nothing found, though. So I had the service search the next ten years, and this is what they came up with."

The certificate showed that James Carlton McDonald had died of kidney failure on April 9, 1950—just a few days before his sixty-fifth birthday.

"He's buried in Spokane, Washington," Edward said. "Is that far from Colorado?"

"Not all that far," Daniel said quietly.

Edward pushed the box toward him and jumped to his feet.

"Help yourself to whatever you can find in there. I'll get the sausage on the grill."

* * *

Scottish sausage turned out to be like hamburger spiced with mace and lots of pepper. Daniel slathered his soft kaiser bun with relish, ketchup, and red onion and wondered why food always tasted so good when he was traveling. He was embarrassed at eating two, but Edward had three, topped off with a liter of root beer. He also had a bowl of corn chips as they returned to their information swapping. Daniel wondered how his cousin had remained so thin.

"So it's your turn. Tell me what you've managed to find out about the rest of James's children," Edward directed, pulling out a pen and a pad of yellow legal paper.

So Daniel started at the beginning and told him all he'd found, about his trips to Montana and Wisconsin, and even how his anxiety about becoming a father had triggered this whole search. Edward listened with interest and wrote a great deal at first, but after a while he laid his pen down, folded his fingers together in his lap, and just listened. Daniel didn't realize how long he'd been talking until he stretched, looked up, and saw that it was pitch-dark outside.

"What time is it?" he asked in horror. "I'm sorry I bent your ear so long."

"It's eleven," Edward said. "No problem. To you it's only, what, nine? I'm glad to hear it all. It confirms some of what I've been finding out, and it fills in a lot of holes. So now the only one left to find is your dad."

"Yes."

"Tomorrow is Friday. I have to work. We're putting in a huge Japanese garden for a client, a pharmaceutical company. It's good to put plants in while it's cold, but not quite this cold, eh? Anyway, you make yourself at home while I'm gone. Go through the rest of these papers. Look around Oakville. You can borrow my car if you want, and I'll get a ride in with one of my crew. I'll give you my cell number in case you need anything or get lost."

"Thanks."

"I'll be back about five. It's too dark after that to do anything."

"Okay."

"On Saturday I have to put in a half day. But that afternoon I can take you to do some sightseeing in Toronto—there won't be time for anything else. And then on Sunday we'll head up north to Creemore and Collingwood. Sound good?"

"Sounds wonderful."

* * *

That night, Daniel dreamt the same recurring dream, that he was running down a dirt road past barbed wire fences. But no matter how hard and fast he ran, the road stretched out before him, endless, and the red-haired woman never came.

When he awoke the next morning, Edward was getting ready to head out the door. He wore a thick tartan jacket with a hooded sweatshirt beneath it, and his boots were thick yellow-brown leather. He tossed Daniel a set of keys.

"The Subaru's all yours," he said. "You can't get too lost in Oakville. It isn't that big. But here's a map book in case you need it."

Daniel took the thick, coil-bound book with some trepidation. Seeing his expression, Edward laughed.

"Don't worry, that's not all Oakville. That's the whole stretch of the shoreline from Toronto to St. Catharines. Here." He flipped to a section of the book and marked it with a sticky note torn from a pad by the phone. "This part is Oakville. There are some nice shops and places to walk along the lake. There's a quay where you can watch the boats come in and out and some good parks."

"All right." Daniel thought about finding the shops and getting a souvenir for Rose, maybe something for the baby. He pocketed the keys and set the map book on the table.

"I made scrambled eggs like I promised. They're in the pan on the stove." Edward straightened from tying his boots. "Will you be all right on your own today?"

"Sure. Thanks," Daniel said, already looking forward to the eggs. "I'll probably look around town and then take a nap. I've been going at it hard lately."

Edward nodded. "That's how I feel once winter comes and work slows down. I could sleep until April. See you tonight."

* * *

Daniel spent the morning happily poking through the box of Edward's research and the rest of the day perusing some antique shops he found in downtown Oakville. He purchased a couple of paperback novels at a used bookstore and found a pretty, antique lace tablecloth for Rose and a silver bank shaped like a teddy bear for the baby. He couldn't help smiling to himself as he took the bag from the clerk. His first real gift for the baby. It felt strange but good.

Daniel took himself to Wendy's for a hamburger lunch (not as good as Scottish sausage) and spent a while walking through one of the garden centers they'd passed on Trafalgar Road. He'd always enjoyed walking through greenhouses, especially in the winter time. The air was muggy and moist and smelled of damp earth and growing things. This greenhouse had an indoor koi pond with a small waterfall running into it. Potted palms and papyrus plants grew around it. If he closed his eyes, he could imagine himself in Hawaii. He pictured Rose walking beside him, how she'd admire the still-blooming hibiscus and the web-covered little cactus. He missed her a lot. It would be better if she were here to share this with him.

When Edward returned from work, he found Daniel busy in the kitchen whipping up his specialty—fried pork chops and potato salad. He dropped his muddy boots on the mat just inside the door and went to wash up, calling back over his shoulder, "I knew you'd be good for something. Sure you can't stay longer?"

As they ate, Daniel reported on how he'd spent his day. Afterward they went out to a movie, something full of action and testosterone and pyrotechnics, but Daniel didn't pay much attention. His mind was already running ahead to Sunday. He felt far from home, and yet he also felt as if he were getting closer and closer to home. It was an odd sensation.

Saturday morning he slept in, and he only had time to shower and make himself some toast before Edward was back from work. He brought Gwen with him, a cheerful girl the size of a ten-year-old with hair cropped short and spiky and dyed an impossible maroon. She had three earrings in one ear and four in the other, and she wore a smiley-face T-shirt and parachute pants under her heavy winter coat. Her boots were furry and reached her knees, making her look like she'd borrowed the legs off a Wookie. She grabbed Daniel's hand and pumped it as if his coming were the most terrific thing that had ever happened to her.

"Edward has been so excited to have you come," she said. She had a deep voice, loud for someone her size, and when she grinned two dimples appeared around her mouth. "Ever since he found your ad in the paper he's been on the moon. You can't know what this means to him, connecting to more of the family."

"I imagine I'm feeling about the same as he is," Daniel told her, charmed by her sincere smile. "Congratulations. I hear you're getting married."

Gwen dug her elbow into Edward's side and chuckled. "He's just hoping I'll give him a discount at the greenhouse."

"There's not a lot of daylight left, but you can't come to Toronto without seeing the CN Tower," Edward said as they climbed into his car. "I think it's the world's tallest free-standing structure. It's got a glass floor you can walk out on and look down."

"Scares you spitless," Gwen agreed. "But it's a good photo op, eh?"

It was also half an hour away on the busiest freeway Daniel had ever seen. Edward drove with his usual flair, blissfully ignoring the traffic, zipping in and out of lanes with only a click or two of his signal light, and riding the tail of the car in front of him. As he drove, Edward kept up a steady conversation, whistling snatches of songs between sentences with his flexible mouth pursed exaggeratedly and his smile always at the ready. Daniel noticed that everyone else seemed to be tailgating too, flowing along at one hundred kilometers per hour with twenty-four inches between their bumpers. He concentrated on reading billboards, looking out at the gray, flat lake, and not watching the road.

They arrived in one piece and walked down a long tunnel called the Skywalk to the base of the CN Tower. The admission fee was astronomical, but Edward shooed away Daniel's offer to pay his own way.

"How often do I get to treat a cousin?" he asked, whipping out his wallet.

The elevator left Daniel's stomach somewhere in his shoes, and he was glad to step out into the room at the top. Wide windows gave a three-hundred-and-sixty-degree panoramic view of Toronto, laid out at their feet like a set of Legos. Daniel soon lost his fear as he peered down at the city, trying to locate the landmarks Edward and Gwen pointed out. The skyscrapers seemed incredibly slim, as if they'd topple at any moment. Lake Ontario looked flat as a cookie sheet and was the color of blue marble. The city seemed to go on forever, beyond the horizon.

"What's that funny-shaped building there?" he asked, pointing to what looked like a boiled egg below them.

"The Skydome. Only they call it the Rogers Centre or something stupid like that now, because Rogers bought it out, but Skydome sounds so much more poetic."

"And that building?"

"St. Michael's Cathedral. They have an amazing boys' choir."

"And that building way over there? By the lake?"

"The nuclear power plant," Edward murmured. "Welcome to our fair city."

* * *

At last Sunday came. Daniel and Edward were up early and heading north as the sun was rising. The traffic wasn't so bad on a Sunday, and the roads stretched out invitingly before them. It didn't take long to leave the city behind and enter rolling farmland. The fields were empty now, starched with frost, prickly with the stubs of corn stalks. They passed an occasional cow, but most animals had been taken in for the winter.

"We can't leave them outside or they'll freeze," Edward explained. "There's no such thing as an outdoor pet here. All dogs and cats are brought indoors."

"Patricia—she's the woman who raised me—would have been horrified. No pets were allowed in our house while I was growing up."

"That's sad. We always had two or three dogs, at least. Gwen has already agreed to let me buy a Saint Bernard when we get married."

"A dog that big could knock Gwen right over."

Edward shot him a grin. "Nothing can knock Gwen over. She's a rock."

* * *

Creemore was a tiny village on the highway, nothing more than a jumble of houses and a few stores surrounded by outlying farms.

"It took me a while to find out which farm was James and Hannah's," Edward said when they stopped for gasoline at a corner station. "There were two surveys done, and I had the right concession and lot numbers but the wrong survey plan. I'll drive you by it, but there are no buildings there now. The house must have been torn down."

They drove along a paved road with ditches on each side of it, past barbed wire fences and a couple of sagging wooden barns. Daniel noticed there was no litter by the roadside and no billboards to speak of. There were only bare, rolling fields and fresh air. At last Edward stopped the car by the side of the road. He and Daniel climbed out and stood looking at a stretch of empty land, harvested and now lying fallow. The rough grass was a tawny brown, lightening in ripples where the wind stirred it. It reminded Daniel of how crushed velvet changed colors when you ran your hand over it. On the far edges of the field, he could see a boundary line made of piled stones and a couple of stubby trees. The air was sharp with the smell of frost and—distantly—cows.

"According to the survey, the house would have been close to the road, along here somewhere," Edward said. "They farmed a hundred acres. I walked along the fence line one summer and found a little stream and a duck pond about twenty feet across. It's at the back of the property. Grandma told me they used to lower the big metal milk cans into the pond to keep them cold. They didn't have a fridge, eh? They were only here from about 1923 to 1927."

"Why didn't they stay?"

"James wasn't really a farmer at heart. He didn't stay with it for long," Edward said. "They eventually followed the railroad line up north, following the work. Collingwood was a port city on Georgian Bay, and there was a bit of a boom on back then. A brick mason could get work if he looked for it. I don't know how hard James looked."

"Mary said she and William would smuggle Hannah their wages whenever James wasn't looking," Daniel told him.

Edward nodded, then said, "I wish Grandma had a photo of the place, but she didn't. She really didn't get to know Hannah until she moved to Collingwood. She didn't visit her in Creemore."

"How much farther to Collingwood?" Daniel asked.

"Not far—less than an hour."

Daniel took some snapshots of the empty field, the distant trees, the perspective staring down the straight road. Then they got back in the car, and Daniel watched the fields fly by, for once enjoying the speed Edward seemed to favor. It was exhilarating, so long as there wasn't traffic. Creemore was soon left far behind.

Collingwood was larger, a satisfyingly modern-looking town with wide streets and pretty buildings. Edward stopped at a Dairy Queen and bought them burgers for lunch (Daniel began to wonder how many burgers a person could eat in three days without clogging his arteries). He opted for onion rings instead of fries. Rose would have pointed out that he hadn't had any vegetables in three days. They ate as they drove.

"The hospital is over here—the yellow brick building," Edward pointed out. "Hannah died two days after Alex was born. Hemorrhaged. Alex was premature and very small. Grandma said no one expected him to live."

He obligingly stopped the car again while Daniel took more pictures. The building was not remarkable in any way, but he felt a tension in his chest thinking about Hannah dying there, her newborn son left behind.

"Mary said James never collected Alex from the hospital. She went and got him and took care of him herself." Daniel hesitated, wanting to ask a question that had been nagging at him, but unsure of how to frame it without giving offense. "Your grandmother knew Hannah. She didn't live that far away. Why didn't she help with Alex? Why didn't she take the children in?"

"I asked her the same thing once. She said she wanted to," Edward said, slouching down in his seat and pushing a French fry around in a paper cup of ketchup. "She had five children of her own by then, one of them with cerebral palsy. She had her hands full." He shrugged, looking embarrassed. "I can't judge her. I don't know how it was. I don't expect she could have taken in all of Hannah's children. But it does seem to me she could have done something."

* * *

The frame house stood under a massive willow tree. There was a row of townhouses on one side and a RadioShack on the other, but the lot between remained basically untouched. Daniel stood on the curb with his cold hands shoved into his pockets and tried to visualize his grandmother and her family living here. Hannah picnicking on a quilt with her children under that tree. Baby Jimmy toddling down those steps with his watchful sister Mary holding his chubby fist. A clothesline stretched between house and tree, where Hannah hung out the laundry she washed for other people. James sitting on the porch with his rifle across his lap.

"It could use some paint," Edward observed next to him.

It could indeed. Though someone had obviously put some effort into repairs over the years, replacing the missing porch railing with mismatched pieces and installing new windows and roof, the house still had a run-down air. It looked droopy, as if one side were shorter than the other. Perhaps it had settled. Perhaps it had never been straight.

"I wonder who lives here now." Edward peered at the mailbox. "Tucker. Want to knock on the door and invite ourselves in?"

"No, no. There's no need to bother anybody. I just wanted to see where they lived."

"Bet now you wish you hadn't."

But Daniel shook his head. "It's not that bad. Small, yes, but it wouldn't have been so ramshackle back in the thirties. It might have been kind of cozy."

Edward nodded, though he didn't look convinced. Daniel took a couple of pictures, but the sadness and hopelessness of the place crept into his throat and made his chest hurt. After a while he pocketed his camera. He glanced back at the house once more as they returned to the car. He couldn't believe that Hannah's whole life had been as bleak as this house appeared. Surely the family had had some moments of happiness, he insisted to himself. Maybe not when James had been drinking, but surely sometimes.

* * *

The cemetery was just as the photo had shown, though the grass was a dull brown now and there were no leaves on the maple tree. Daniel stood in silence, gazing at the area where, somewhere, his grandmother was buried. He almost expected her to appear at his elbow and say something, or at least ruffle his hair in passing. But of course nothing happened. Did she know he was here? Did she know how far he had come in his search? The only sound was a distant tractor grinding up the road. Edward stood to one side, giving Daniel a moment alone.

After a while, Daniel turned to his cousin.

"Where is William buried?"

Edward pushed his long chin to the north. "He and his wife are buried along there, on the other side of the cemetery. Charlotte is over there under that spruce."

Charlotte! Somehow it hadn't occurred to Daniel that the little girl would be here. But of course, she'd died in Collingwood. He found the stone, a simple white slab half sunk in the grass. Weather and time had made it difficult to read the inscription:

Charlotte McDonald, 1923–1928.

"That's it? That's all they wrote?" he asked, unable to keep the dismay from his voice.

Edward shrugged, looking down at the spot with a sad expression on his face. "What else can you say? It says it all, really."

Daniel spotted a plastic pot of dried mums sitting to one side of the grave. He touched it gently with his foot.

"Who put these here?"

"I did. It was her birthday a few weeks ago." Edward shrugged again, and his ears turned pinker than the cold could explain.

Daniel nudged him with his elbow. "Thanks," he said.

"It probably sounds stupid," Edward said as they turned away and trudged back toward the car, hands in pockets. "But I've always felt something for her. The forgotten little girl. The one they covered up the truth about. I'm sure it broke Hannah's heart to lose her. When I'm in town I like to drop by for a visit."

"It's not stupid at all," Daniel told him. "It's nice of you."

Edward drew in a long breath, gazing out over the street, now deserted as the air grew colder.

"Sometimes—now, mind you, don't tell Gwen this, because she'll think I'm a flake—but sometimes I feel like Charlotte's not entirely gone. Maybe it was the suddenness of her going. Or the violence of it, or the sadness of it.

Either way, sometimes I feel like she's still hanging around a little—not unhappy, not like that. Just waiting. For something. I don't know what."

"I think," Daniel said slowly, "maybe I know what she's waiting for. I get the same feeling about Hannah. I think they're waiting and hoping for the same thing, for the family to be together again."

"That's just it," Edward said, and his face was truly troubled. "They can't be together ever again. That's what's so sad about it."

"Yes they can," Daniel said quietly. "Let me tell you about it."

CHAPTER 20

He returned home to Denver that Wednesday, his suitcase full of photocopies and his heart full of things to share with Rose. But he didn't have a chance to tell her anything. As soon as the taxi dropped him off in front of the house, she was pulling him inside, tripping over her tongue and laughing at her own excitement.

"Don't be mad or anything, but while you were out running around the continent, I thought I'd do a little sleuthing myself."

"Oh?"

"I have something to tell you. Come in and take off your coat. Daniel, I talked to your sister yesterday."

"That's okay. Why do you sound so guilty? You can talk to Isabel anytime you want to." He dropped his coat on the couch and sank into a chair, fleetingly wishing that it were as comfortably ancient as Edward's had been. He toed off his shoes out of his newly formed habit.

"Well, she opened up to me, Daniel." Rose dropped to her knees in front of him, her hands grasping his. "Maybe because I'm female, I don't know. We got to talking about labor and babies, like all women do when they get together, you know. Delivery room war stories. And that led us to the topic of families and parents and her dad in particular. And . . . well, she admitted to me that she got a Christmas card from Charlie two years ago."

"She *what*?"

"The return address was in Seattle, Washington. She didn't keep the card. She was upset and threw it out. But she remembers it was Seattle. Don't be mad."

"But that's wonderful! I'm not mad. How did you worm that out of her? Why didn't she tell me he sent a card?" Another thought struck him.

"How did Charlie get her address? I mean, she's listed under her married name. How would he have found her? He left home a long time before she married."

Rose's eyes slid away. "Well, that's another thing she didn't tell you. After he left home in 1977, he kept in touch with her, just occasional letters maybe once or twice a year. He knew about her getting married. He knew she'd moved to Boulder. But then about ten years ago he stopped writing, and she figured he'd lost interest in keeping up the relationship. There was no word until the card two years ago."

Daniel scrubbed his face with his hands, trying to take in the fact that Isabel had communicated with Charlie and hadn't told *him*. "But when she got his card, she didn't write back to him or even keep his address? Why not?"

Rose spread her arms out. "Because she was angry, Daniel. You've got to understand. As far as she's concerned, Charlie left you two, just like your father did." She raised her hand to keep him from interrupting. "I know it wasn't the same and that he kept in touch for a while, however infrequently. But she was eleven when he left, and she wanted her big brother, and in her eyes he ditched her. I know it isn't rational, but she was angry, Daniel. So she didn't tell you. She thought you'd be better off not knowing."

"I can't believe she kept that from me. I asked her right out."

"You see? You are mad."

"Well, sure. She heard from Charlie, and she kept it from me."

Rose touched his arm. "But look at the bright side. You know he was alive and well and living in Seattle two years ago. It's a lead."

Daniel let his breath out in a long stream and gave her hands a squeeze.

"You're right," he said. "It's a lead."

* * *

Daniel was beginning to feel like an old friend of Directory Assistance. There were thirty-eight McDonalds living in Seattle. With how many minutes he'd gone over this month, his cell phone bill was going to be higher than his mortgage payment. Not to mention the cost of all the airline tickets.

"I'll call some of them for you," Rose offered. "Let me help."

"Maybe I should just put an ad in the paper again." Daniel sighed. "It might be easier than weeding out all the wrong numbers. We don't even know that Charlie's still in Seattle."

"You're so close. You can't give up now."

"I'm not close to giving up," he told her. "I'm just wishing my last name was more unusual. Why McDonald, for heaven's sake?"

Once again Daniel began the long process of phoning. By nine o'clock that night he'd had no luck and finally had to stop out of sheer exhaustion. Who knew that explaining himself to strangers over and over again could be so tiring?

"Don't talk to me about exhaustion," Rose yawned, one hand on her stomach. "I can't lie down, or Junior starts tap-dancing on my bladder. How do women have twins? I think they'd burst something."

"Imagine quintuplets."

"Oh, my, yes, don't even say it," Rose groaned, crawling into bed. "One little Junior at a time is quite enough." She rolled over, one eye peeking out from beneath her disheveled hair. "We haven't decided on a name yet, you know. We're getting down to the wire."

"It's not even December yet. You're not due until February."

"But I need to know the name."

"Why?"

"Because I'm cross-stitching a sampler for the baby's room, and I want to leave enough space for the name. I mean, if you're going to insist on something like Aloysius or Murgatroyd, I'm going to need to leave more space than if you're dead set on Sam or John."

"I think I can guarantee that his name won't be Murgatroyd," Daniel murmured, already half asleep.

"I just want to decide now and not have to choose on the spot," Rose said.

"We could choose a perfectly good name right now, and you still might change your mind when you see him. And might I remind you that it could be a girl."

"It's a boy," Rose said firmly. "I just know it is."

"Did the doctor tell you so?"

"No. But when I called Grandma on Sunday, she said she was knitting a blue sweater set. She knits for every baby, and she hasn't been wrong about the color yet."

* * *

It was the second week of December. A light snow had fallen overnight, and Rose was in a Christmassy mood. She had Daniel haul up the boxes of decorations from the basement, and she began draping fake greenery over windows and entwining red ribbon through the stair banister. Burl Ives sang carols on the CD player (holidays always put Rose in a nostalgic mood), and strings of lights sat by the door, waiting for Daniel to trudge out and hang them on the front of the house.

"Saturday we'll go pick out our tree," Rose said, hammering a nail into the wall to hold a grapevine wreath. It was a project from one of her craft classes and one of Daniel's favorite decorations.

"It's too early to get a tree. It'll be dried out by Christmas," he pointed out.

"But I like having one early. I don't really feel ready until the tree is up."

"Then let's get a fake one," Daniel suggested, as he did every year. "It snaps together like a puzzle, no fuss, no drying out, no needles on the carpet."

"That's no fun. It doesn't smell like a real tree."

"There are realistic-smelling candles," Daniel said.

Rose ignored him and set about constructing the wooden stable that held the crèche. Her figurines were olive wood, imported from Jerusalem, and she loved to stroke their smooth-as-wax amber surfaces. Daniel noticed that she held the figure of the baby Jesus for an extra-long time, cradling it in the palm of her hand, examining its tiny carved features, before slipping it into place. Patricia had always waited until Christmas Eve to place the baby in the manger, but Daniel knew it was more than his life was worth to suggest Rose hold off displaying the baby.

He put up the lights with much mumbling, vowing as he did every year to put them up earlier next year before it got cold. Why couldn't architects simply build Christmas lights into the eaves of houses? A flip of the switch and they'd be on. He'd bet Theresa's nursing home had something like that.

When the lights were hung, Daniel went into his den to work for a while. He had an assignment due on Monday that couldn't be put off any longer. It was a piece about the local food bank, and the newspaper gave them a free plug every Christmas. It was a worthy cause, and ordinarily Daniel would be happy to write an upbeat piece. But this year he was too distracted, and the stories of the people he'd interviewed who used the food bank were depressing. After an hour he set the article aside unfinished.

Burl Ives had been replaced by Bing Crosby, and Rose was crooning along with him to "White Christmas." Daniel could smell something delicious and spicy simmering on the stove. He hoped it would turn out to be something he was allowed to eat; more often than not it was a craft of some sort—beeswax candles or potpourri sachets—that Rose was creating. He leaned back in his chair to stretch and saw a piece of paper on the corner of his desk. The unfinished phone list of McDonalds in Seattle. He had given up after the twentieth number, the second Charles he'd located but not the right Charles. He was amazed by how many other names started with C.

He reached for the paper now, thinking to get in a few more calls before dinner. The next number on the list turned out to be a Catherine, not a Charles. The number after that had been disconnected. He glanced at his watch and decided to try one more before going to help Rose cook. This time Charlie answered.

It took both of them a minute to grasp the fact that they were actually talking to each other. Then the voice on the other end of the line erupted in enthusiasm.

"Danny? My brother Danny? Man alive, I never thought I'd hear from you!"

"I can't believe it's really you either," Daniel said, feeling his throat tighten with tears. He forced them back. "You can't know how good it is to hear your voice."

"You sound all grown up. I mean, I know that's a dumb thing to say. You're how old now?"

"Thirty-five."

"Wow. That old? The last time I saw you, you were about seven."

"Yes. I imagine you're old now too."

"Forty-five. Man, that sounds old as dirt. Where are you calling from, Danny?"

"Denver."

"After all this time, I'd given up ever hearing from you."

"How could I have called you? I didn't know where you were."

"What do you mean? I've been in Washington this whole time. You know that."

"No, I didn't have a clue where you were until just a few days ago, when Isabel let slip that she'd gotten a card from you two years ago and that it had a Seattle return address on it. I didn't know until then."

There was a pause. "What do you mean, she let it slip?"

How could he explain? Daniel took a deep breath. "Isabel never told me you wrote to her and kept in touch after you left. She never once told me she'd heard from you. I thought you'd disappeared without a backward glance."

"But—but I wrote to you too. Didn't you get my letters?"

"No. But Isabel was always the one who collected the mail. She never told me there were any letters from you."

"The little brat. Why didn't she?"

"I don't know. Maybe she wanted to keep you all to herself. Maybe she was angry you'd left at all. I was only seven. Maybe she was trying to spare me from feeling bad. Maybe in some weird way she was afraid I'd go after you and she'd be left alone. Who knows with Isabel? Getting information from her is like getting blood from a turnip."

"I did write to you, Danny, quite a few times after I left. Just little notes saying things like where I'd been and what I'd seen. That I missed you. Hi to Patricia. All that sort of stuff."

"You never wrote to Patricia, though. She would have told me."

"No, just you and Isabel. I didn't get along so well with Patricia and Mark. Maybe you don't remember. I gave them a bit of trouble."

"I only vaguely remember. But Isabel said your letters stopped ten years ago, and she hadn't heard anything more until that Christmas card two years ago."

There was another pause. When Charlie spoke again, his voice was rough with emotion.

"I was too ashamed to write, Danny. Ten years ago I was arrested on drug charges and did some time in prison. Eight years. It wasn't my first offense."

"Oh." Daniel didn't know what he had expected, but it hadn't been this. He didn't know what to say.

"After I got out, I decided to make a clean start. And I wrote that card to Isabel telling her everything and asking her to forgive me. Not just for the prison time, but for leaving you two to grow up alone all those years. I felt like I should have come back and not been away so long."

"I never knew," Daniel said. "She—she threw out your card."

"I thought so. She didn't write back. I figured it was the final straw for her, and she'd cut me off completely. But I never imagined she hadn't told you about it. When I didn't hear from you either . . . I guess I thought you just weren't interested in keeping up the relationship."

Daniel felt a wave of anger toward his sister. "She had no right to make that decision for me. She had no right to keep you from me."

"Danny . . ."

"I loved you, Charlie. I missed you so bad. I remember once I started crying right in the middle of school and had to go home. I felt like an idiot. Mostly because I thought I was crying for a brother who didn't care enough to keep in touch with me."

Daniel hadn't meant to say so much. He swiped his hand across his eyes and struggled to control his voice.

"Oh, Danny. I'm so sorry. I'm sorry I wasn't there. And I'm sorry I ended up such a useless big brother. I didn't set much of an example."

"That doesn't matter now," Daniel told him. "I'm just glad I've found you now. I should have believed in you. I should have known you wouldn't have just up and disappeared without a word like Dad did. You weren't like him."

He heard the rasping intake of Charlie's breath. "You don't know why Dad left, Danny. He had his reasons. You can't judge him for what he did. You haven't been in his shoes."

"That's true. I haven't. I've only been in the shoes of a five-year-old boy whose father didn't want him anymore."

"It wasn't like that. He didn't leave because he didn't want you. He left to protect you."

Daniel gripped the phone so hard he thought he would snap it in half.

"Protect me? From what, for heaven's sake?"

"From himself. It's too long a story to go into on the phone. But Danny, he did it because he cared about you."

"How can you know that? You can't say that."

"If you don't believe me, you can ask him yourself."

Daniel felt as if he'd been hit in the face with cold water. "What do you mean?"

"Dad's here, Danny. He lives in Seattle."

Daniel couldn't speak. He couldn't breathe. He laid his forehead on the top of his desk and let the tears come.

CHAPTER 21

"One more trip," Daniel said and kissed Rose on the forehead. "Last one until after the baby—I promise."

She smiled up at him, bumping her stomach gently against him as she reached up to hug him. "I'll hold you to that," she said. "You're lucky Dave didn't fire you."

"Dave knows he's lucky to have me."

"So am I. Be home by Christmas," she murmured.

"Of course. We have days yet."

"Safe trip."

"Love you."

"You too."

* * *

Daniel went to the waiting taxi and climbed in, sliding his bag across the seat. He directed the driver to the airport and leaned his head back and closed his eyes. He'd turned in his article on the food bank yesterday. He'd hardly thought about what to pack, randomly tossing in sweaters and jeans and making such a mess of it that Rose had quietly taken over and repacked for him. He had called Isabel and told her where he was going. He hadn't confronted her about her deception, hadn't scolded her for with-holding the information. But he'd asked her to come with him, and she had refused. He hadn't pressed her. He'd only said, "I love you, Isabel. I'll see you when I get back." He could tell she was crying when he hung up the phone.

The flight wasn't long, but it seemed to take forever, and it was even more exhausting than the flight to Toronto had been. When he disembarked, an airline employee in uniform directed him to a shuttle bus that smelled of stale cigarettes and let the cold air in. Now he was crawling along through traffic toward Seattle, down toward the ocean. He could feel the difference in the air, in the altitude, in the taste of the humidity on his lips.

At the shuttle stop he caught a taxi that took him to a neighborhood of pretty houses and tree-studded yards. They pulled up in front of a one-story white house with green shutters. The yard was plain, with little land-scaping—only a lawn mown short and a hedge in need of trimming. A winter-yellow hydrangea half obscured the steps. Daniel went up the stairs, hearing the taxi pull away behind him, and for a moment he wanted to race after it. He was suddenly nervous and afraid; he was five years old all over again.

He knocked and shifted his bag to his other hand. It felt like rain, and he was glad for the thick sweater he wore under his coat. He heard shuf-fling, and then the door opened with a squeak. Charlie stood in the light of the hallway.

Daniel said the only thing that came to mind. "You're not as tall as you used to be."

Charlie laughed, and Daniel's restraint and nervousness were gone as suddenly as they had come. That was the laugh he remembered. This was his brother. He dropped his bag on the porch, and they threw their arms around each other.

* * *

It was some time before either brother could speak coherently. Daniel found himself sitting on a sagging sofa in the living room with Charlie in a chair opposite him and a large slobbery dog draped across his feet. The room was as simple as the yard, with a sofa, two tables with lamps, and a half-empty bookshelf. The green carpet and gold wallpaper were straight from the 80s. There weren't a lot of personal things, he noted—no photos, no framed prints, only a drooping houseplant he couldn't name and a chewed tennis ball obviously belonging to the dog.

"That's Tiny. Don't mind him. If he bothers you I can put him out."

"No, it's fine. I like dogs," Daniel said. It struck him as sad that his brother didn't know he liked dogs.

"Can I get you anything? I don't have any beer in the house. I've given it up. But—"

"No, thanks, that's fine. I don't drink it either."

"Something to eat?"

"I'm okay. I don't think I could eat anything right now." Daniel gave a wry smile. "To tell you the truth, I feel kind of jittery, like I might be sick."

Charlie laughed again. "I feel the same way. I've felt like that since your phone call. I wasn't sure what to expect. You're taller than I imagined, taller than I am."

"Yeah. I always wondered if I would be."

"Does Isabel know you're here?"

"Yes. I asked her to come with me, but . . ." He shrugged.

Charlie nodded. "Ah."

"I don't know if she'll ever come around," Daniel said honestly.

"Give her some time."

Daniel wanted to point out that Isabel had had time, more time than he'd had. But he let it go. He shifted on the sofa, trying to get more comfortable, and the dog sighed and rolled its liquid eyes at him.

"So what have you been doing since you got out?" Daniel asked, trying to sound casual, as if everyone he knew spent time in prison.

Charlie ran his hand through his hair, making it stand up in graying spikes. His tall, lean frame had filled out a bit, and his cheeks looked as if he'd just shaved a moment before. He wore a blue dress shirt and tan slacks, and his face, familiar and yet not, held wrinkles that belonged on an older man. He sat with his legs stretched out and crossed at the ankle, a relaxed pose, but his foot vibrated nonstop. He reflected every tension Daniel felt himself.

"I took a course. There are programs for ex-cons, you know. Now I'm a gas fitter. I work for a heating and air-conditioning company. And once a month I go out with a social worker and give presentations to kids in schools. You know, 'you don't want to end up like me' speeches." He shrugged. "I enjoy it all right. It's not where I thought I'd end up, but truth be told, I never really thought much about where I wanted to end up. So here I am." He shrugged a shoulder and smiled.

"Never married?"

"No. Never met anybody. There was one girl I thought of marrying, but she didn't wait around for me to get out. I don't think much of marriage anyway. It's not like we had a great example, huh? How about you?"

"Yes, I'm married. My wife is due to have a baby soon."

"Good of her to let you come."

"That's one of the reasons I started searching out our family," Daniel told him. "I didn't feel ready to be a father. Like you said, it's not like we had a great example of fatherhood, growing up. And I wanted to have . . . something to give the baby. I guess I just needed to understand it all better, what happened and why, so I could put it to rest and get on with living *now*. You know? I can't explain it very well."

Charlie rubbed his nose thoughtfully. "I think I know what you mean." He snapped his fingers at the dog. Tiny heaved himself to his feet, then went over and dropped onto Charlie's feet with a sigh. He looked like an oil spill.

"What kind of dog is he?" Daniel asked, amused. Edward would like this dog.

"Half basset hound, half throw rug, apparently." Charlie sighed and looked up at Daniel. After a moment, he said, "I won't get into details or make excuses for Dad. You can see him tomorrow and hear all that from him when we go to the nursing home."

Daniel nodded. "He's in a nursing home?"

"He has been for the last few years. He's only seventy-five, which isn't really that old, but mentally he's started to go, you know? I mean, he recognizes me when I visit, and he remembers everything just fine and talks up a storm, but he can't find his way from the bedroom to the kitchen by himself."

"Oh. Do you think it'll upset him, seeing me?"

"I don't know. He was pretty mad when I found him back in 1980."

"Didn't want you tagging along after him, I guess," Daniel said, trying to play it off as a joke but not succeeding.

"He was upset when I found him because he didn't think any good could come from it. But I was older by then, and I could fend for myself, and I was just as stubborn as he was. I've stayed around here since then, just keeping an eye on him, you know? I just . . . needed to."

"I'm glad you did. Does he know I'm here?" Daniel asked.

"No. I didn't call, because I know he would make life miserable for the attendants at the nursing home between now and tomorrow. I think when we get there I'll call him from the front desk before we go to his room. Prepare him, like. But not give him enough time to get worked up."

Daniel couldn't help wincing. "Is he that temperamental? What am I walking into?"

Charlie grinned, his face splitting from ear to ear. The mischief Daniel remembered returned to his face, and suddenly he looked more like a pirate than a gas fitter. "You'll see," he said, chuckling. "You'll see what you've been missing out on all these years."

* * *

They spent the evening chatting at the table over canned chili and corn-bread, keeping the conversation purposefully light and not discussing the past any further. As Charlie had said, Daniel would learn everything for himself tomorrow. For tonight he was just happy to be with his brother again. Time had changed Charlie, made him quieter and a bit gruff, but he was still Charlie underneath, with the same sharp wit and contagious laugh. Daniel told him about meeting Rose, about Isabel and her kids, about Mark's death, and about his work at the paper, particularly the information he was still compiling about nursing homes. Charlie listened to his description of Theresa Zahlmann's home and wryly shook his head.

"Dad's rest home isn't quite like that," he said, chuckling. "It's state run and cost-cutting. And somehow I just can't see Dad sitting on his front porch and shooting the breeze with the codger next door."

But when Daniel pressed him about what Jimmy was like, Charlie only shook his head again. "Time enough for that tomorrow," was all he said.

Daniel didn't sleep well on the lumpy couch. It was too short and smelled of dog. He wished he had held out for a hotel, but Charlie wouldn't hear of it. Daniel's night was punctuated by half-dreams, but none of them were of Hannah. He wished he could dream of her. After all, he thought irritably, he was about to find her last missing child. Shouldn't she be here? He woke feeling wrinkled and grumpy and more than a little sick to his stomach. He was going to meet his father today. He brushed his teeth and splashed water over his face, wishing Rose were with him to rub his shoulders and tell him everything was going to be all right. He debated about what to wear. He wanted to make a good impression, but he didn't want to come across as too fancy. He settled for a blue wool sweater over a white shirt and faded, comfortable jeans.

Charlie had also spruced up for the occasion. Hair slicked wetly down, dressed in a long-sleeved rugby shirt and khakis, he looked younger, like a teenager on his way to school. He explained to Daniel that he didn't have a driver's license, but they could take the bus. It was only a few miles to the nursing home. He offered Daniel breakfast, but all Daniel could manage was a piece of toast.

As they rode the bus through the unfamiliar streets, Daniel tried to compose himself and think about what he should say. He didn't want to upset anyone, but he also wanted to hear the truth. He wanted to know what had sent his father away—and kept him away—for so many years.

The nursing home was indeed several steps down from Theresa Zahlmann's. The parking lot needed repaving, and the junipers on each side of the door looked pinched and dead in the cold. The low stucco building had long hallways and the stifling ammonia smell reminiscent of all rest homes, mingled with the choking stench of old cigarettes. Apparently patients and staff alike were allowed to smoke on the patio, and the odor drifted in through the half-open sliding glass doors. The nurse at the front desk recognized Charlie, which let Daniel know that his brother visited often. The idea made him glad. Charlie borrowed the phone to call his father's room.

"Dad? Charlie. You up to a visit?"

Daniel strained to hear the reply but heard nothing. Charlie glanced at Daniel and gave him a thumbs-up.

"Hey, Dad, I brought somebody with me. You'll never guess who's come to visit you. It's Danny."

There was a long pause, and then Charlie repeated, "Danny. Your kid. My kid brother. You know."

After another pause, Charlie simply nodded, as if Jimmy could see him, and hung up. He gave Daniel an encouraging thump on the back.

"Let's get down there before he wakes up the neighborhood."

They strode down the hall, passing a bald gentleman slumped in his wheelchair next to the wall like a car run out of gas. He didn't look up as they passed. They turned the corner, past a row of identical wide doorways, and then Charlie went into a room, pushing the heavy door open with his shoulder. Daniel hung back a little, his mouth dry, angry with himself for being nervous. This was just an old man, someone he'd come to interview. Nothing to worry about. He stepped inside.

CHAPTER 22

The room was bare but for the hospital bed, a straight-backed metal chair, a metal breakfast cart, and a gray footlocker. The only hint that a person actually inhabited the cold space was a plastic breakfast tray on the cart and a paperback lying facedown on the top of the footlocker.

The man sitting upright in the bed was covered by a blue blanket from the waist down, a white nightshirt showing above it. Two blue-veined hands lay on the covers—large hands, once strong and capable. Daniel took a steadying breath and forced himself to look into his father's face.

Daniel's first thought was that he'd changed so much, and his second thought was that he hadn't changed at all. The McDonald eyes were fixed on him, the eyebrows lowered and jutting, the jaw lean and tight, the planes of his face sharp and defined like jagged granite. His hair was still thick and steel gray. Daniel could tell the shape of his father's skull through the papery skin. Jimmy was at once familiar and totally unexpected. For a moment they stared at each other, and then Daniel said quietly, "Hi, Dad. It's Daniel."

"What are you doing here? What, did you bring a whole busload of people to come stare at me?" Jimmy barked, turning to Charlie.

"No, Dad, just Danny. He looked me up the other day, and he's come to visit for a little while. So I thought I'd bring him round to see you."

"What for?" Jimmy turned his glare back on Daniel, who felt himself actually square his shoulders. He felt like he was being drilled by the sheriff.

"I wanted to see you," he said simply.

"It's been too long," Jimmy growled. His hands moved impatiently on the blanket.

"Yes, it has. All the more reason to come."

Jimmy flung his arms out to his sides, jerky like a marionette. "Well, take a good look. This is it. This is all there is to see. Satisfied?"

Daniel cleared his throat. He moved forward a few steps into the room, his shoes clicking on the linoleum. He put his own arms out to his sides and turned slowly.

"What are you doing?" Jimmy demanded.

"Letting you get a good look at me too," Daniel replied. "What do you think? Did I turn out okay?"

Charlie gave a snicker, and Jimmy scowled at him.

"Rude pup, aren't you?"

"I came clear from Denver to see you, Dad."

"What for? I can't do anything for you now."

"I don't know. Maybe you can."

"What?"

"You can talk to me." Daniel felt his voice catch, and he cleared his throat again.

Jimmy leaned back on his pillow and pursed his lips. After a moment he said, "I don't have anything to say."

"You can say hello. You can say it's good to see me again. You can ask what I've been up to for the past thirty years."

"I don't care what you've been up to. Why? What have you been up to?" His voice rose in suspicion.

Daniel couldn't help smiling.

"Good things. I'm a journalist. Went to college. I'm married to a really nice girl named Rose."

"What do you want, a medal?"

Daniel glanced at Charlie, who shifted on his feet.

"I'm going to go down to the cafeteria," Charlie said. "Want me to bring you two anything?"

"No, thanks," Daniel said hesitantly. He wasn't sure he wanted to be left alone with this man. He fluctuated between resentment at Charlie's defection and appreciation for his sensitivity.

"One of those Fruitopia things. Red," Jimmy said.

Charlie nodded, gave Daniel an encouraging little punch in the arm, and went out. Daniel turned back to the bed, struggling to keep his composure. He hadn't expected to be welcomed with open arms, but he hadn't expected such antagonism either.

"I've spent the last few months looking up your family."

"My family?"

"Your brothers and sisters."

"What did you do that for?"

Daniel considered sitting on the chair but decided against it. He wanted to be taller than the man in the bed. He didn't bother to analyze why.

"It was important to me to find out who they were and what happened to them. I've found them all. Do you want me to tell you about them?"

"What good would it do now? They're probably all dead by now anyway."

"Not all of them. Mary and Alex and Matthew are still around. Do you remember them?"

Jimmy lifted a hand to rub his face. He looked tired. "Look, what do you want? I don't want to hear this. What makes you think I wanted you to barge in here and talk about this? No good can come of it."

Daniel finally sat on the chair, his hands limp on his knees. He felt defeated and sad. "All right," he said. "I won't talk about it, then. I just thought you might like to know."

"They all left me," Jimmy snapped. "Why should I care about what happened to them?"

"They didn't leave you. Your dad left them. He left your brothers and sisters behind and took you with him to Montana."

"What do you know about Montana?" Jimmy's voice rose in pitch.

"I didn't mean to upset you," Daniel said quickly. "This isn't how I wanted this to go at all. I just wanted to talk to you. I just wanted to see you." Daniel felt dangerously close to tears. Why didn't Charlie come back so they could leave?

"You don't know a thing about me or my father or Montana. It's none of your business. Just leave it alone."

"Okay."

Jimmy picked irritably at the sleeve of his nightshirt and shot Daniel a disapproving glance. "You turned out skinny."

"I got that from you."

"Charlie shouldn't have brought you. He should have known better." His voice had changed; it was almost a wail now. Daniel stood and stepped close to the bed. Jimmy looked away. His skin looked weathered, like old flannel that had been rubbed too long.

"I'm sorry, Dad. As soon as Charlie comes back I'll go." Daniel hesitated and then added, "I have to say, this hasn't turned out at all like I imagined."

"I suppose you expected it to be like something in a movie. The prodigal son and all that."

"No. I know that isn't realistic. But I did think we could at least be civil to each other."

"What's the matter? Did I hurt your feelings?" Jimmy sneered.

"Yes," Daniel said flatly.

The honest response seemed to surprise Jimmy. He slumped against the pillow, looking more wary. Daniel went back to his chair and folded his arms, determined not to say anything else until Charlie came back. This whole trip had been a bad idea, doomed from the start.

"Mary," Jimmy said slowly.

Daniel looked up.

"Yeah, I think I remember Mary. Not the others. I don't remember all their names. But the name Mary sounds familiar."

Daniel swallowed. "She's been looking for you for a long time. She loved you like a mother."

"And you found her?"

"Yes. I went out to visit her and Alex in Wisconsin."

"Alex."

"The baby. He's old now." Daniel stopped, feeling foolish.

Jimmy shook his head, his hair falling across his forehead. Daniel found himself wondering if anyone in his family had ever gone bald. Or did that come through the mother's side? What had his mother's father looked like? He bit his lips together, wondering why his mind was wandering now of all times, and wondering what was keeping Charlie. Was the cafeteria on the other side of the world?

"It was all a long time ago," Jimmy said finally. His voice was low now, back to normal range. "Nothing to be done about it now. My father abandoned me, you see."

"Yes, I know."

"How do you know? I didn't ever tell you," Jimmy said sharply.

"I found out on my own."

"Nosy little brat, aren't you?"

"I also know that your father died in 1950 of kidney failure. Did you know that?"

Jimmy looked away toward the window. The metal blind blocked most of the sunlight, and Daniel saw a potted cactus perched on the sill. Probably the only kind of plant that could survive in Jimmy's prickly presence, he thought. Had his father always been this nasty? He couldn't remember.

"Why should I care? He took off without me. I always hated him for it."

"If so, then why did you turn around and do the exact same thing to us?" Daniel exploded. He hadn't meant to blurt it out.

"What? I didn't. I mean, that wasn't the same thing at all."

"Come on, Dad. It was exactly the same thing. You knew what it was like to grow up without a father. So why did you do it to me and Charlie and Isabel?"

"That was totally different," Jimmy barked. He sat upright, knocking the book from the locker. His blue eyes blazed like gas jets.

"If you hated your father so much, why did you turn out just like him?" Daniel knew they could be heard all up and down the hall, but he didn't care. He expected a nurse to come running in any moment now.

"You don't know what you're talking about. You know nothing about it."

"Then explain it to me, Dad. This is your chance. I doubt I'll be coming back to see you anytime soon. This is your chance to explain it to me. That's why I came. I wanted to hear it from you."

Daniel braced himself for a good rousing fight, welcoming the release of it. But Jimmy subsided again and turned his face away, quiet. Frustrated, Daniel strode over to the window and looked out, seeing nothing between the slats of the blinds but the parking lot. His heartbeat pounded behind his eyes. The whole dismal room depressed him, the metal and the linoleum, the fuzzy blue blanket. He wanted to cry. He gritted his teeth. "Charlie said you left to protect us."

"Charlie's a bigmouth."

"Maybe so. But what did he mean, Dad?"

There was silence, and he was sure Jimmy wasn't going to answer. Then he heard the rasping old voice.

"I knew I had to get away from you. You kids and your mother. I—I wasn't any good for any of you. I didn't want to hurt you."

Daniel turned around to face him. Jimmy was picking at his sleeve again, engrossed in a loose thread. He didn't look up.

"What do you mean?"

"I had a temper back then." At Daniel's snort, he finally looked up, scowling. "Don't be rude. I mean a bad temper, worse than I have now. This is nothing. This is just . . . assertiveness."

Daniel wiped the smile from his lips. "Okay," he said.

Jimmy shrugged, splaying his spotted old-man hands. "I'd seen what a temper could do. I'd seen my own father . . ."

"I know about that. You remember that?"

"How could you know?" Jimmy demanded.

"I told you, I looked it up. I found out. I talked to Mary."

"She told you?"

"Probably even more than you remember."

"Well, then. There's your answer. He—he wasn't a nice man."

"Were you afraid you'd turn out like him?"

"I *was* like him back then. I knew it could only end in something bad. I fought it, don't think I didn't. I held it back for sixteen years. You can't say I didn't give it a good shot."

"But I don't remember you being like that," Daniel said quietly. "I don't remember that at all."

"Good. That means I left in time, before you were old enough to have it affect you." He looked away again. "Your mother was probably relieved to see me go."

"No. I don't think so," Daniel said softly.

"It was for the best, all around."

"I don't buy that. I grew up without a dad."

"Better no father than a bad one."

"You weren't a bad father."

"You just said you don't remember. Be grateful for it and get on with your life."

Daniel had to clear his throat before he could speak again. "Did you miss us at all, Dad?" He felt his face grow hot at the wistfulness in his voice.

Jimmy coughed. "That's a stupid question. It's too late to think about that. Can't do anything about that now."

"I want to know."

"Of course I did. A few times I nearly turned around and went back. But it wouldn't have been any good, I told you that. So I talked myself out of it. And then after a while it was just . . . too late to go back."

Daniel dropped into the chair, looking at his shoes, thinking. His father lay silently in the bed. After a while, Jimmy said, "Don't just sit there. Pick up my book."

Daniel picked it up and placed it back on the locker. It was a John Grisham novel, dog-eared, with a candy wrapper as the bookmark.

"I like Grisham too," Daniel said.

"Maybe you turned out all right," Jimmy said gruffly after a while. "You said you were a journalist and married and all. So no harm done."

"No harm!" Daniel swallowed back the response that sprang to his lips. He breathed in sharply through his nose and let the air out slowly through his mouth. No, Jimmy was right. He supposed that all in all, in the grand scheme of things, he'd turned out all right. Maybe Charlie had seen what Daniel hadn't. In his own way, Jimmy must have cared about his family. He hadn't wanted to hurt them, so he'd gone. It had hurt them anyway, just differently perhaps.

"My wife's having a baby in a couple of months," he said for lack of anything else to say. He expected Jimmy to reply with "What do you want, a medal?" again, but instead Jimmy just nodded.

"That's good. You be good to them."

"I will."

"I know you will."

Daniel brought his head up quickly. "How do you know?"

"You've got your mother in you. She was a fine person."

"Thanks," Daniel said quietly.

Jimmy's eyes slid sideways at him. "You'll be a better father than I was. After all, that's what you came here to hear, isn't it? That you don't have to turn out like me?" His face suddenly split into a hundred wrinkles, and he gave a choking cackle that Daniel supposed was his version of a laugh.

"No . . ."

"I may be old, but I'm not stupid. It's the same question I ran into, isn't it?"

"But you said you *did* turn out to be like your father."

"At first. But I stopped it, didn't I?" His chin jerked out, defiant.

Daniel eyed him a moment, then slowly nodded. "I suppose so. Yes, you did. But there are other ways to stop it than by running away."

Jimmy cocked one eyebrow at him. "Yep, there probably are. Well, so, there's your answer."

Daniel shook his head, a smile beginning to form. "I guess you're right."

"Yep."

"I guess you think I'm the stupid one."

"Yep."

"Well, thanks for saying so."

"Anything else you want me to say before you go back to Denver?"

Daniel hesitated. *I loved you. I still love you. I want us to be father and son again.* "No, I think that about does it," he said aloud, then put out a hand. "I'm glad I came to see you," he said solemnly. "Maybe I'll come again."

Jimmy eyed him a moment, then shook his hand. His grasp was stronger than Daniel had expected. Jimmy smiled again, gleeful at Daniel's surprised look.

"I'm not dead yet," he declared.

"No, you certainly aren't."

At that moment, Charlie, returning with trepidation after what he deemed to be a suitable length of time, entered the room and was astounded to find his father and brother clasping hands and laughing.

* * *

There was one more stop to make before he went home to Denver. In a pocket of his suitcase Daniel carried the slip of paper on which Edward had written the directions to and plot number of James Carlton McDonald's grave. He arrived in Spokane on a chilly, rainy morning and had the taxi take him directly to the cemetery. It wasn't a large place, and he found the plot without much difficulty, since the number markers were laid out in logical grid fashion. But the actual grave site had no headstone. He counted out the markers again to make sure, but the space between the neighboring stones was the correct one. There was no stone, no tree, no bush to mark the place or soften the flat ground.

When Daniel inquired at the cemetery office, the portly man at the counter looked up the record and informed him that James McDonald had purchased his own plot a few months before his death, but had ordered no marker. There had been no family to erect one. Daniel thanked him and turned to go, then stopped with a thought. "Do your records say who arranged his burial?"

"It says he made his own arrangements ahead of time. Must have known it was coming and wanted to be prepared. But he was residing at the Sun River Retirement Home at the time of his death."

"I see. Did James McDonald name a next of kin?"

"Sometimes they do. Let me see." The man looked at the record again. "It says here Laura G. McDonald. You know who that is?"

"Yes," Daniel said quietly. "I know who that is. Thank you."

He walked through the rain back to the grave site and stood looking down at the wet grass. Fifty-five years ago a man had been buried here with no one to mourn him or erect a stone. James McDonald had started all of this—the whole family legacy of addiction and abandonment. There was always a reason for things, Daniel thought, though maybe not always the reason you expected. He thought he understood a little better now what had started everything in motion. It broke his heart to think that when his grandfather had found himself dying, he'd bought his own plot and named as his next of kin not his living family, nor the woman who'd borne him eight children, but the love of his youth, the wife who had died forty years before him. The wife who lay buried beneath a six-foot stone in Canada.

Daniel turned back toward the road where the patient taxi waited, the meter softly clicking. His pants were wet to the knee, and the rain had soaked his hair, running in rivulets down his neck under his collar, but he didn't feel chilled. He felt warm. He paused at the curb and looked back at the grave site, but it was lost to view behind other stones. In his mind's eye, he saw his red-haired grandmother. As in the photograph, Hannah stood holding an infant peacefully in her arms. She was standing in the rain beside the grave. Though she was turned slightly from him, looking down at the grass, somehow he knew she was smiling. As he turned away, so was he.

Daniel opened the door of the taxi and climbed in. It was time to go home. He knew he wouldn't be a perfect father. He'd make mistakes too, just as other fathers did. But he was ready to go home and give it the very best effort he could. If he fell short, he would just have to trust God to make up the rest. It was time to pass a new legacy down to the next McDonald.

* * *

Rose had reached the point where she could no longer tie her shoes. Laughingly she asked Daniel to do it, and he knelt before her. He had a dreamy smile on his face, and Rose poked him in the shoulder.

"What is it?"

"What?" he asked.

"You look like you have a funny secret."

"No secret. But I have been thinking. About a name for Junior."

"Finally," she said. "What have you come up with?"

"I thought," he said, tipping his head back to look up at her, "maybe we could call the baby Charles. And if it's a girl, Charlotte, so we could call her Charlie."

"Not Aloysius?" Rose smiled and touched his cheek with her finger.

"Not Aloysius."

She put her arms around his neck and stood when he stood. She smiled up at him. "Charlie it is, then."

CHAPTER 23

2006

The soft glow from the Winnie the Pooh lamp spread over the pale blue walls of the nursery, pouring down the sides of the maple bookcase to the Eeyore rug on the floor. The bookcase was already stuffed with books waiting for their small owner to reach the age when he could really appreciate them. *Green Eggs and Ham. Mike Mulligan and His Steam Shovel. Chicken Soup with Rice.* Good solid books that wouldn't have to be read in a squeaky voice. Rose had taken the Winnie the Pooh theme and run with it, stenciling the dresser drawers with pots of honey and sewing orange-and-blue curtains with iron-ons of Tigger. Sleepers and bibs with Rabbit and Piglet lay snuggled in the drawers. Even the clock softly ticking on the dresser had Pooh's pudgy face smiling out from between its hands.

Daniel carefully shifted the warm, heavy bundle that was slowly cutting off the circulation in his arm. Charlie didn't stir, his eyes screwed closed as if in deep thought. Even in sleep he looked coiled and ready to spring into action, one hand in a fist, the other splayed out on his blanket like a starfish. His red hair, a quarter-inch long, stuck out as if electricity ran through it. He was going to be all energy, this boy—Daniel could tell. He was already looking forward to baseball and riding a two-wheeler, swimming lessons and camping, soccer games and the Pinewood Derby. He imagined this little boy grown tall and gangly, dressed in suit and tie to pass the sacrament, or taller still and heading off on his mission. Daniel lifted his free hand and gently traced the outline of his son's profile, the softly rounded forehead, the bridgeless nose. When he touched the tiny pink lips, Charlie twitched and smiled.

"You and me, kid," Daniel whispered. "We'll do all of those things."

"Hey." Rose poked her head in, her smile reflecting Charlie's. "Asleep?"

"He finished the whole bottle," Daniel whispered as he swiveled the chair to let her see Charlie's lashes, long on his cheeks. "Out like a light."

"Good. Maybe we'll make it through the whole night this time." Rose crossed her fingers and held them up.

"Wouldn't you know, just when insomnia would have been handy, I get over it?" Daniel chuckled. "I think I could sleep standing up now."

"Me too."

"Who was that on the phone earlier?"

Rose came into the room and lowered herself to sit cross-legged beside Daniel's feet, resting her head on his unoccupied knee. She kept her voice low, but he could hear the pleasure in her voice. "Edward. He and Gwen arrive on the 10:35 flight Friday night. I wrote it all down. We'll need to pick them up at the airport, but not until they call us, in case the flight's delayed or something. It'll take them a while to collect their luggage and go through Customs anyway."

Daniel laid his hand on her head with a contented sigh. "I'm glad they decided to come for Charlie's blessing. I explained it to them, what it means for us, and how it's different from a christening. I guess Edward's been thinking over everything I told him about the Church. He said he has some questions for us when he comes."

"That's encouraging."

"Somehow I didn't realize when I started this journey just how much it would affect other people too, not just me."

Rose carefully smoothed the flannel blanket over Charlie's outstretched hand, warming it. "I'm glad. And I'm glad you found them and that they want to stay connected with us too."

"It will be good to have family here, and they'll love meeting Mary, Alex, and Matthew."

Rose yawned. "Speaking of which, I'd better go put the sheets in the dryer, or your aunt and uncles won't have anything to sleep on when they get here."

"Thanks for letting me load the house with relatives so soon after Charlie's arrival," Daniel added.

"No problem. Oh, and my mom and dad called earlier. They just wanted to say thanks again for asking them to be proxies in the temple. It was the highlight of their week. I think it meant a lot to them that you asked them to be involved."

Daniel stroked his hand down her hair, letting it flow through his fingers like honey in the lamplight. Rose had been beautiful that day, radiant in her temple dress (which she rejoiced to fit into once again). As she'd knelt across from him in Hannah's place, he'd felt an almost physical *click* as the pieces of his life, of Hannah's life, had come smoothly and perfectly together. He leaned down now and kissed Rose's cheek.

"Have I told you lately that you're an incredible person?"

"Mm, yes, but feel free to do it again." Rose tipped her head back to look up at him, upside down. "Can you get Charlie settled?"

"Sure," he replied.

She took the empty baby bottle and left the room. Daniel sat a moment longer, gazing down at the peaceful little face held in the crook of his arm. Then he carefully rose and placed the baby in his crib, tucking in the blanket, making sure Charlie was in just the position he preferred. Charlie had begun to breathe so heavily that a less doting parent might have said he was snoring.

Daniel turned off the Winnie the Pooh lamp and paused, one hand cupping his son's fuzzy head. Then he stepped softly to the door and went out.

About the Author

Photo by Melanie Templeman

Kristen Garner McKendry began writing in her teens, and her work has been published in Canada and the United States. She received a bachelor's degree in linguistics from Brigham Young University and has always been a voracious reader. Kristen has a strong interest in education, urban agriculture, and environmental issues. A native of Utah, she now resides with her family in Canada. This book was developed while Kristen and her husband were researching their family history over the course of several years.